"You're God's most inspired creation."

Erich cradled her in his arms. "You have the body of a siren and the face of an angel."

"How about my mind?" she teased. "Did you notice I have one?"

"It's one of your many attractions."

"But how would you know?"

He tipped her chin up and gazed at her. "I know a lot about you."

Kelley stirred uneasily. She couldn't put off telling Erich the truth any longer. There was no reason to be nervous about his reaction. He was almost sure to think the mix-up funny. "You don't *really* know a lot about me," she began tentatively.

He chuckled, gliding his hand over her body. "I'd say I knew you intimately. What surprises do you have in store for me?" He dipped his head to kiss her breasts. "Tell me everything."

Kelley felt herself melting under his sensuous exploration. "It can wait...." she whispered.

Dear Reader,

Welcome to Silhouette *Special Edition* . . . welcome to romance.

Last year I requested your opinions on the books that we publish. Thank you for the many thoughtful comments. For the next couple of months, I'd like to share quotes with you from those letters. This seems very appropriate while we are in the midst of our THAT SPECIAL WOMAN! promotion. Each one of our readers is a very *special* woman, as heroic as the heroines in our books.

This month, our THAT SPECIAL WOMAN! is Kelley McCormick, a woman who takes the trip of a lifetime and meets the man of her dreams. You'll meet Kelley and her Prince Charming in *Grand Prize Winner!* by Tracy Sinclair.

Also in store for you this month is *The Way of a Man,* the third book in Laurie Paige's WILD RIVER TRILOGY. And not to be missed are terrific books from other favorite authors—Kathleen Eagle, Pamela Toth, Victoria Pade and Judith Bowen.

I hope you enjoy this book, and all of the stories to come!

Sincerely,

Tara Gavin
Senior Editor

QUOTE OF THE MONTH:

"I enjoy characters I can relate to—female characters who are wonderful people packaged in very ordinary coverings and men who see beyond looks and who are willing to work at a relationship. I enjoy stories of couples who stick with each other and work through difficult times. Thank you, Special Edition, for the many, many hours of enjoyment."

—M. Greenleaf, Maryland

TRACY SINCLAIR

GRAND PRIZE WINNER!

Silhouette®

SPECIAL EDITION®

Published by Silhouette Books

America's Publisher of Contemporary Romance

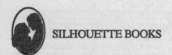 SILHOUETTE BOOKS

ISBN 0-373-09847-2

GRAND PRIZE WINNER!

Copyright © 1993 by Tracy Sinclair

Books by Tracy Sinclair

TRACY SINCLAIR,

author of more than thirty-five Silhouette novels, also contributes to various magazines and newspapers. An extensive traveler and a dedicated volunteer worker, this California resident has accumulated countless fascinating experiences, settings and acquaintances to draw on in plotting her romances.

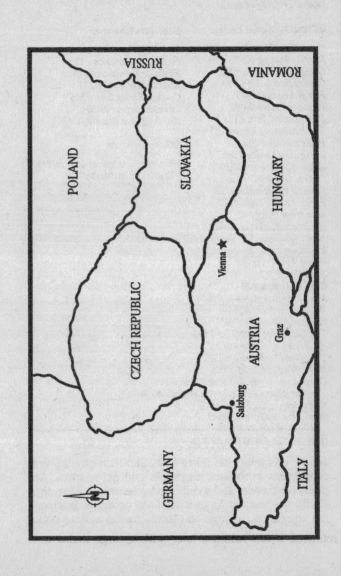

Chapter One

The passengers in the airline waiting room began to gather their luggage expectantly when the ticket agent picked up a microphone.

"Good morning, ladies and gentlemen," she said in a professionally cheerful voice. "Flight 621 to Vienna is now ready for boarding. First-class passengers may proceed to the gate. In just a few moments we'll be calling rows twenty-one through fifty. Please have your boarding passes ready at that time. Thank you and have a nice flight."

Kelley McCormick joined the small group of people straggling toward the open door leading to a ramp. It was hard to believe she was actually on her way to Europe! This seemed as unreal as the day she'd won the lottery.

The first-class cabin held only a dozen passengers, and each seat was as roomy as an armchair. A flight attendant welcomed Kelley aboard and hung her coat in a closet. She returned a few minutes later with a large menu and a smaller one. Offering them to Kelley she said, "We'll be serving cocktails soon after takeoff."

The luncheon menu listed six courses, starting with an assortment of appetizers that included caviar, smoked salmon and pheasant paté. After soup and salad, three entrées were listed, followed by cheese and fruit, strawberry cream cake, coffee and petits fours.

Kelley was happily scanning the choices when a man sat down next to her. He was blond, with blue eyes, aquiline features and broad shoulders accentuated by an impeccably tailored camel-hair jacket.

The plane hadn't even started its engines yet and already Kelley knew she'd made the right decision. Everybody had told her it was insane to pay so much extra for first class. A coach ticket would get her to Vienna in the same amount of time and cost a quarter of what she was paying.

But Kelley was determined, for once in her life, to indulge herself. At twenty-seven, she had no dependents, no debts, and until now, a fairly humdrum existence. This was going to be a fantasy trip—the best hotels, the finest restaurants, shopping frenzies, the works.

"You only won fifty thousand dollars. It isn't as if you were the grand prize winner," her friend Marina had scolded. "You'd be smart to use the money for a down payment on a condo. Or invest it in something that will pay dividends, like tax-free municipal bonds. How can you be so irresponsible?"

"Because for the first time, I can afford to be." Kelley had laughed. "Haven't you ever wanted to walk away from your nine-to-five existence and see what happens?"

"I guess everybody thinks about it, but nobody actually does it."

"Some people do. They're the ones who discover new continents."

"I hate to break the news to you, but all the continents have already been discovered. You'll spend all that money and have nothing concrete to show for it."

Kelley hadn't bothered to argue. She knew this trip would change her life. If nothing else, she'd have the opportunity to live for a while in a dream world. That was something everybody was entitled to.

The man next to her was regarding Kelley with the same lively interest she'd shown in him. He didn't try to conceal his admiration as he inspected her heart-shaped face framed by long glossy black hair and dominated by thickly fringed, violet blue eyes. His gaze was more discreet but no less appreciative, when it flicked over her slender figure and long slim legs.

Kelley was glad she'd bought the new coral-colored knit dress to travel in. Not that she expected anything to develop from a casual encounter on an airplane, but it was nice to make an impression on such an obviously sophisticated man.

"It should be a smooth trip," he remarked. "I was told we have a good forecast all the way across."

"That's good news," Kelley answered, although even bad weather couldn't have spoiled her enjoyment.

"It does make a tedious journey easier, doesn't it? I usually fly the Concorde so I don't lose valuable time. There's nothing like it, but on this trip, their schedule didn't coincide with mine."

"What a shame," she murmured.

"Not really." His eyes kindled. "You're a delightful change from the dowagers I usually find myself sitting next to. Permit me to introduce myself—Baron Kurt Ludendorf, at your service."

Kelley hoped she didn't look as ecstatic as she felt. A baron, a real live baron! So far, everything was exactly the way she'd hoped it would be.

"Is this a business or a pleasure trip?" he asked, after Kelley had supplied her own name.

"Pure pleasure. I've never been to Vienna before."

"That's shocking." His smile softened the criticism. "Once you've seen Vienna you'll wonder why you wasted your time in Paris and London."

Before Kelley had to admit she'd never been to those places, either, the plane started to move down the runway. Excitement fizzed through her veins as she peered out the window, watching Los Angeles turn into a miniature city. When it was only a blurred landscape far below, the flight attendant returned to take their drink orders.

Kelley gave hers promptly. "I'll have a glass of champagne."

Kurt glanced at the smaller menu and frowned. "I don't see any imported champagne."

"We're serving an excellent American brand," the flight attendant replied. "It's very nice. Perhaps you'd like to try it."

He made a face and requested an expensive scotch. When she left, he remarked to Kelley, "It's unconscionable the way the airlines are cutting corners lately."

"It seems quite luxurious to me."

He raised an eyebrow. "You're very charitable."

"Oh, well," Kelley answered vaguely, dismissing the unimportant topic. "Tell me what I should see in Vienna besides the Schonbrunn Palace and the Vienna Woods."

"You don't want to waste your time on tourist attractions. They're overrun by people in appalling clothes with cameras slung over their shoulders."

Kelley glanced at the tote bag that held her brand-new camera. "I'll just have to grin and bear it," she said dryly. "I can't very well go home without seeing those places, but what else would you recommend?"

"Well, the opera, of course, and the shops along the Ringstrasse. I presume you're staying at the Metropole Grande." He named one of the best hotels in Vienna. When she nodded, he said, "All you have to do is walk out the door and you'll find the finest merchandise Europe has to offer."

The flight attendant arrived with their drinks and Kurt held up his glass in a toast. "To a memorable visit in Vienna."

Kelley smiled. "I'll drink to that." She took a deep swallow of the bubbling champagne.

"How long do you plan to stay?" he asked.

"I don't have any definite plans. I'd like to go on to Paris and Rome eventually, but that depends on how long I decide to stay in Vienna."

"I hope it's a very long time," he murmured.

"I have all the time in the world," she answered happily.

"You're very fortunate. Not everyone can afford the luxury of doing whatever they desire."

"I'm certainly aware of that." She drained her glass as the flight attendant appeared to refill it. "That's why this trip is a dream come true. For the first time, I'm as free as a bird."

"You recently severed a relationship?" he asked delicately.

"Possibly, but not the way you mean. I took an indefinite leave of absence from my job. Everybody was positively aghast. It *is* a good job, but it's so terribly dull. I want to visit exciting places and do extravagant things."

Kelley didn't usually open up this freely to strangers, but the unaccustomed champagne was overcoming her usual reserve.

Kurt gazed at her with a slight frown. "What kind of work do you do?"

"I'm a loan officer at a bank."

"I see." His interest was definitely chilled by her answer.

"What do *you* do?"

"A number of things." When she waited expectantly, he added with reluctance, "I deal in antiques, for one thing."

"That must be great fun. I love to poke around in antique shops—the dustier the better."

"That's not my forte. I specialize in rare furniture. It's more of an avocation, actually. I scout around for exceptional pieces for my friends."

"We have some very good antique shops in Los Angeles. Did you get to visit any of them?"

"Yes, this was a buying trip for me. I picked up an exquisite Louis XVI chest for my good friend, the countess Von Dornberger. It's decorated with Sèvres porcelain plaques and ormolu, truly one of a kind, like the countess."

"I've read about her," Kelley remarked. "She's the one with the fabulous art collection. Isn't she an American heiress?"

"That's correct. Henrietta has done a remarkable restoration of the count's family castle."

"I'll bet it's fabulous." Kelley's eyes shone. "I'd love to see the inside of a castle."

"A few are open to the public. I believe there are tours you can take."

"That's the sort of thing I want to do. Can you also suggest some good restaurants?"

"Not offhand, but I imagine you can find some nice, moderately priced ones away from the Ringstrasse."

Kurt's snobbery had been evident almost from the moment he sat down, but Kelley had no intention of letting him patronize *her*.

"I'm not looking for a bargain," she said coolly.

He had the grace to be embarrassed. "I'm sorry. I just naturally assumed that since you're a working woman..." His voice trailed off.

"That's the wonderful thing about America, the land of opportunity," she answered ironically. "Anyone can make a fortune—or win it in the lottery."

He regarded her uncertainly. "You're joking, aren't you?"

"Nope." She grinned. "I'm living proof that somebody does win those things."

"I've heard your lotteries pay millions of dollars!"

"You heard right." Kelley saw no reason to tell him she hadn't won the grand prize. If he made that assumption, it wasn't *her* fault.

"I feel like such a fool for suggesting a sight-seeing bus," he said with chagrin. "You should have a car and driver. Or if you would permit me the honor, I will take you on a tour myself."

"Are you serious?"

"Most assuredly. It would be my pleasure."

"Well, gee, that would be lovely, if you have the time," she said slowly.

"I will *make* the time," he answered, gazing into her eyes.

Kelley felt a twinge of conscience, but only a fleeting one. This was too good an opportunity to pass up—the chance to see Vienna with a native.

The flight attendant appeared with a tray of hors d'oeuvres that looked wonderful. She handed them each a linen napkin and served their selections on small china plates.

"This isn't like any airline food I've ever had," Kelley proclaimed after taking a bite of a tiny puff filled with minced lobster and shrimp. "It's delicious."

"Wait until you've tasted the food in Vienna," Kurt told her. "Our restaurants are world famous."

"Perhaps you can write down some of the names for me."

"I'll do better than that. I'll take you to them."

"I couldn't ask you to do that." Kelley's conscience was definitely bothering her now. "You must have a busy social life."

"I *am* out almost every night. Vienna is a very social city. As a matter of fact, I cut short my trip to Los Angeles so I'd be back for a charity ball tomorrow night." Kurt snapped his fingers. "There's an idea! Why don't you come with me?"

"I'd love to! But don't you have a date already?"

"Let me worry about that," he said dismissively. "It's formal, of course. The crème de la crème will be there, including Henrietta. You two will have a lot in common."

"I'd be thrilled to meet her. This is so nice of you, Kurt. You're starting my visit off with a bang."

"I'm the fortunate one to have met *you.*"

Kelley wasn't taken in by Kurt's sudden interest. She realized he wouldn't have wasted his time on an ordinary working woman, no matter how attractive. But he was so charming during the rest of the flight that she was willing to forgive him for being a snob. Maybe all nobles were like that.

The hours flew by as they dined elegantly while Kurt regaled Kelley with fascinating stories about European royalty. He also managed to refer to his own family castle in a very low-key fashion.

Afterward they reclined their seats and watched a movie. Although she didn't want to miss a moment of this fairy-tale experience, Kelley was so comfortable, wrapped in a blanket with a pillow behind her head, that she fell asleep at the conclusion of the movie.

When they arrived in Vienna the next morning she was bubbling with excitement. Who knew what further adventures awaited her? She felt like Alice entering Wonderland.

The Metropole Grande Hotel was everything the travel agent had promised. Kelley's spacious room and bath were stocked with every comfort to pamper a guest. The bathroom had a built-in hair dryer, a basket of toiletries and a long white terry-cloth robe. In the bedroom, a large armoire housed a television set with a bar underneath stocked with small bottles of liquor, soft drinks and various snacks.

After delightedly inspecting the unaccustomed luxuries, Kelley unpacked hurriedly. There were all sorts of fascinating places to see, but first she had to buy a dress for that evening. It still seemed unbelievable. On her first night in Vienna she was going to a formal ball!

Erich Von Graile Und Tassburg didn't share Kelley's enthusiasm. The telephone call he received reminding him of the event came as an unwelcome surprise. "I'd forgotten it was tonight, Henrietta. I'm afraid I made other plans."

"You can't do this to me, Erich," Henrietta Von Dorn-berger stated. "You're one of the sponsors."

"That only means I helped underwrite the ball," he said dismissively. "It doesn't matter if I'm there or not."

"Yes, it does," she insisted. "You're a grand duke. Why do you think people pay a fortune to come to these things? They expect to see celebrities."

"You're confusing me with a rock star. I'm just an ordinary citizen."

"Don't hand me that! You're about as ordinary as an orchid on a cactus plant," Henrietta said in her native Texas drawl.

Her assessment was accurate. Erich was movie-star handsome, tall and lean, with dark hair and unusual green eyes. A vast fortune and noble lineage that went back hundreds of years didn't detract from his desirability. But even without them, his magnetic personality and great charm would have made him outstanding.

"Half the women at the ball will be hoping you'll ask them to dance," Henrietta continued. "You can't let me down. I'm the chairwoman of this shindig and I promised you'd be there."

"All right." He gave in with a sigh, knowing her tenacity. "I'll show up, but I won't guarantee to stay long."

"Don't be so negative. You might enjoy yourself."

"I'll bet," Erich muttered as he hung up the phone.

The shops along the Ringstrasse held a glittering display of merchandise, all enticing. These were the kinds of clothes pictured in fashion magazines. Kelley had always admired their high style, but until now they were priced way beyond her means.

As she strolled along happily window-shopping, her only problem was which boutique to choose. Suddenly she spied *the* dress. It had a very full, leopard-printed chiffon skirt topped by a halter-neck white pique vest. The unlikely combination of fabrics had the unmistakable stamp of a top designer. The gown was probably wildly expensive, besides being impractical. When would she ever wear it again after tonight? But Kelley knew she had to have that dress.

A short time later she was standing in a dressing room inspecting herself in a three-way mirror. From every angle the gown was magnificent. The long gauzy skirt had layers of tulle petticoats underneath. It made her slim waist look even smaller, while the low-cut halter top emphasized her high rounded breasts.

"It could have been made for you," the saleslady said admiringly. "Even the length is perfect."

"That's good, because I want to wear it tonight," Kelley answered.

"Do you have all your accessories? Earrings? An evening bag?"

"My earrings aren't very impressive," Kelley mused.

"Let me bring a few things to show you."

In addition to long pearl and rhinestone earrings, the woman returned with a pants suit and a short white sheath. "I thought these might interest you."

Kelley was hooked the moment she saw both garments. The long-sleeve dress was simply cut, but it was embroidered from neck to hem in a floral pattern of golden roses and leaves. Even the tailored gray pants suit was glamorous. Underneath the jacket was a silver lace bodysuit with a mock turtleneck.

Kelley tried mightily to resist temptation. "I really don't need either one," she murmured.

"They're both classic designs. You can wear them for years."

"Well . . . maybe the pants suit." Kelley's resolve weakened. "I definitely don't need the dress."

"It's perfect for dinner, either at home or in a restaurant."

Kurt *had* mentioned taking her to dinner, and nothing she had with her was suitable. It wasn't hard to convince herself after she'd tried on both outfits and they fit perfectly.

Kelley's bill came to a sizable amount, but she left the shop happy. Spending money had never been this much fun.

Kurt's reaction that night was very satisfying. His eyes glowed as they swept over Kelley. "You're a vision of loveliness," he proclaimed.

"I'm glad you like it." She spread out the bouffant skirt. "I bought it today."

"It's exquisite and so are you. I'm going to have trouble keeping you all to myself tonight."

"I rather doubt that. I won't know anyone there. You might have to dance with me all evening."

"That's what I'm hoping for." He raised her hand to his lips, charming Kelley with the courtly gesture.

The ballroom of the large hotel was already crowded when they arrived. People were standing in groups around the dance floor, chatting and drinking champagne. It was a glamorous crowd. All the men wore well-cut dinner jackets, and the bejeweled women were dressed in the latest fashions.

"There's Henrietta," Kurt said. "I want you to meet her."

He guided Kelley over to a tall blond woman. She was no longer young, but her face was relatively unlined and her figure was still trim. The black velvet gown she wore was like a jeweler's background for a gorgeous ruby and diamond necklace and matching bracelet. In spite of all this elegance, however, Kelley got the impression that the countess Von Dornberger would be equally at home in jeans and a flannel shirt, sitting astride a horse. She gave Kelley a steady gaze and a firm handshake.

Kurt made the introductions, adding, "Kelley is a countrywoman of yours."

The Countess's eyes lit up. "You're a Texan?"

"No, I'm from California," Kelley answered.

"That's close enough. We must have a long talk about the States sometime soon. I still miss my old hometown."

"Don't you get back for visits?" Kelley asked.

"Not as often as I'd like. Heinrich, my husband, is like a fish out of water on the ranch. Of course it takes an act of parliament to get him to leave his precious rose garden for more than a few days."

"As I mentioned to you, Henrietta has done a magnificent job of restoring the count's ancestral castle and grounds," Kurt said to Kelley.

Henrietta grinned. "Nothing God couldn't have done if he'd had money to work with." Her glance touched on someone in the crowd. "There's Erich. You'll have to excuse me. I must make sure he doesn't simply circle the room and disappear. Erich!" she called, waving to catch his attention.

Kelley's interest quickened as she watched Henrietta greet a tall, broad-shouldered man with high cheekbones and a generous mouth. He was laughing at something and white teeth gleamed in his handsome tanned face, giving him the look of a merry pirate.

"Who is Erich?" she asked.

Kurt's lip curled. "No one you'd care to know."

"Oh? Now I *am* intrigued."

"Don't be. He's bad news to women."

"You're determined to arouse my interest," she said teasingly. "Tell me why he's dangerous."

"Erich is one of those men who think women were put here for his amusement. He uses them and then casts them aside—occasionally with something to remember him by."

"What do you mean?"

"One of his liaisons ended in a paternity suit."

"I see." Kelley's smile faded. The man was handsome enough to beat women off with a stick, but at least he could be responsible.

"Just because he's heir to a huge fortune and inherited the exalted title that goes with it, he thinks he owns the world," Kurt continued resentfully. "The rest of us could be just as sought after if we were born into the right family."

Kelley didn't think money and position were the only keys to Erich's success, but she sensed this wasn't the time to say so. "Your family must be just as noble," she said consolingly. "You have a title, too."

"The difference is, I have the integrity that should go with it. *I* don't treat women as sex objects."

"That's very admirable," Kelley murmured, slanting a glance at Erich.

A beautiful woman was clinging to his arm, gazing up at him adoringly. He wore an amused expression, but he was listening politely. What made wickedness so much more interesting than virtue? Kelley pondered. The man might be a womanizer, but he was devilishly attractive.

Henrietta returned with apologies. "I didn't mean to run off like that, but Erich is a slippery character. He doesn't like these affairs."

Kelley glanced over again to see him in the middle of a group. "He seems to be enjoying himself."

"You'd never know if he wasn't," Henrietta said. "Erich has exquisite manners."

Kurt's expression was darkening by the moment. "Didn't you want to talk to Kelley about the States?" he asked abruptly.

"I'm dying to, but not here. If I don't circulate and speak to everybody, someone's sure to have hurt feelings. Don't ever let yourself get roped into being chairwoman of one of these things," she advised Kelley.

"I'll remember that." Kelley smiled, thinking how unlikely it was.

"Maybe we can talk on Wednesday. I'm having a little luncheon at home. Would you be able to come?"

"I'd be delighted." Kelley accepted happily.

They were joined by a young woman in her early twenties. She was very attractive, with dark blond hair and big brown eyes.

"Lovely party," she said to Henrietta. "You should raise pots of money for the homeless children."

"I certainly hope so. I didn't put in all this effort just to stand around in high heels all night. My feet are killing me already." Henrietta introduced the newcomer as Emmy Rothstein. "She's one of my favorite people, even if she did refuse to serve on my committee."

"I'm hopeless at selling tickets." Emmy turned a laughing face to Kelley. "That's my problem. I'm no good at any kind of work."

"Uh-oh, there's the baroness Manheim," Henrietta said. "I'd better say hello before she gets her nose out of joint."

"If you'll excuse me for just a moment, I must say hello to someone, too." Kurt left them and made his way through the throng toward a stunning brunette.

The woman's scarlet mouth was sulky and her eyes glittered with anger. She barely waited until Kurt reached her before unleashing a torrent of words. Kurt answered at length, evidently trying to placate her.

"Do you know who that woman is?" Kelley asked Emmy.

Emmy hesitated imperceptibly before answering, "Her name is Magda Schiller."

"She appears to be annoyed with Kurt about something," Kelley persisted.

"Yes, well, Magda is a little...volatile. I love your dress." Emmy changed the subject.

"Thanks. I bought it this morning at a little shop on the Ringstrasse."

Emmy smiled. "The stores got rich on this ball. Every woman here had to have a new dress."

"It was a necessity in my case. I just arrived this morning and I didn't bring anything formal with me. I had no idea I'd need it, since I don't know anyone in Vienna."

Emmy gave her a puzzled look. "I got the impression that you were with Kurt."

"I am, but we only met on the plane."

"I see." Emmy looked at her more closely, inspecting the sparkling earrings speculatively.

"He's been awfully nice to me— Everyone has. I really like Henrietta. I'd heard about her of course, but I had no idea she'd be so down-to-earth."

"Yes, she's really special," Emmy said fondly. "Some people think Heinrich married her for her fortune, but that's just plain nonsense. Theirs is a real love match, no matter how ill suited they seem. He likes to putter around at home, and she loves being with people."

"He must have money of his own," Kelley said. "He's a count."

Emmy grinned. "You have a lot to learn about European nobility. Most of them keep up a front by borrowing from Peter to pay Paul."

"Kurt indicated that all his friends lived in castles," Kelley said uncertainly.

"He didn't mention that most of the wings are closed off because they can't afford to heat the place or hire people to clean it."

"You're destroying my illusions," Kelley protested. "I had visions of spacious rooms filled with silver services polished by an army of servants."

"Henrietta's country estate lives up to those expectations. She put central heating and modern plumbing into a thirteenth-century castle, so it combines the best of both worlds."

"These people here tonight certainly *look* affluent." Kelley was reluctant to give up her romantic fantasy.

"Some of them are. I didn't mean to give the impression that everybody is living on the edge. One of our leading citizens, a grand duke named Erich Von Graile Und Tassburg is rolling in money."

"What an impressive name! I caught a glimpse of him," Kelley said. "Kurt says he's a ladies' man."

"If you've seen him, how could you doubt it?" Emmy laughed. "He doesn't have to do much chasing, though. Women are drawn to Erich like flies."

"Did I hear my name?" The subject of their discussion joined them, putting his arm around Emmy and kissing her cheek.

"I was warning Kelley that she'd have to stand in line for you." Emmy introduced them.

Erich kissed Kelley's hand, sending a thrill up her entire arm. She knew it was simply an accepted custom, but the same gesture from Kurt hadn't affected her that way. Even the fleeting touch of Erich's lips felt seductive.

"Don't believe everything you hear about me." His laughing eyes had the brilliance of emeralds. "Very little of it is true."

"If everything they said about you was true, you wouldn't need to own any pajamas," Emmy teased.

"Is that any way for a proper young lady to talk? I'm shocked." He didn't look it.

"I'm only joking," she told Kelley. "Erich is the best friend you could ever have."

"Don't overdo it," he said wryly, slanting an appreciative glance at Kelley. "No man wants a beautiful woman to think he's a saint."

"I can't speak for other women, but I'd be uncomfortable with a saint," she answered demurely.

"I'm glad." A little smile curved his firm mouth as he gazed at her. "A halo would give me a headache."

After glancing from one to the other, Emmy remarked casually, "I think Henrietta needs me."

"Would you care to dance?" Erich asked Kelley when they were alone.

"Well . . . I don't know if I should. I'm here with someone." She looked over to where Kurt was still engaged in earnest conversation.

"Any man who would leave you alone doesn't deserve you."

His invitation was irresistible. "I agree." She gave him a dazzling smile. "I'd love to dance."

When Erich took her in his arms on the crowded floor, Kelley was acutely aware of his lean muscular body. He was a magnificent male in his prime, with the effortless grace of a tiger. The thought of how he'd make love didn't bear dwelling on!

"Isn't this a lovely party?" she asked breathlessly.

"It suddenly got better," he murmured, his lips brushing her temple.

She tilted her head to look up at him. "You don't waste any time, do you?"

"Your date might reclaim you at any moment. Who *is* the lucky fellow?"

"Kurt Ludendorf brought me."

"Have you known him long?" Erich asked neutrally.

"Actually we only met yesterday—on the flight over here. I mentioned that I didn't know anyone in Vienna, and Kurt invited me to the ball. I feel like Cinderella." She laughed.

"If you disappear at midnight, where will I find you?"

"You're supposed to come looking for me."

"Count on it." His hand curved around her neck and a long forefinger stroked the sensitive skin behind her ear.

Kelley steeled herself against the incredibly erotic feeling. "From what I've heard, you don't have to pursue women. It's the other way around."

"Has Kurt been warning you against me?" he asked evenly.

She could tell neither man thought much of the other. "I wouldn't call it a warning," she said carefully. "I could see for myself how popular you are."

He chuckled. "Isn't that a recommendation?"

"If you don't mind being part of a cheering section."

"No sensible man would need one if he had you." His voice was like warm honey.

She could see why Erich was so successful. When a woman was cradled against his splendid body, imagining the limitless pleasure it could bring, she wanted to believe he was sincere. This man was so dangerous he ought to carry a warning label!

"I'd heard Viennese men were charming," she said lightly. "I'm certainly not disappointed."

"I'm glad." His eyes held amusement, as though he'd read her mind. "I wouldn't want to disappoint a lady."

"I'm sure you never have," Kelley answered without thinking.

"I'll be happy to let you judge for yourself," he teased.

"I don't know how I could have said that," she muttered.

"Don't worry about it. Frankness is refreshing. So few women say what they really mean."

"And hardly *any* men."

"I'm one of the minority."

"You'll pardon me if I doubt that," she said skeptically.

"Shall I prove it?" He drew her closer and trailed his fingers down her cheek in a feathery caress. "How's this for honesty? I want very much to make love to you. I'd like to remove that beautiful gown and cover every inch of your delectable body with kisses."

The unnerving thought made Kelley draw in her breath sharply. "You needn't be so graphic."

"I was merely demonstrating my honesty."

"All right, you've made your point," she said uncomfortably. "Evidently I misjudged you."

"You can make up for it by going out with me."

"After the remarks you just made? No, thanks. I'm not interested in becoming another notch on your bedpost."

"Somebody's been giving you the wrong impression of me, and I can guess who it is." Erich's jaw set. "Don't believe everything Kurt tells you."

"He has nothing to do with it. *You* were the one who said you wanted to make love to me."

"A lot of men must have entertained the fantasy. I didn't say I expected to be that fortunate." He smiled. "All I'm asking for is the pleasure of your company."

Kelley felt a little foolish for overreacting. Erich certainly didn't have to force himself on any woman. He was a glamorous, sophisticated man, and she'd be crazy to pass up the invitation. Her highest expectations for this trip hadn't included a date with a grand duke!

"You said you didn't know anyone in Vienna. Let me show you the real city," he coaxed. "Not just the part tourists see."

"You people don't appreciate your city's attractions," she protested. "When I told Kurt I wanted to visit the Vienna Woods, he advised me to go shopping on the Ringstrasse instead."

"How would you like to have lunch on the largest Ferris wheel in the world?"

"You're joking," she answered uncertainly.

"Be ready at noon. We'll start at the Prater amusement park and go from there. Is it a date?"

She laughed delightedly. "How can I refuse lunch on a Ferris wheel?"

"I wish I were the attraction, but I'll settle for whatever I can get. We'll have—" He paused as someone tapped him on the shoulder.

Kurt looked disgruntled. "In case you're not aware of it, the lady is with me."

"Then you owe her an apology." Erich gazed at him with distaste. "A gentleman doesn't abandon his date."

"I didn't! I only— I had to speak to someone for a moment."

"Your priorities are seriously skewed," Erich said caustically.

"It's all right." Kelley moved out of his arms, hoping to avoid a scene.

Erich's expression softened. "Thank you for the dance."

"I enjoyed it," she murmured.

"I'll see you tomorrow. Where are you staying?"

"The Metropole Grande." She didn't look at Kurt.

His reaction was predictable. When they were alone he asked in outrage, "You made a date with Erich after what I told you about him?"

"I don't believe in listening to gossip. He was very pleasant."

"That's what he's known for. Women are so dazzled by his pseudo charm that they're putty in his hands. I suppose he told you he's a grand duke."

"No, he didn't mention it. Someone else told me."

"Don't be taken in by a title," Kurt warned darkly. "You could be very sorry."

"If I were that suspicious I never would have met *you*. How do I know you didn't have some ulterior motive in asking me out tonight?"

"You can't really believe that! My reputation is spotless—unlike some other people. I'm not usually an impetuous man, but I was attracted to you instantly. That was my only reason for wanting to be with you."

"I was only joking, Kurt. I'm really very grateful to you for bringing me. I'm having a wonderful time."

"Starting with your meeting with Erich?" he asked sulkily.

"He offered to take me sightseeing and I accepted," she explained patiently. "That's all there was to it."

"I would have taken you."

"I can't expect to monopolize your time. You've been very kind to me already."

"I hope to see more of you," he murmured. "Will you have dinner with me tomorrow night? Or has Erich beaten me to that, too?"

"He didn't say anything about dinner."

"Good, then we have a date—if that's all right with you."

"It sounds lovely."

Kelley accepted with a small degree of reluctance, which was silly. She had no reason to think Erich would ask her. Besides, Kurt was pleasant, even if he wasn't as nerve tinglingly attractive. All in all, tomorrow was shaping up as quite a day.

Chapter Two

Kelley was glad she'd bought the gray pants suit. It was perfect for her date with Erich, although she had second thoughts the next day about the lace bodysuit. It was semitransparent, and the delicate fabric clung to her breasts and midriff provocatively. Perhaps she'd better change to a nice safe blouse. As she hesitated indecisively, the phone rang.

"I'm in the lobby whenever you're ready," Erich announced.

That settled the matter. Kelley slipped into her jacket and went downstairs.

Erich looked just as elegant in casual clothes as he had in formal attire. The navy cashmere jacket was perfectly tailored to his broad shoulders, and he wore an ascot knotted inside the throat of a pale-blue silk shirt.

He returned her admiring glance. "How lovely you look."

"I was thinking the same thing about you."

Erich laughed. "You're very generous with your compliments."

"I think we've established that I say what I'm thinking," she answered wryly.

"You're a delight. I've never met a completely honest woman before."

"It's probably not a good thing to be. Men like women to be mysterious and unpredictable."

His emerald eyes glowed. "I wouldn't change a single thing about you."

Erich's seductive voice made Kelley's pulse race, even though she knew this was something he did effortlessly. She was careful to seem unmoved. "Hadn't we better be going?"

He glanced at the thin gold watch on his wrist. "We're right on schedule. The wine should be properly chilled by the time we arrive."

"Are we really having lunch on a Ferris wheel? How is that possible?"

"I'm a wizard." He put his arm around her shoulders and led her out of the hotel. "I have the power to make enchanting things happen."

As Kelley gazed into his darkly handsome face, she didn't doubt it for a moment.

The Prater was much more than an amusement park. It was actually an extensive forest right in the city. Scattered throughout the acres of grounds were riding schools, swimming pools and a large stadium where international soccer matches were held.

The famous Reisenrad was different from most Ferris wheels. Instead of open, swinging seats, people rode in boxy little rectangles that resembled miniature train cars.

As many as a dozen passengers could stand at the windows and gaze at the vast panorama of Vienna spread out below.

All of the cars were occupied except the one Erich had reserved. It held two chairs, and a small table covered with a linen tablecloth and set with china and crystal. Champagne cooled in a silver bucket and a large wicker picnic basket sat on a ledge.

Kelley shook her head in amazement. "This is incredible."

"I was going to bring somebody to serve, but I didn't want anyone hovering over us," Erich said.

"Totally unnecessary," she agreed. "I'll put out the food."

"You're my guest." He pulled out a chair for her. "I'll take care of everything."

"That's not exactly your forte. You've been waited on all your life."

"So have you." He opened the champagne and filled her glass.

"What gave you that idea?"

"A number of things." He raised his glass to her in a silent toast.

"Like what?" she persisted curiously.

Erich busied himself setting out the food, two small roasted pheasants, pasta salad studded with mushrooms and sweet red peppers, and flaky croissants.

"There." He placed a wedge of Brie on the table and sat down. "How does that look?"

"Fantastic, but you haven't answered my question. Why do you think I'm part of the privileged class?"

"You dress exquisitely and you carry yourself like a princess." He gave her a melting smile.

His compliments were gratifying, but Kelley had the feeling something more had formed his opinion. "And what else?"

Erich hesitated, then answered reluctantly, "Perhaps your friendship with Kurt. I don't mean to detract from your very real attractions, but he judges people by their supposed importance."

"I realize Kurt is a snob," Kelley said calmly. "But he's made my visit memorable. I can forgive him for not being interested until he found out I got lucky in the lottery."

"You're joking!"

"That's everybody's reaction, but some people do win."

"It must have been a great thrill."

"You have no idea. Two days ago I was a loan officer in a bank, and suddenly I'm hobnobbing with royalty."

"That sounds a lot grander than it really is. A title doesn't automatically mean the bearer is trustworthy."

Kelley laughed. "That's funny. Kurt told me the same thing."

"I never thought I'd say this, but you'd be wise to listen to him."

"He's been a perfect gentleman."

A mischievous smile replaced Erich's frown. "You mean, he never said he'd like to make love to you? That proves he's a fool."

"Or less direct in his approach," she answered dryly.

A little smile curved Erich's firm mouth as he gazed at her. "Would you really want a cautious lover?"

"Actually I'm not looking for any kind," she said lightly.

"One doesn't look for love. It happens spontaneously when a man and a woman are irresistibly attracted to each other."

"You're talking about sex. That's different from love."

"It shouldn't be. When a man holds a woman in his arms and they bring each other exquisite pleasure, it should be a sublime experience, not merely a physical act."

Her entire body warmed in response to the vivid word picture he was painting. Erich would make love divinely. They would merge together until they were one person, throbbing pleasure coursing between them in a fiery stream.

"Surely you agree?"

His voice broke the spell. Kelley drew in her breath sharply. "It isn't something I care to discuss over lunch." She picked up her fork.

"You're right, of course. The subject is more appropriate for dinner." His eyes twinkled.

"The food is delicious," she said determinedly. "Does the amusement park supply it?"

"No, I had my chef prepare it."

"Do you live in Vienna?" Kelley thought it best to take charge of the conversation.

"I have a town house in the city, but I spend quite a lot of time at my country place. It has trees and flowers, even a little stream. I'd like to show it to you."

"I haven't seen Vienna yet."

"We're going to remedy that after lunch. Is there anything special you had in mind?"

"The crown jewels and the Spanish Riding School, for starters."

"You're in luck. They're next door to each other."

Kelley gradually relaxed as they talked about Vienna's many attractions. Nothing controversial was mentioned again, including Kurt's shallow penchant for cultivating celebrities. It occurred to Kelley that she hadn't corrected Erich's impression of her as independently wealthy, but it wasn't important. He had no reason to care, one way or the other.

When they'd finished lunch, Erich repacked everything into the wicker basket, refusing Kelley's offer to help.

"Stand over there by the window and look at the view," he told her. "I haven't given you much of a chance."

Their car was climbing to the very top of the circle, so she had a spectacular view of the city. An ancient cathedral dominated a circular area that included dozens of equally old buildings.

"Tell me what all these places are," she called.

Erich joined her at the window. "The church with the tall spire is St. Stephan's Cathedral. Over there is the Opera House, and to the right is the Hofburg, the imperial palace. That's where we're going."

"Where? I don't see a palace."

"It's that whole group of buildings." He put his arm around her shoulders and turned her in the direction he was pointing. "See?"

"Oh, yes. Is that where the crown jewels are kept?" As she turned her head to look at him, their lips were only inches apart.

For a long moment when time seemed to stand still, they stared at each other. Then Erich's arm tightened and he drew her against his taut body. He lowered his head almost in slow motion and their lips met. It was a sensuous, drugging kiss that sapped Kelley's will to resist. She'd wondered what it would be like, and now she knew. His mouth offered limitless bliss, while his lithe body reinforced the promise.

He lifted his head to gaze into her dazzled eyes. "I've wanted to do that from the minute I saw you. You're utterly enchanting."

Kelley was determined not to overreact this time, even though her heart was racing. "That's quite a compliment, coming from a connoisseur of women."

Erich frowned slightly. "You don't think I'm being sincere?"

"It doesn't really matter. I'm having a wonderful time. You planned this lovely luncheon for me and I appreciate it."

"Is that why you kissed me?"

"No, certainly not!"

"You feel the chemistry between us, too, don't you?" he asked softly.

"You're a very attractive man, Erich, but I'll save you a lot of time and effort. I don't indulge in casual affairs."

"And you're convinced that I do?"

"It's different with men," she explained carefully. "Sexual attraction is enough for them."

"Can I assume from your answer that you *are* attracted to me? Or are you merely trying to soothe my ego?"

"You can assume whatever you like."

"As long as I have your permission, I prefer to hope you'll ignore mean-spirited gossip and find out for yourself what's involved here."

"I wouldn't bet on it," she said tersely.

"I only wager on unimportant things."

A little ripple traveled up Kelley's spine. At that moment, Erich resembled a stalking, green-eyed tiger.

The impression vanished when he gave her a charming smile. "At least there won't be any misunderstandings between us. We both know what we want."

"Or don't want."

"Possibly." He stroked a wisp of hair off her forehead with a caressing touch. "It should be interesting to see which one of us convinces the other."

The Ferris wheel had completed its circle, bringing their car back to the starting gate. Erich picked up the basket and helped Kelley out.

By the time they were settled in his low, racy sports car, the subject was dropped, if not forgotten—at least by Kelley.

Erich wasn't the first man with a slick line who had targeted her and struck out. She was adept at thwarting advances without damaging egos. That was why Kurt's warning had fallen on deaf ears.

Now Kelley was beginning to have second thoughts. Had she met her match? Erich was right about the awesome chemistry between them, but it was more than that for her. He was the kind of man women dream about. Who knew what her response might have been if Erich had expressed an interest in more than a brief fling?

Kelley's poignant regrets were shelved when they reached their destination. The former Imperial Palace was a vast sprawling group of buildings, the oldest parts dating from the thirteenth century. The center section was built in a U-shape around a large plaza called the Josefplatz.

The museum that housed the jewels was located in one corner of the ancient gray stone edifice. It was dimly lit and the entry was stark.

"It doesn't look very palatial," Kelley said tentatively.

"Wait until you get upstairs," Erich answered.

She revised her opinion when they reached the first of a series of rooms containing a dazzling collection of antiquities. One crown was more resplendent than the next. Some were larger than others, but all were set with huge precious stones, many the size of robins' eggs. Rubies, emeralds and sapphires competed with diamonds in brilliance.

Erich smiled at her rapt face. "Do these meet with your expectations?"

"I've never seen anything so magnificent! Look at this one over here." She tugged at his hand.

The glass display cases contained many other priceless objects. There were golden chalices, heavily embroidered ceremonial robes and massive swords in scabbards, all encrusted with precious gems.

Kelley lingered in front of a small gold pitcher studded with rubies. "Just one of these stones would make a spectacular ring."

"Are rubies your favorite?"

She grinned. "I'm partial to them, but I wouldn't turn down that sapphire-and-diamond pendant."

"You like jewelry, don't you?"

"Most women do." Her attention shifted to a white satin robe embroidered with gold flowers centered by pink tourmalines. "Oh, Erich, isn't this elegant?"

Kelley could have lingered over the collection for hours. It deserved more than a cursory look. She realized, however, that he didn't share her fascination.

"Okay, I guess we've seen everything," she said finally. "On to the next attraction—although I don't think anything could top this."

"Wait and see."

The Spanish Riding School was located across the courtyard at the opposite end of the palace. Inside was a cavernous rectangle filled with activity. Men in black jackets and knee boots over white breeches were putting snow-white horses through their paces.

Spectators stood on a second-floor balcony, where they had a sweeping view of the choreographed drill. The beautiful horses arched their necks and sidestepped in intricate routines, following their riders' commands.

"They're like poetry in motion," Kelley exclaimed. "Did you ever see anything so lovely?"

"Only once or twice." Erich's attention was focused on her softly parted lips.

She didn't even hear him. "Those gold bridles are elegant, and look at their long plumy tails. They look like spun silk."

"I was sure you wouldn't be disappointed."

"Today has been a joy from start to finish," she declared.

"It isn't over yet," he murmured.

As Erich was gazing at her, a small boy jostled him. The youngster was trying to climb up on the railing. Erich smiled when he turned and noticed him.

"That's not a very good idea," he said.

"I can't see," the little boy complained.

"I think we can do something about that." Erich lifted the child in his arms. "Is this better?"

"Oh, yes! They're dancing." The boy laughed delightedly, putting one arm around Erich's neck. "Look at that one standing on his hind legs. Why doesn't the man fall off?"

"Because he's holding on with his knees. That's the way you ride a horse."

"Could you teach me how? I want to ride a big white horse like that one."

"First you have to start with a pony," Erich told him. "Then when you get older you'll know how to handle a horse."

"I'm four already," the youngster protested.

"Really? You're a very big boy for your age. I thought you were at least five or six," Erich said with a straight face.

As the child gave him a pleased grin, a young woman rushed up to them. "I've been looking everywhere for you, Emil!" She was torn between relief and anger. "You know you're not supposed to wander off. I'm very cross with you."

The child's lower lip trembled. "I only wanted to see the horses."

"He's a fine young man." Erich interceded tactfully. "We were having an interesting conversation."

The woman smiled ruefully. "Emil is quite a talker. I hope he didn't bother you."

"Not in the slightest." He lowered the boy to the floor. "Mind your mother, Emil, and remember to grip with your knees."

Kelley was surprised by Erich's genuine interest in the small child. It was a side of him she never would have suspected. "You really like children, don't you?" she asked slowly.

"They're wonderful. I appreciate their directness. They never say anything they don't mean—unlike adults."

"We can't always be brutally frank. A lot of hurt feelings would result."

"I suppose so, but it's a pity."

As they walked toward the exit Kelley asked casually, "Have you ever wanted to have children of your own?"

"I intend to someday. Several, I hope."

"When you find the proper wife and are ready to settle down?"

He frowned slightly. "I'm not sure I know what you mean by proper."

Kelley realized she was on shaky ground. Erich didn't know she knew about his paternity suit. He would be angry at Kurt for telling her, and she wasn't proud of listening to gossip.

"I meant someone with a noble lineage like yours," she said hastily.

"Loveless marriages are a thing of the past, thank God."

"You intend to marry for love?"

"It's the only reason."

"You must have a lot of fun looking for it," she commented cynically.

As they walked outside Erich said evenly, "I don't dangle the promise of marriage as an incentive to get what I want, if that's what you're implying."

Kelley knew she should back off, but she couldn't. Erich seemed so flawless in every other respect. Why did he deny his own child? "Even if marriage wasn't implied, it still seems to me two people should share a responsibility."

He stopped and looked at her directly. "What's this all about, Kelley? What are you accusing me of?"

"Nothing," she mumbled, regretting her impulsiveness. Erich's private life was none of her business. "I was simply speaking in generalities."

"I don't think so. Somebody has been poisoning your mind against me and it's not difficult to guess who. What did Kurt tell you? About the paternity suit?"

"Well . . . he sort of mentioned it."

"I'll bet! Did he also tell you it was dropped? In case you think I applied pressure, my only coercion was to ask for a blood test. I hadn't seen the lady in months. She knew I wasn't the father." His face set in stern lines.

"I'm sorry," Kelley faltered. "I shouldn't have brought it up."

"Why not, since you were thinking it?" He jammed balled fists into his pockets. "It's difficult to defend myself without sounding like a cad, but when you're wealthy you become a window of opportunity for people seeking status and security. Men don't enjoy being used any more than women do. How would you like to wonder if someone really cares about you or simply wants to be the next Grand Duchess Von Graile Und Tassburg?''

"That's quite a mouthful." She smiled. "I doubt if it would fit on a credit card."

"You wouldn't think it was so funny if you were in a similar situation," he said grimly.

"I have a simple solution for you—date only women who already have their own titles."

His expression softened. "If I did that, I'd never have gotten to know *you.*"

Kelley had an uneasy twinge. Would Erich be as trusting if he knew she wasn't independently wealthy? "You don't really know anything about me," she said hesitantly.

"I'm looking forward to finding out." His warm tone suddenly cooled. "Unless you still believe I refuse to acknowledge my own child."

"No, I'm sure you wouldn't do such a thing." She was thoroughly convinced. Erich loved children. He would cherish his own child, legitimate or not.

"I'm glad we cleared that up. I don't pretend to be a saint. I'm a mature man, not a schoolboy. But I've had caring relationships, not tawdry affairs. And when they were over we parted as friends. I've tried never to hurt anyone."

Kelley was sure that was his intent, but it would be difficult to walk away from a man like him unscathed. Once a woman had been the center of his universe—however briefly—could any other man ever measure up? It was too big a risk to take. Erich admitted his relationships didn't last.

"I appreciate your honesty," she said soberly.

His smile returned. "See how much we have in common?"

She glanced at her watch without answering. "Goodness, I had no idea it was so late."

"That's because you couldn't drag yourself away from the jewels," he teased. "Where would you like to go next?"

"I'm afraid I have to go back to the hotel."

"I thought we'd have dinner together."

"I'm sorry, but I already have a dinner date." She really did regret it, but it was too late now.

"With Kurt, I presume?"

"Yes."

"Make sure you take your credit card," Erich said contemptuously. "He has a way of forgetting his wallet."

"I'm sure Kurt wouldn't do a thing like that on purpose," she protested.

"He thrives on trusting women like you."

"I realize there's no love lost between you, but don't you think that's a little unworthy of you?" she asked impatiently.

"I don't like fortune hunters—female *or* male."

"What are you talking about? Kurt is a baron."

"The two aren't mutually exclusive."

"I don't understand. I just naturally assumed he was well-off. I mean, he knows all the people you do, and he mentioned a family castle. Maybe we have different definitions of wealth."

"Europe is filled with impoverished nobility. They're anachronisms from a bygone era. Some of them find jobs and get on with their lives. Others—like Kurt—wheel and deal, hoping to strike it rich off somebody else's labors."

"You think he expects *me* to replenish his fortune?" Kelley laughed, picturing how disappointed Kurt would be if he knew the truth.

"I'm sure his interest in you is exactly what it seems. Even Kurt lets his emotions take over once in a while." Erich gave her an admiring look. "You're enough to make any man forget about the mortgage payments."

"Can you really take out a mortgage on a castle? What would you do with it if you had to foreclose? I don't imagine many people are in the market for a fifty-room fixer upper."

"You've pinpointed the problem. A lot of nobles in straitened circumstances can't afford to maintain the old homestead, not to mention heating and staffing it. Mostly they live in just a few rooms, warming themselves on memories of former glory."

"Emmy Rothstein told me the same thing, but I didn't believe her. That's really sad."

"It's worse than that, it's unrealistic," Erich said impatiently. "You have to live in the present."

"Aren't you being a little unfeeling? Your ancestors managed their resources wisely—or maybe they were just lucky. You don't know what it's like to be poor. Maybe you'd try to hang on, too."

"Not passively. I'd go out and get a job, and I'd work like the devil to succeed through my own efforts. I can't imagine sitting still and waiting for somebody to hand me something."

She could believe it. Even strolling along slowly as they were doing, Erich's lean body had a leashed energy, like that of an athlete's, eager to compete. He would never have anything to worry about.

"Everybody doesn't have your drive or your ability," she said quietly.

His intensity was replaced with a grin. "You're too credulous. How do you know I'm good at anything except making love?"

"I'll even have to take your word for that," she answered lightly.

"Not necessarily. My offer is good anytime."

"I'll keep that in mind. Now, I really must get back."

"All right, if you're determined to spend a dull evening." They'd reached his car and he held the door open for her. "Where is Kurt taking you?"

"I don't know and I wouldn't tell you if I did. You'd do something irresponsible, like telling the management Kurt intended to skip out without paying the check."

Erich's face was thoughtful as he pulled away from the curb. "I never thought of that one."

"Don't," she ordered.

He slanted a glance at her. "You really like him, don't you?"

"He's been very nice to me—for whatever reason. If it weren't for Kurt I'd have spent today sightseeing all alone and I'd be facing a solitary dinner someplace mediocre. This trip is more than I ever hoped for, and I owe it all to Kurt."

"Okay, honey, I understand." Erich reached out and squeezed her hand. "I hope tonight lives up to your expectations."

When they pulled up in front of her hotel she attempted to thank him for the eventful day, but he cut her off.

"You couldn't have had as good a time as I did." He leaned over and kissed her cheek.

Kelley walked slowly across the lobby, feeling slightly deflated. After making a big play for her all afternoon, Erich hadn't said anything about seeing her again. Was this

his usual line, or did he think she was more interested in Kurt? If so, he certainly gave up easily.

As she showered and dressed, Kelley tried to tell herself it was for the best. Erich was exciting to be with—maybe *too* exciting. She could quite conceivably fall in love with him, and that would be disastrous. Erich was the unattainable dream. It was much wiser to remember their day together as one perfect episode in her life.

Kelley's self-esteem was bolstered by Kurt's reaction when he arrived for their date. His admiring gaze paid tribute to her lovely face and slim figure. She had on the gold embroidered white dress and the pearl earrings.

"You look stunning, as usual." He kissed her hand.

"I'm going to find it difficult to go home." She smiled. "The men I know aren't nearly as courtly."

"Then why go home? Stay here and share in our traditions." He clasped both of her hands between his.

"I'm having such a wonderful time, I might just do that," she said lightly, extricating her hands.

"You spent the day with Erich, didn't you? Is he the reason for your 'wonderful time'?" Kurt stressed the two words sarcastically.

"Certainly not the only one."

"But he's part of it," Kurt persisted.

She controlled her mounting irritation, keeping her voice neutral. "We had an interesting day."

"Where did he take you? To one of his private clubs, I presume."

"No, we went to see the crown jewels and then to the Spanish Riding School." Kelley didn't know why she omitted mentioning lunch on the Ferris wheel. Because it had been so sexually charged?

"He doesn't have much imagination," Kurt sneered.

"They were places I wanted to see."

"Erich is certainly a fast worker. He managed to brainwash you in only one day."

"What makes you say that?"

"You don't want to hear any criticism of him."

"You're not exactly a reliable source," she answered coolly. "You told me about the paternity suit against Erich, but you didn't mention it was dropped for lack of evidence."

"He probably paid the woman off," Kurt said dismissively.

"Do you know that for a fact?"

"Well, no, but it would be easy for him to do. He can surely afford it."

The bitterness in Kurt's voice convinced her that arguing with him was a waste of time. He was so eaten up by jealousy of Erich that he didn't want to hear the truth.

"Correct me if I'm wrong, but I thought you asked me out to dinner," she said crisply. "I didn't get all dressed up to stand around a hotel lobby, speculating on someone else's love life."

"I'm sorry." Kurt was instantly contrite. "I know how attractive Erich is to women. I guess I just wanted reassurance that I'm still in the running."

Kelley's annoyance faded. Poor Kurt. It must be humiliating to realize he couldn't compete. "I wouldn't be here if I didn't like you," she said gently.

"You won't regret it, I promise! We have resèrvations at the best restaurant in Vienna. I want this night to be special."

"I'm sure it will be," she replied politely.

The restaurant was everything Kurt had promised. Haughty waiters presided over tables set with china and an array of wineglasses. A busboy filled their water goblets, and a sommelier with a gold chain around his neck presented Kurt with an extensive wine list.

When they were finally alone, Kurt leaned forward and looked deeply into Kelley's eyes. "I've been looking forward to this all day. I finally have you all to myself."

"The ball last night was nice, too," she said brightly. "I especially enjoyed meeting Henrietta."

"I thought you would. She's one of the most influential women in town. Henrietta can really launch you into society if she likes you."

"It's too bad her husband doesn't enjoy going to all the events with her."

"If you lived in a castle like his, you might not want to leave it, either. Henrietta scoured Europe for the best craftsmen to restore the place."

"You have a castle, too, don't you?" Kelley asked in a casual tone.

"Nothing like theirs."

"Is yours livable?"

"Well, most of it is closed off. I only use a few of the rooms when I go down there. It's much too big for one person," he added hastily.

So what she'd heard was true. "I suppose it costs a fortune to restore those ancient places."

"It's worth it, though. You should see what can be done inside. My drawing room has windows fourteen feet tall, and the inlaid floor was copied from a duke's palace." His face was alive with animation.

"So, you've restored your castle, too."

"Well, more or less. It still needs a little work, but I'm waiting until I have someone to share it with me." He slanted a glance at her. "A man gets awfully lonely rattling around by himself. I'd like to see the rooms filled with children.''

"Growing up in a castle must be great fun," Kelley mused. "All those rooms to play hide-and-seek in.''

"I knew you felt the same as I did!'' He reached across the table and gripped her hand. "I felt the irresistible attraction between us the minute I sat down next to you on the plane.''

That wasn't the way Kelley remembered it. She withdrew her hand. "We scarcely know each other, Kurt. Don't you think you're being a trifle premature?''

"I know it's too soon, but I'm afraid you might get restless and move on without ever knowing how I feel.''

"I'm not going anywhere for the present. I love what I've seen of Vienna and I want to see more.''

"I'll show you all of it," Kurt declared fervently.

"Right now I'd like to see a menu. I'm starved.''

Kelley worked so hard to keep the conversation general that she couldn't appreciate the truly excellent food. Kurt seized every opportunity to advance his cause during a very long, multicourse dinner. They were having dessert when she brushed her hair back wearily and discovered she was missing an earring.

"Damn," she muttered. "I lost one of my earrings, and I just bought them yesterday.''

"Maybe it's on the floor." Kurt lifted the tablecloth and peered underneath.

Kelley stood and inspected the area around her chair with an equal lack of success. "I'm afraid it's gone. I could have lost it anywhere between here and the hotel.''

"I'm so sorry. They looked expensive.''

"I never paid that much for earrings," she said wryly.

"Perhaps you can have the other one copied.''

"It's no big deal. I'll just buy another pair.''

"That's the right attitude. You shouldn't deny yourself anything you really want."

"I've never had the resources before, but I must admit I enjoy spending money."

"As long as you have it, why not?"

The waiter appeared at their table. "Can I bring you anything else, sir?"

Kurt looked inquiringly at Kelley. "Would you like to have an after dinner drink here, or go somewhere else?"

"Truthfully, I'm a little tired. Could I have a rain check?"

"Of course. How about lunch tomorrow, and then we'll go sightseeing?"

"Thanks, but Henrietta invited me to a luncheon."

"I'd forgotten about that. Did she say who else is coming?"

"No. I wouldn't know any of them anyway."

"Henrietta's luncheon invitations are really sought after. You're bound to meet important people."

"I'd rather they'd be interesting." She glanced at her watch. "Would you mind taking me home now, Kurt? It's been a long day."

"Certainly." He signaled for the check. "You'll have to tell me all about the luncheon. How about dinner tomorrow night?"

"I'm still feeling the effects of jet lag. Why don't we make it another time? Give me a call," she said vaguely. Kelley felt a little guilty, but Kurt wasn't very stimulating company. She wasn't keen on seeing him two nights in a row.

He looked at her reproachfully. "Did Erich monopolize all your time?"

"He has nothing to do with it. I don't even expect to see him again."

Kurt looked gratified. "You're showing good judgment. Erich pours on the charm, but his interest in a woman never lasts."

That brief period leaves lasting memories, though, Kelley thought wistfully.

Chapter Three

When Kelley was alone in her hotel room she halfway regretted her excuse about being tired. Vienna was supposed to have extensive nightlife. If only Kurt wasn't so dull! All that talk about his titled friends was terribly boring, and his ridiculous attempts at courtship weren't any better.

Kelley sighed and kicked off her shoes. As she reached for her zipper, the phone rang.

"Oh, no!" she muttered. "What more can he possibly have to say?" It wasn't Kurt's voice that greeted her, however.

"I thought you'd be home early." Erich sounded smug.

Kelley felt a jolt of excitement that she tried to keep from showing. "It isn't early. It's almost eleven."

"The best part of the evening. Where would you like to go?"

"To bed," she answered curtly. The nerve of the man! After dropping her off today without a word about seeing her again, he just assumed she'd be waiting with open arms!

"That would be my first choice, too," he said softly.

"I meant *alone.*"

"That's no fun." He chuckled. "If you don't want me to join you, let's go dancing. At least I can hold you in my arms."

"Is that all you ever think of?"

He laughed outright. "No harm ever came from using your imagination. Shall I come up and get you?"

"No!"

"All right, I'll meet you by the elevator."

"I don't know if it's an ethical thing to do," she said hesitantly. "I told Kurt I was tired."

"Okay, we won't go dancing. We'll go to the casino instead."

She fought a losing battle with her conscience. "I'll be right down."

Erich's eyes lit up when Kelley got off the elevator. "You look more beautiful every time I see you."

"I'll have to go shopping again tomorrow. This is the last of my new wardrobe. All the things I brought with me are strictly utilitarian."

"You'd look lovely in anything," he said fondly.

"You might not say that if you saw me in jeans and a sweatshirt."

"With a figure like yours, you'd look sexy in a burlap bag."

"Wouldn't you be shocked if I turned up in one?" she teased.

"I'm not easily shocked." A little smile curved his firm mouth. "Feel free to act out all your fantasies with me."

Kelley's blood warmed as she remembered a few she'd had involving him. "I'll consider it," she answered lightly.

The casino was filled with well-dressed men and women sitting or standing around green felt tables. They were concentrating fiercely on cards or dice or the little white ball clattering around a wheel.

"Everybody looks so serious," Kelley remarked. "I thought gambling was supposed to be fun."

"It is, if you win." Erich grinned. "What's your pleasure?"

"I'd like to try roulette if the stakes aren't too high. It seems so continental."

"Whatever pleases you." He pulled out a chair for her at one of the roulette tables. Taking the chair next to hers, he handed the croupier some bills and said something in German.

Until now everyone Kelley had met had spoken English when they found out she didn't understand German. Evidently the croupier wasn't bilingual.

"What did you say to him?" she asked Erich.

"I just told him to give us some chips." He put two stacks in front of her.

"How much are they?"

"It's all taken care of."

"I have to know how much I'm betting," she insisted.

"Don't worry about it. We're partners. We'll split our winnings."

"I'm worried about losing, not winning."

"You have to get your bet down before you can do either one."

Erich was placing chips all over the board. Just before the whirling ball settled into a slot, Kelley put one chip on number sixteen.

"Thirty-five red, the winner." The croupier pointed to the numbered square and swept all the other chips in front of him. Then he paid off the winners, not including Kelley or Erich.

"That wasn't a lot of fun." She grumbled. "In the movies, everybody wins a fortune."

Erich laughed. "Welcome to the real world."

Kelley continued to bet one chip at a time while he distributed his all over the table. He usually won something on every spin, but luck eluded her. Finally she hit a number, then another one. Suddenly she had stacks of chips in front of her, and Erich had even more.

"Why don't we quit while we're ahead?" she suggested.

"You're not the last of the big-time gamblers, are you?" he teased.

"I agree with whoever said, winning isn't everything, but losing is for the birds. Or something like that."

"Okay, honey." Erich shoved their chips forward and received a sheaf of bills in exchange. He handed them to Kelley.

"It's your money," she objected. "You paid for the chips."

"I want you to have it," he said, leading her away from the table.

"At least take back your investment."

To appease her, he reluctantly took one bill, although she'd seen him pay more than that. Kelley took a closer look at the money in her hand and made a rapid mental calculation.

"How much did those chips cost?" she asked suspiciously.

"Does it matter?" He guided her into a small cocktail lounge that was relatively quiet. "Let's have a drink."

Kelley refused to be distracted. "That's why you spoke to the croupier in German, isn't it? You didn't want me to know what we were playing for."

"I thought we might as well make it interesting." He seated her and signaled for a waiter.

"How much was each chip worth?" she asked adamantly.

"Five hundred A.S.," he replied unwillingly. That meant Austrian schillings.

"You're joking! We could have lost a fortune!"

"But we didn't." He grinned. When Erich saw she was really upset, he took both of her hands. "I realize you've probably had to be frugal all your life, but you shouldn't give money undue importance."

"That's easy for you to say. You've always been able to do anything you want."

"So can you, now. Indulge yourself. Buy a castle in Spain, endow a wing of a university. It's a great feeling."

"We need to talk, Erich," she said carefully. "There's something you don't know about me."

"There are a lot of things, and I want to hear all of them—where you grew up, what your hobbies are. Do you have any brothers and sisters?"

"I have one brother. He and my parents live in North Dakota, so I don't get to see them as often as I'd like."

"Why did you leave North Dakota?"

"When I graduated from college I wanted more excitement than our little town had to offer, so I went to Los Angeles, the glamour capital of the country."

"And did you find what you were looking for?"

She smiled wryly. "I could have gotten the same dull job in North Dakota. Being a loan officer in a bank isn't exactly challenging."

"Why did you stay?"

"I'm an incurable optimist. I kept hoping one day something magical would happen."

"And it did."

"Well, yes, in a way." She hesitated, looking for the right words to explain how a misunderstanding had occurred. She didn't want Erich to think she'd deceived him on purpose.

He didn't give her a chance to continue. "I've always believed if you want something badly enough you'll get it."

"Not necessarily," she murmured, gazing at his handsome face.

"*You* did."

"Yes, but I didn't specifically wish I'd win the lottery. It just happened out of the blue."

"That's the way momentous events occur. Like seeing you across a crowded ballroom."

"Don't pretend you were wishing to meet someone."

"In our case it was fate." He leaned forward and touched her cheek in a feathery caress. "Whether you're ready to admit it or not, we were meant to be."

His deep voice wove a spell around her. Kelley felt her defenses crumbling. She wanted to feel his mouth on hers, his arms molding her to that hard body.

Using great willpower, she leaned back in her chair. "It's very late and I have to get up early in the morning. We'd better go."

Erich didn't try to change her mind, but when they were in the car he said, "There is one more place I want to show you. It's especially beautiful in the moonlight."

"I've seen so many things today. I don't know if I can do full justice to anything else."

"I guarantee you'll be charmed."

In the middle of the city, across from a large hotel, was a park. Giant trees shaded a path that wound past flower beds, their vibrant colors muted in the pale light.

As they walked down the path Kelley asked tentatively, "Wouldn't it be prettier in the daylight?"

"Not what I'm going to show you."

They entered a clearing where a graceful statue of a musician stood under an archway decorated with stone cherubs. He had a violin tucked under his chin and a bow in his raised right hand. In the shifting moonlight he seemed almost alive, a joyous figure playing for pure pleasure.

"You're right, it *is* charming," she exclaimed. "Who is he?"

"Johann Strauss. I always think he embodies Vienna's musical heritage."

Kelley swayed back and forth. "I think I can hear the music."

"May I have this dance?" Erich bowed, then took her in his arms and whirled her around in a waltz, humming the melody.

She laughed delightedly. "What a perfect ending to a wonderful day."

His pace slowed and he drew her closer. "It doesn't have to end."

Kelley tensed. "Don't spoil everything, Erich."

"That's the last thing I want to do." His lips slid down her cheek to the corner of her mouth. "I want to make you happy."

"*Me,* or yourself?"

"A man who doesn't think first of his partner isn't much of a man." His hands moved over her back while he nibbled delicately on her earlobe.

"Don't do that," she said weakly, raising her shoulder to dislodge his tormenting mouth.

"How about this?" His lips brushed tantalizingly across hers. "Can I do this?"

She gripped his shoulders, gazing up at him wordlessly. Kelley knew this was the moment to call a halt, but she couldn't. Her entire body ached for him.

Erich's eyes glittered as he lowered his head and parted her lips. That was too much to resist. With a sigh of surrender, she twined her arms around his neck and returned his kiss fervently.

Uttering a low sound of satisfaction at her response, his embrace tightened. She was welded to his taut frame, made aware of every hard, straining muscle.

"My beautiful, passionate Kelley." Erich dragged his mouth away and strewed kisses over her rapt face. "I want to make love to you a hundred different ways."

She quivered when his hand cupped her breast and his mouth possessed hers once more. Any doubts were swept away by his probing tongue and enflaming hands. She was like a finely tuned instrument, responding to an expert musician's touch.

Erich was the one who finally drew away. Framing her face between his palms he said softly, "You won't have any regrets, I promise."

His words sounded a faint warning in her drugged brain, and when they walked out of the park and a car screeched to a halt at a red light, sanity returned. She was like a sleepwalker awakening from a dream. How had she allowed this to happen?

Erich had his arm around her shoulders. "My house is just a short drive from here."

Kelley moved out of his embrace. "I'm not going with you," she mumbled. "Please take me back to my hotel."

"That's not what you really want." He turned her to face him. "You want me as much as I want you."

"That has nothing to do with it. I explained how I feel about casual sex."

"Is that how you'd describe the way we felt about each other just now?"

"You're very expert at arousing a woman," she answered carefully. "I'd heard that, and you lived up to your reputation."

"Are you saying I attempted to seduce you?" he asked evenly.

"I don't know what else to call it. You knew I didn't want to go to bed with you."

"That wasn't the impression I got," he answered sardonically. "My mistake was in wanting a lovely, meaningful experience, not a quick tumble on the grass."

"Don't be crude." She turned away to hide her burning cheeks, knowing Erich was right. He could have taken her and she would have complied eagerly.

"I'm sorry," he said more gently.

"I'm sorry, too. I wasn't leading you on," she said in a small voice.

"I know that." He put his arms around her and pulled her rigid body close. "We both felt the same magic, that's the pity of it. But someday you're going to stop denying yourself and follow your instincts." He stroked her long hair. "When you do, I'll be waiting."

"You're not angry?" she murmured.

"Disappointed, not angry. I'm a big boy."

Erich bore as much resemblance to a boy as a telephone did to a tom-tom! In spite of knowing she'd made the right decision, Kelley felt an aching regret.

"Come on, I'll take you home," he said.

Kelley undressed listlessly, facing the fact that Erich was gone for good. It had to be this way. If they'd continued to see each other, it would only be a matter of time until she gave in. And then she'd feel even worse when he walked away.

"Tomorrow I'll go out and buy a whole new wardrobe," she announced to her reflection in the mirror. "Erich was right about one thing. I should learn to be less frugal."

Only then did Kelley remember she'd never gotten around to telling him the truth about her lottery winnings. Well, it didn't matter anymore.

In spite of her late night, Kelley didn't sleep much. She was up and out early, shopping for something to wear to Henrietta's luncheon that day.

The saleswoman greeted her cordially, although she raised an eyebrow at Kelley's jeans and sweatshirt. "What may I show you today? Some tailored pants, perhaps?"

Kelley hid her amusement. "I'm really looking for a suit or a simple dress. Something to wear to a luncheon."

"I have some lovely things to show you," the woman promised.

For the next hour Kelley tried on clothes for every occasion—pants, dresses, accessories. Since she was a true six, everything fit perfectly. It was difficult to choose between all of the wonderful outfits.

"Please don't show me anything else," she finally pleaded weakly. "I've already spent more than I planned to."

"You've assembled a versatile wardrobe, though. The white jacket will go over either a skirt or pants, and the gray skirt can be worn with the lace bodysuit you bought the other day. That means you don't need this pink blouse." The saleswoman took back the least expensive garment. "Shall I show you our ball gown collection now? We just got in some stunning things."

"I don't have time," Kelley said firmly. "I'll take the gray skirt with me and you can send the rest of the things to my hotel."

As she left the shop, Kelley realized she'd been too busy all morning to think about Erich—which was a good sign. In time, she'd forget the deep masculine sound of his voice, and the way his superb body moved so effortlessly.

Shaking her head to dislodge the disturbing memories, she hurried back to the hotel to change for lunch.

Henrietta's city residence was a beautifully furnished town house. A uniformed maid admitted Kelley and directed her to the drawing room. A babble of female voices told her it was a larger gathering than she'd expected.

As Kelley paused uncertainly on the threshold, Henrietta came to greet her. "So nice to see you again, my dear," the older woman said. "I'm glad you could make it."

"I'm delighted to be here. Your home is lovely," Kelley remarked politely.

"It's sure a far cry from Texas." Henrietta grinned. "Come on, I'll introduce you around."

There were about twenty women in the room, and Henrietta led her from group to group. After the first five or six introductions, Kelley gave up trying to remember all the names. Before they'd completed a circuit of the room, Henrietta was called to the telephone.

She beckoned to a butler carrying a tray of glasses. "Have some champagne and make yourself at home," she told Kelley. "I'll be right back."

Kelley took a glass and wandered over to a window, where she studied the gracious room. It was very formal. Couches and chairs were covered in expensive damask, and the silk covered walls were decorated with heavy gold framed oil paintings and crystal sconces.

Emmy Rothstein joined her. "You look a little dazed. These charity luncheons have that effect on me, too." She grinned.

"I didn't know this was a fund-raiser," Kelley said.

"Don't worry, Henrietta has too much class to pass the hat. She uses these things to browbeat women into serving on her committees."

"That couldn't be why she invited *me.*"

"Me, either," Emmy said. "She's given up on me."

"Then why are we here?"

"Consider yourself lucky. You're in the select group of people Henrietta likes."

"She doesn't really know me."

"You have a slight edge." Emmy smiled. "You're an American. Henrietta has made a comfortable life for herself here, but she still misses her own country."

"It must be difficult to give up your old friends and move to a foreign country," Kelley observed.

Emmy's merry face sobered. "Sometimes you don't have a choice."

"How could that be? With her fortune she could do anything she wanted. Besides, you told me Henrietta married for love."

"She did. She's one of the fortunate ones."

Their hostess joined them. "I'm sorry I had to run off. Heinrich always finds it easier to phone me than to look for something himself. I'm glad Emmy's taking care of you."

"Don't be." Emmy laughed. "I was telling Kelley how you twist everyone's arm in the name of charity."

"Only the ones who can afford it." Henrietta gave her a speculative look. "When is your rich boyfriend coming to town again?"

"Don't count on Stavros for a donation. He expects a tangible reward for his money." Emmy's smile was a little strained.

The older woman gazed at her shrewdly. "That always tells me something about a person."

Emmy changed the subject. "I was surprised to see Erich at the ball the other night. What did you threaten him with to make him attend?"

"Erich is a pussycat if you know how to handle him."

Emmy laughed. "A lot of women would pay a fortune for that information. You met him, Kelley. Isn't he gorgeous?"

"He's quite nice," Kelley replied tepidly.

"That's the word that describes him," Henrietta said. "Everyone thinks he's a Don Juan, but it isn't Erich's fault that women make fools of themselves over him."

Kelley couldn't let that pass. "I imagine he does his share of the pursuing," she said coolly.

Henrietta shrugged. "He's a man, isn't he? They're born with the hunting instinct. I must say Erich is more honorable than a lot of men, though. I've never known him to take advantage of anybody. The woman who finally ropes that maverick will be one lucky lady."

"I can't imagine Erich ever settling down with one woman," Emmy commented.

"They all get tired of the dating game eventually. He'll pick somebody with a suitable title and they'll produce a lot of little dukes and duchesses. That's the accepted thing to do."

"*You* didn't have a title," Kelley blurted out.

"In my case, it didn't matter. Heinrich already had children to carry on the bloodline."

Kelley didn't care to hear any speculation about Erich's future bride. "Do you have children of your own?" she asked quickly.

"Three big strappin' boys. One of them runs the ranch down home."

"Henrietta always gets her drawl back when she talks about Texas," Emmy teased.

"I have to keep in practice." The older woman smiled. "Folks can hardly understand me when I come to town. Are the Texas Rangers hot this year?" she asked Kelley.

A maid approached. "Cook said to tell you luncheon is served, Countess."

"Wouldn't you know it?" Henrietta sighed. "Just when we were getting around to the interesting stuff. Oh well, we'll talk later." She went to round up the other guests.

The dining room was as elegant as the living room. A tremendous crystal chandelier hung from the ceiling, and the tall French windows were elaborately draped with a richly woven fabric. Floral arrangements were spaced every three feet down the center of an antique mahogany table that extended almost the length of the room. On the polished surface, embroidered linen place mats held an array of heavy sterling flatware and crystal goblets.

"I hope we're sitting together," Kelley told Emmy as they scanned the white place cards displayed on small Lalique easels.

Emmy grinned impishly. "If we're not, I'll switch the cards." She didn't have to. Their seats were next to each other.

"If this is luncheon, I wonder what her dinners are like," Kelley murmured.

"Everybody reclines on couches while beautiful maidens pop grapes in their mouths," Emmy joked.

"It wouldn't surprise me a bit."

White-gloved waiters were circling the table, serving dark green acorn squashes on small china plates. As Kelley was wondering what to do with hers, the waiter removed the top. Steam rose from the sherried consomme inside.

"Can you imagine scooping out all these squashes?" Kelley exclaimed. "No, of course you can't. You probably don't even know where your kitchen is located."

"Don't be too sure. Not all of us live like Henrietta."

"Very few people do. But you and I still come from different worlds. I work for a living."

"You're fortunate." It wasn't a polite comment. Emmy's voice vibrated with suppressed emotion. "I wish I knew how to do something useful."

"What would you like to do?"

"I don't know. Like most of my friends, I was never trained for anything."

"You could go back to school and learn a profession."

"It would take too long, and I couldn't expect to be successful in the foreseeable future." Emmy's soft mouth drooped.

Kelley felt slightly impatient with her. "That's a defeatist attitude. If you're not happy with your life, change it."

"I'm considering it." Emmy fiddled with her spoon. "I'll probably get married."

"You don't seem too enthusiastic over the prospect," Kelley commented. "Maybe you'd better give it more thought."

"I have to make a decision. Stavros won't wait much longer."

Kelley paused until the waiter had removed their soup. "Is he the rich boyfriend Henrietta mentioned?"

Emmy nodded. "Stavros Theopolis. He's a Greek shipping tycoon."

"He must be quite a bit older than you," Kelley said slowly, slanting a glance at her.

"I'm twenty-one." Emmy answered the unspoken question. "Stavros is fifty-three."

"That's old enough to be your—" Kelley stopped abruptly.

Emmy gave her a sardonic smile. "There are compensations. He's very rich."

"I see," Kelley murmured as the waiter served plates containing individual vol-au-vents filled with lobster thermidor.

"No, you don't," Emmy answered. "You're like all Americans. You think anyone with a title is wealthy."

"I didn't even know you had a title."

"Baroness Emmy Marlene Rothstein." Her voice held mockery. "It's the lowest rung on the ladder, but it means something to my parents."

"I thought a baron was higher than a count."

"It's the other way around. Not that any of it matters today except to the old guard."

"We don't have titles in America, so all of them sound glamorous to me."

"You wouldn't think it was so glamorous if you had to scrabble around every month to make ends meet," Emmy answered tersely.

Her parents must belong to the impoverished group Erich had talked about. But Emmy seemed so levelheaded. Would she really marry for money?

Kelley chose her words carefully. "I'm sure it's not easy to give up things you're used to, but you have options. Even if you've never worked before, you could get some kind of job. There's a sense of satisfaction in knowing you can support yourself."

"Don't you think I know that? I'd kill for the chance to work at any sort of job and make it on my own!" Emmy's cheeks were flushed with intensity.

"Then why on earth don't you?"

Emmy's passion died. "Do you have parents?"

"Yes, of course."

"What does your father do?"

"He's a high school science teacher."

"Do they have a home they've lived in for a long time?"

"My brother and I grew up in it." Kelley smiled reminiscently. "They bought it when Mother was pregnant with Stan. It's a little too big for them now that we're both gone, but I don't think they'll ever move. Their roots are there."

"Then you should understand how *my* parents feel about a home that's been in their family for centuries."

"In a way I can, but it's not the same thing. A castle takes tremendous upkeep. Wouldn't they be better off living in a comfortable apartment instead of an old place that's crumbling around them?"

"Not when it would mean admitting to their friends that they were bankrupt."

"*Friends* would be sympathetic," Kelley said pointedly.

"You really don't understand. Keeping up appearances is very important to the older aristocrats. Society forgives everything except failure," Emmy said mockingly.

"So you intend to shore up the family fortunes by sacrificing your own future. Do you think your parents would want you to do that?"

Emmy concentrated on her plate, although she'd barely touched her lunch. "They think Stavros will be a steadying influence on me."

Kelley was appalled. Emmy's parents were willing to sacrifice her for some outdated traditions that didn't mean diddly squat today. And she was so brainwashed that she was letting them get away with it!

"What they think isn't the point. You're the one who's going to pay the price. How do *you* feel about marrying a man older than your own father?"

Emmy didn't answer directly. "Could you refuse to give your parents another chance? I'm their only hope. My father went through his inheritance because he has no head for business. All they have left is pride. If I don't help, they'll grow more and more hopeless."

Kelley couldn't manage much sympathy for people whose worst problem was a run-down castle. Emmy was as misguided as her parents; they all needed to join the twentieth century. The days when daughters were regarded as a salable commodity were long gone. But Kelley didn't know her well enough to say so.

Emmy gave an embarrassed little laugh. "I don't know why I'm baring my soul to you."

"I guess I have a sympathetic face," Kelley said lightly. "Although the people who come to me for a loan might not agree."

"Do you sit on a charity disbursement board?"

"Hardly. I'm a loan officer at a bank."

"It must pay well. I was shown that gown you wore to the ball, but it was too rich for my pocketbook."

"Don't judge by that." Kelley laughed. "I bought it during a momentary fit of insanity."

Emmy's practiced eye assessed Kelley's present outfit. "The one thing I do know about is clothes. You don't shop in bargain basements."

"I used to—or at least, I had to wait for sales. Until I bought a lottery ticket on a whim and joined the moneyed classes."

Emmy's face registered the surprise everyone felt at the news. "How wonderful! It must have felt like suddenly acquiring a fairy godmother."

"That's an apt description." Kelley smiled. "I might not have found a prince, but I got to go to the ball in a fancy new dress."

"You're an inspiration. I never believed in fairy tales before. Maybe I should buy a lottery ticket."

"I wouldn't wait around for magic to strike if I were you."

Emmy's expression sobered. "No, I'm not expecting miracles." She sat back in her chair. "I'm afraid I've been monopolizing you. Lunch is almost over and I haven't given you a chance to talk to anyone else."

It was graciously put, but Kelley realized that Emmy was regretting her candor. For the remainder of the meal they both chatted with other people.

After dessert—tulip-shaped chocolate cups filled with raspberry ice—coffee was served in the drawing room. When some of the guests started to leave a little later, Kelley decided she should, too. The ones who stayed were mostly Henrietta's committee members. They were grouped together, discussing the next fund-raiser.

Kelley managed to get her hostess's attention so she could say goodbye. "Thanks so much for inviting me. I really enjoyed myself."

"It was nice having you. I'm glad you and Emmy hit it off so well."

"I liked her as soon as I met her the other night. She's a very outgoing person."

"Emmy is a dear girl. I just hope—" Henrietta stopped short. "Well, never mind. Do you really have to leave? We still haven't had a chance to talk."

"You have other guests to take care of. I understand."

"They don't show any signs of leaving, either." Henrietta sighed. "I can't even ask you to wait around. I'm due at a cocktail party at five."

"Don't give it another thought. I know how busy you are."

"It's always like this in the city. I'm beginning to understand why my husband prefers the country. Heinrich hates formality. He gets a big hoot out of occasionally being mistaken for the gardener."

"He sounds nice. I'm sorry I didn't get a chance to meet him," Kelley remarked politely.

"Now there's an idea! Why didn't I think of that? We're having a few people for the weekend and I'd love to have you join us."

"I wasn't hinting for an invitation," Kelley protested.

"I know that. It's an excellent idea, though. We're very relaxed down there. Everyone does exactly what he feels like. You and I can sit around and get to know each other. Unless you have other plans, of course."

"No, I hadn't made any."

"Good. Emmy is coming, too." Henrietta glanced around the room and beckoned. When Emmy came over, Henrietta said, "Kelley will be joining us for the weekend. Can you bring her with you?"

"I'd be happy to, but I'll be coming from my parents' house. I'm going down there tonight."

"Is there a train I could take?" Kelley asked.

"It doesn't run very close," Henrietta answered. "We're in the middle of nowhere."

"I could pick her up at the train station," Emmy volunteered.

"I don't want to be a bother." Kelley was starting to feel like a liability. "Maybe I could rent a car and drive myself."

"Wait a minute, I have an idea." Henrietta's expression cleared. "I'll invite Kurt. I want him to find me a console table for the hall, and this will give him an opportunity to take some measurements. I just hope he hasn't already made plans for the weekend."

"Don't worry. If he has, I'm sure he'll change them," Emmy said ironically.

"Yes, he did seem quite taken with Kelley. It should be a lovely weekend. I enjoy having young people around."

"Who else is coming?"

"We'll just be a small group. Erich said he'd try to make it. I'm not counting on him, but I'll call him one more time. If he does come with a date, there will be eight of us."

"Who's the eighth person?" Emmy asked.

"Niles Westbury, an exchange student from Oxford. He's a charming young man."

"At least you're hoping I'll think so," Emmy answered dryly.

"I always hope *all* my guests are compatible." The older woman's expression was bland. "Everything's settled, then. Plan to get there early on Saturday."

"It should be an interesting weekend if Erich does show up," Emmy commented to Kelley as they left together. "He and Kurt detest each other."

"Doesn't Henrietta know that?"

"It probably didn't occur to her. She gets along with everybody, even the ones she's not crazy about, and I guess she thinks other people should, too."

Kelley was having second thoughts about the upcoming weekend. Spending a couple of days under the same roof with Erich would be difficult enough. Watching him turn that devilish charm on another woman would be downright painful. Maybe he wouldn't come. Henrietta *had* sounded doubtful.

Kelley set her chin grimly. She had to stop acting like a schoolgirl with a crush. How many people got invited to stay in a castle? This was the chance of a lifetime, and she didn't intend to let Erich spoil it for her.

Chapter Four

Kelley might have had doubts about the weekend, but Kurt was delighted. "I couldn't believe my good fortune when Henrietta phoned," he enthused as they drove through the countryside. "A chance to spend two whole days with you."

"Along with other people," she reminded him.

"I wonder who else is coming. Not that it matters. You're the important one." He turned his head to give her a melting smile.

She ignored it. "Emmy will be there, and a young man from England. Henrietta doesn't seem like the type to play Cupid, but I think she's matchmaking."

Kurt frowned. "I thought Emmy was practically engaged to that millionaire from Greece. She better not let him catch her fooling around or she'll lose him."

"You really think that would be a suitable match?"

"Are you joking? The man is worth a fortune! He could solve all her problems."

"*She* doesn't have any," Kelley said pointedly. "But if Emmy feels she has to marry for money, at least she should look for a younger man—someone like Erich," she added deliberately, because she was annoyed with him.

"You think *he'd* make a good husband? A woman would have to be out of her mind to marry him!"

"He's rich. You seem to think that's the most important qualification."

Kurt slanted an uncomfortable glance at her. "Emmy's case is different. Personally I wouldn't consider marrying for anything but love. That's why I've waited so long."

"Well, hang in there. You'll find your soul mate someday," Kelley said lightly.

"I think I already have," he murmured.

"I thought we settled that the other night, Kurt. It's nothing personal. I just don't want to get involved with anyone right now."

"Not even Erich?" he asked sulkily.

"I haven't seen Erich since the night—" She stopped short, remembering the circumstances. "I told you I don't expect him to call again."

"But you're hoping he will."

"I won't even dignify that with an answer," she said impatiently. "Let's just drop the subject, okay?"

"I'm sorry." He took her hand and held on when she tried to withdraw it. "I know I'm overreacting, but it's frustrating to realize I can't compete with Erich. He has more money, a grander title—everything that impresses women."

That wasn't the secret of Erich's success, but Kelley didn't say so. "No woman worth having would judge a man solely by those yardsticks. You should stop competing with Erich and start realizing you have a lot to offer, too.''

"I wish *you* thought so."

"I do. I just told you so."

"You're merely being kind." Kurt sighed. "I appreciate the intent, but I can see the difference in you. You've changed in just a few days."

"That's nonsense, but I won't bother trying to convince you. You're paranoid about Erich."

"It isn't only him. When we first met you were happy to accept my invitations. And then I introduced you to my friends. Now I can't even get a date with you," he said dolefully. "You always find some excuse."

Kelley felt guilty, because he was right. Kurt wasn't stimulating company, but he *was* responsible for making her visit memorable. It wasn't very nice to drop him after he'd served his purpose.

"I'm sorry you got that impression," she said gently. "I was really pleased when Henrietta suggested we drive down together." That was at least partially true. She was happy to have a way to get there.

"You couldn't have been as overjoyed as I was." He gave her hand a final squeeze before turning off the highway onto a winding road. "We're going to have a wonderful time this weekend."

"I'm really looking forward to it. How much farther do we have to go?"

"We're on Heinrich's property now."

They were driving through wooded acres with no signs of life except birds and an occasional squirrel that raced up a tree and disappeared.

Kelley gazed through the windshield. "I thought castles were huge. Shouldn't we be able to see it?"

"The grounds are extensive, although it isn't this wooded when you get nearer to the castle. The land surrounding it was kept clear so invaders could be spotted before they got too close."

"It's hard to believe men with lances and spears trouped through this actual spot," Kelley observed.

"Over and over again. Dornberger Castle served as a major fortress for many centuries. It stood against Germanic tribes, a challenge by the Venetians, and a Turkish assault that closed down the Danube completely. Throughout all that time the Dornberger family managed to retain possession of the castle. The remarkable thing is that it hasn't changed much. Heinrich is dedicated to preserving it the way it was."

"I hope that doesn't mean a ban on indoor plumbing."

Kurt laughed. "He's a traditionalist, but he's not fanatic about it."

They emerged from the woods to a scene of incomparable beauty. A massive gray stone castle sat majestically in the center of lush green lawns, looking like the cover of a romantic period novel. Ivy softened the stark turrets pierced by narrow slit windows, and flower beds provided a touch of color that prevented the building from looking forbidding.

"Well, what do you think?" Kurt asked as he drove around the circular driveway and stopped in front of a pair of massive front doors. "Does it live up to your expectations?"

"I feel as if I've stepped into the past," she breathed. "I expect pages in silk tunics to come out and welcome us with a fanfare."

He chuckled. "Henrietta drew the line at buglers, although you won't find anything else missing."

A servant came out to take their luggage and they followed him into an entry hall that made Kelley's mouth drop open. A broad staircase led to a gallery that circled the hall. It was hung with heavy gilt-framed portraits of bygone Dornbergers. The men had elaborate hairdos and ornate costumes that rivaled the ladies' décolleté satin gowns. Interspersed among the paintings were suits of armor, studded maces and swords in jeweled scabbards.

"Don't let all that junk scare you off." Henrietta came into the hall to greet them. "We don't sit on wooden benches and spear our meat with a knife. The rest of the place is quite livable."

"I can't wait to see it," Kelley said eagerly.

"Heinrich will be glad to give you the grand tour. He's in the rose garden with Emmy. Come and meet him."

The count was a tall handsome man with a dry sense of humor. He and Henrietta sparred back and forth, but it was obvious they were very fond of each other.

"I'm so happy you could come," he told Kelley. "My wife said you were lovely, and she was right."

"You could have met her sooner if you'd come to the ball with me," Henrietta remarked.

"I don't have your tolerance for pain, my dear." Heinrich smiled at his wife. "Besides, you always weed out the bores and bring the best and the brightest down here."

Emmy laughed. "Isn't he charming? You'd never know he'd rather be feeding his roses."

"They're simply gorgeous," Kelley said. "I've never seen any that color."

She indicated a bush covered with spectacular blooms. The yellow center petals blended into white edged in cherry red. Those were the showiest blossoms, but a profusion of other bushes displayed flowers in almost every color of the rainbow.

"That one is called Double Delight," Heinrich told her. "It was the all-American rose winner in 1974."

"Let her get unpacked before you further her education," Henrietta said. "I've put Kelley in the blue room," she told Kurt. "Will you show her the way? You're down the hall in your usual place."

Kelley's room was fit for royalty. A canopied bed had side hangings of gold embroidered blue damask that matched the draperies framing the tall windows. At the other end of the room, a tufted settee faced a fireplace with a carved mantel. Flanking the couch were two exquisite gilded chairs. The elaborate furnishings might have seemed intimidating, but bowls of fresh flowers and numerous small knickknacks made the room inviting.

"This is fabulous!" Kelley exclaimed.

"There are some excellent pieces in here," Kurt said. "I located that Biedermeier table at an estate sale in Germany. It's one of the finest examples of its kind."

"You travel all over the world looking for furniture, don't you? That sounds like more than a hobby."

"I enjoy doing it," he answered dismissively. "I'll be back in fifteen minutes. Will that give you enough time to unpack?"

"Plenty," she assured him.

Kelley hurriedly put away her clothes so she'd have time to examine her luxurious surroundings more thoroughly. The bathroom was incredible. Although it had modern plumbing, the character of a bygone era had been preserved. A large marble tub with gilded claw feet occupied the center of the room, and the sink was shaped like a giant shell decorated with bluebells twined among green leaves. Thick white towels bearing the Dornberger crest in gold were stacked on a table beside the tub, along with shampoo, bubble bath and body lotion.

She wasn't nearly finished with her inspection when Kurt knocked on the door.

The volume of voices coming from the garden indicated more guests had arrived. Kelley had forgotten about Erich temporarily. She braced herself, hoping her apprehension was unjustified. It wasn't.

Erich was lounging in a chair facing the door, looking like a picture in an upscale magazine. He was dressed casually in cream-colored flannel slacks and a silk shirt with an ascot knotted at the open neck. The sun turned his hair to deep chestnut and glinted in his laughing green eyes.

A beautiful dark-haired woman was sitting beside him, the woman Kurt had argued with at the ball. She certainly got around. Kelley didn't notice that Kurt was as rigid as she was.

"Did you find everything you needed?" Henrietta rose to greet them.

"Yes, my room is lovely." Kelley avoided looking at the others.

"I hope you'll be comfortable. Come and meet everyone. You already know Erich, I believe."

"Not very well," he said with a smile, getting to his feet.

"And this is Magda Schiller," Henrietta continued.

The dark-haired woman barely acknowledged the introduction before turning to Kurt. "I didn't expect to see *you* this weekend." Her mouth curved sardonically. "Didn't you say you had to fly to Budapest?"

"Well, I . . . that is, my plans changed at the last minute."

"So I see." Magda looked pointedly at Kelley.

"What would you two like to drink?" Henrietta asked. "They're all having aperitifs, but you can join me in a good old American Bloody Mary, if you like," she said to Kelley.

"That would be fine," Kelley answered mechanically.

"Are you enjoying your stay?" Erich asked her.

"Very much," Kelley answered warily. His question could have been prompted by simple courtesy, but she didn't trust the gleam in his eyes.

"What stands out most in your memory?"

Her jaw set grimly. "No one special event," she managed to answer coolly.

"That's unfortunate," he murmured. "Perhaps you're not taking advantage of everything Vienna has to offer."

After assessing the situation Emmy said hastily, "Kelley is the luckiest person I know. She won the lottery, and now she can do anything she wants. Isn't that smashing?"

"It's very interesting," Heinrich remarked. "One hears about these things, but one never expects to meet someone it's happened to."

Every time the subject came up, Kelley wanted to set the record straight, but this was an awkward place to do it. Would they think she'd misrepresented her winnings to make herself more acceptable to them?

As she hesitated, Magda said nastily. "If you're interested in buying a castle you've come to the right place. A lot of them are for sale, aren't they, Kurt?"

"Don't do it," Henrietta advised. "You'll spend a fortune putting in central heating. I don't know how your ancestors survived the winter," she told her husband.

"That's why they went on so many crusades to warmer climates." He smiled.

"I'm sure Miss McCormick would be willing to put up with a little discomfort to get what she wants," Magda drawled.

"Only up to a point," Kelley replied evenly.

"I think this would be a good time to show Kelley your roses, Heinrich," Henrietta remarked.

"I'll go with you." Emmy stood. "I never get tired of looking at them."

Heinrich led the way through an extensive garden, stopping here and there at a special favorite. "This hybrid musk rose was bred in England. As you can see, the clusters of single flowers resemble a hydrangea."

Kelley leaned forward and sniffed deeply. "It smells heavenly, too. I can see why you're so passionate about your hobby. One is more gorgeous than the next."

"Roses have held a special fascination through the ages. Many people have enjoyed the Empress Josephine's rose garden at Malmaison, but did you know the Mary Washington rose was hybridized by your first president, George Washington?"

"No, I'd never heard that."

Before Heinrich could expand on the subject, a servant came to tell him he was wanted on the telephone.

After he'd excused himself and left, Emmy asked, "Are you really interested in roses, or did you just want to get away from that witch, Magda?"

"That's an apt description of her. I don't know why she's on my case. What did I ever do to *her?*"

"She's Kurt's girlfriend," Emmy answered succinctly.

"How can that be? She's here with Erich."

"That *was* a bit of a shocker. I can't imagine why he'd bring her. Magda isn't his type at all."

"What gives you that idea? She's very attractive—if you like all that heavy makeup," Kelley couldn't refrain from adding.

"Magda made a play for Erich years ago but he wasn't interested."

"He evidently changed his mind."

"It's more likely he brought her here to aggravate Kurt. Henrietta must have mentioned Kurt was coming."

She probably gave him the rest of the guest list, too, Kelley thought grimly. Erich decided to settle two scores at once. "I thought he and Henrietta were friends. Disrupting her house party is a rotten thing to do."

"It isn't like him, I agree. Erich detests Kurt, but he's always had exquisite manners. Maybe he really didn't know Kurt was coming."

"That means his interest in Magda *is* personal," Kelley said woodenly.

"I suppose anything's possible, but she's been going with Kurt for ages. It's only a matter of time until they get married."

"What's stopping them?"

"Money. Neither of them has any."

"Things must be different over here," Kelley commented. "In my country, all you need is a few dollars for the license."

"Magda would be willing, but I think Kurt feels a wife would slow him down. He's in big demand as an extra man at parties. That's where he makes his contacts."

"I'm beginning to understand why Magda is so insecure," Kelley said disgustedly. "Although what she wants him for is a mystery to me."

"Don't be too hard on poor old Kurt. He's just trying to survive like the rest of the faded glory crowd."

Kelley remembered Erich's solution to the problem. He would make it on his own. But Kurt wasn't Erich. Maybe she *was* being too hard on Kurt.

"I wish there was some way to tell Magda she has nothing to fear from me," Kelley sighed. "I don't relish having her make snide remarks all weekend."

"Stick close to Henrietta," Emmy advised. "She expects her guests to behave themselves. Magda won't act up around her."

Their hostess approached down the path. "Come and meet Niles. Where's Heinrich, still on the telephone?" She clucked her tongue in annoyance. "He must be talking to a fellow rose fancier about a new discovery. I swear, they're worse than a bunch of bird watchers."

"Count your blessings." Emmy chuckled. "He could have a worse hobby. What if he liked to chase young girls?"

"That wouldn't be a problem." Henrietta smiled. "All he'd get would be a lot of exercise."

When they returned to the rest of the party, a nice looking young man had joined them. While Henrietta was making the introductions, Heinrich came out of the house followed by two servants, who began to set up a buffet table on the terrace.

"Niles is doing graduate work in architecture," Henrietta announced. "Maybe you could introduce him to some of your friends, Emmy. He doesn't know anybody in Vienna."

"I'll be happy to do what I can," she answered politely.

"That would be awfully nice." He had an appealing smile. "Perhaps we could have dinner together one night. It gets rather lonely rattling around by myself."

"Too bad you're the wrong sex." Magda gave a tinkling little laugh. "Kurt loves to show visitors around, but only if they're women."

"You might be able to give Niles some pointers," Erich told Kelley. "Tell him about some of the things *you* enjoyed. Like Stadt Park, for instance. You did enjoy it, didn't you?"

Emmy didn't make things any better when she asked, "Isn't that gold statue of Johann Strauss adorable?"

"I don't remember it." Kelley hoped her cheeks weren't as pink as they felt. "I've seen so many beautiful statues. They tend to blur together."

"That's true. Unless you have some reason for one to stand out in your memory," Erich said softly. "Obviously you don't."

"But that one's famous," Emmy insisted. "You must remember it, Kelley. He's standing on a raised platform and he's so graceful he looks as if he's about to dance."

"It sounds charming," Niles remarked, inadvertently taking the pressure off Kelley. "Would you go with me to see it?"

"I'll do better than that. I'll introduce you to someone who will take you all over. You don't want to waste your time with an engaged woman," she said deliberately.

"Oh...I didn't know."

"Nobody else did, either," Henrietta said bluntly. "When did you make up your mind?" she asked the younger woman.

"I'm sure nobody is interested in my love life," Emmy answered brightly.

Niles smiled wryly. "I've never been irresistible to women, but this is the first time one got engaged to avoid a date with me."

"It has nothing to do with you," Emmy said contritely. "This is something I've been contemplating for a long time."

"And I made up your mind for you?"

"No! You seem like a very nice person. If you still want to go out with me under the circumstances, I'd be happy to have dinner with you."

"Now that that's settled, I believe lunch is ready," Henrietta said with satisfaction. "For those of you who haven't been here before, take a plate and sit wherever you like. We aren't formal in the country."

The buffet was as lavish as its surroundings. A servant carved a whole turkey and a ham, and another servant helped guests to fresh asparagus and large stuffed mushrooms from twin silver chafing dishes. A variety of salads accompanied the main dishes, and a large platter was heaped with fruit.

After filling a plate, Kelley followed Emmy's advice and sat at a table with Henrietta. While Kurt hesitated uncertainly, casting a wary glance at Magda, his dilemma was solved for him. Emmy and Niles took the other two places at the table.

Lunch would have been a pleasant event if Kelley hadn't been so burningly aware of Erich. Every time she looked up from her plate he was in her line of vision, laughing with Magda or discussing something with Heinrich. Erich was completely at ease. Her presence didn't bother *him* in the slightest, Kelley thought bitterly.

After lunch Henrietta made an announcement. "Anyone who likes can play billiards or watch a movie on the VCR, or choose a book from the library. Kelley and I are going for a walk."

As they strolled toward the woods she said, "You see, I told you we'd have some time to ourselves down here."

"It's like a dream world. I can understand why you're happy in this country," Kelley said.

"I don't think the place has anything to do with it. It's nice to be able to live in a castle, but I'd be happy anywhere with Heinrich."

"You're very fortunate," Kelley said wistfully.

"You've never been in love?" The older woman looked at her shrewdly. "Or was it unrequited?"

"I'm not sure I know what love is," Kelley answered slowly. "How do you differentiate between love and infatuation?"

"One lasts and the other doesn't, but that's no help. By the time you discover the difference, you're apt to have done something foolish."

Kelley broke off a twig and concentrated on stripping off the leaves. "Perhaps the foolish thing is to pass up an experience you'd always remember."

"Did you take this trip hoping to get over some faithless boyfriend at home?"

"No." Kelley gave her a lopsided smile. "I came here looking for adventure."

"Did you find it?"

"Beyond my wildest expectations."

Henrietta slanted a glance at her. "A lot of Americans think a title is glamorous, but you have to take the man who comes with it. They aren't all like Heinrich."

"I wouldn't know how to be a duchess, anyway. Or a countess or baroness," Kelley added hastily.

"I see," the other woman murmured.

Kelley was afraid she did. Henrietta was very astute. She changed the subject abruptly. "When was the last time you were back in Texas? It was a hotly contested state in the recent election. Did you follow it over here?"

"I was glued to the television set on election night, waiting for a news break. They didn't give it as wide coverage over here, naturally."

They talked about politics, urban problems and sports as they walked through the woods. When Henrietta discovered how well-informed Kelley was, she kept firing questions at her. Kelley enjoyed the conversation, but when they came to a clearing her attention was distracted. A lovely pond suddenly appeared, with swans floating on it majestically.

"What an idyllic spot!" she exclaimed.

"I thought you'd like it. Shall we sit down for a few minutes?"

"I don't know how you can tear yourself away from here to go into the city."

"Now you sound like Heinrich." Henrietta smiled.

Crunching sounds in the woods preceded Erich's appearance. "I thought I'd find you two here."

Kelley was annoyed at him for spoiling this tranquil moment. "Shouldn't you be with your date?" she asked stiffly.

"She's keeping busy."

"I'm glad you're here, Erich." Henrietta stood. "I must speak to the cook about dinner. See that Kelley doesn't get lost in the woods."

"I'll come with you." Kelley got up hurriedly.

"That would be foolish. Stay here and enjoy yourself."

"You're a great hostess," Erich murmured.

"Better than you deserve." Henrietta smiled reluctantly. "If you weren't such a charming devil I'd cross you off my guest list." With a wave of her hand, she left them.

"I'd better get back, too," Kelley said. "Kurt will be wondering what happened to me."

"Don't go." Erich put his hand on her arm. "I want to apologize for my behavior earlier."

"I don't know what you're talking about," she replied distantly.

"I shouldn't have reminded you of something you'd prefer to forget. The entire day wasn't bad, though, was it? You seemed to enjoy lunch, and the rest of the things we did."

She was reminded of how much thought he'd put into her entertainment. "I enjoyed the day immensely. My mistake was in not quitting while I was ahead." Her mouth curved ruefully. "You're irresistible by moonlight."

He returned her smile. "Evidently not."

Erich was proving to be every bit as irresistible in the daylight. Kelley was achingly aware of his long, lean body so close to her. She knew how those relaxed muscles could tense, the feeling of his arms cradling her against that hard chest.

Turning her head to gaze at the swans gliding across the water with scarcely a ripple she said, "Now that we've cleared the air we can forget about the entire incident."

"Are we friends again?"

"I hope so. You make a formidable enemy."

"What gave you that idea?"

"The vendetta you're carrying on against Kurt, for one thing. It wasn't just an unfortunate coincidence that you brought his girlfriend here this weekend. You did it to make trouble between them."

"Even if that were true, your reasoning eludes me. It was all right for *him* to date someone else, but not for her?"

"It isn't the same thing," Kelley insisted. "Henrietta asked Kurt to bring me."

"If it was only an innocent favor for a friend, why did he tell Magda he had to fly to Budapest?"

"Maybe he intended to, originally. You suspect Kurt of having an ulterior motive for everything he does."

"That's because I know him better than you do," Erich answered grimly.

"You're being terribly unfair and it doesn't become you. Someone in your position can afford to be more tolerant."

Erich stared at her moodily. "The guy really has you taken in."

"I wouldn't call it that. I'm merely less judgmental than you. I'm sure Kurt has faults like everyone else, but he's gone out of his way to be nice to me."

"I can't answer that without sounding like a cad," Erich muttered, almost to himself.

"Then don't. We're never going to agree, so let's just drop the subject."

"You're probably right." He sighed.

"I suppose we'd better go back," Kelley said reluctantly. "Henrietta will think I got lost."

"She knows you're in good hands—figuratively speaking, of course." Erich grinned.

"It's so lovely here. Is your place like this?"

"The grounds are, more or less, but my house was a former hunting lodge—nothing as grand as this."

"I thought you'd have a castle, too."

"You sound disappointed." His expression was unreadable.

"No, just surprised. Since even the impoverished nobility seems to have inherited one, I thought surely *you* must have."

"I did. I turned it into a children's hospice."

"What a generous thing to do!"

He shrugged. "These big old places might have made sense in the old days when they housed extended families. They're anachronisms today. Who needs that many rooms?"

"You're right, of course. But what a wonderful way of life if you can afford it."

"You'd like to live in a castle?"

"I think I could adjust to it." She laughed.

"You shouldn't have any trouble fulfilling your wish. There are a lot of them for sale—if you don't mind paying the price."

Kelley hesitated. "There's something I've been meaning to talk to you about." She paused, hoping he'd understand how her innocent deception had started. "When I first met Kurt on the plane I thought he was a terrible snob. But then he was very charming to me."

Erich's expression wasn't encouraging. "I thought we agreed not to talk about him."

"This isn't about Kurt, actually. It's about me—the way I felt when he gave me a chance to see a glamorous world I'd only read about."

"Too bad you're so dazzled you can't see past the glamour." Erich stood abruptly. "I'll take you back to the house."

"You didn't let me finish."

"It's your life," he said without interest. "Do whatever you like with it. Can we go now? I really must get back to Magda."

"Go ahead. I can find my own way back," she said stiffly. "I don't need you to show me the way."

He stared at her for a long moment, strong emotions playing across his patrician face. "You can't say I didn't offer," he rasped.

Kelley gazed out at the swans after he left, alternating between anger and disappointment. Erich had an unreasoning blind spot when it came to Kurt, but he didn't have to be so cold to *her*. Why did they always end up at each other's throats? Because Erich's only interest was in taking her away from Kurt, she concluded sadly. It was pointless to keep hoping he had any other feelings for her.

The day was spoiled for Kelley after her disagreement with Erich. He and Magda were playing croquet on the lawn when she returned to the house. As she walked toward them, Erich moved behind Magda and put his arms around her, ostensibly to give her a lesson in how to stroke the ball. Kelley would have walked by without speaking, but the other woman called to her.

"Why don't you and Kurt join us?" She looked up archly at Erich. "We're having great fun. I never knew croquet was such a physical sport."

"You have the right teacher," Kelley answered coldly. "Make the most of it. He has a short attention span."

"That depends on how good you are at keeping a man interested," Magda cooed.

"Let's hope you have better luck this time," Kelley drawled.

Magda's expression was murderous, but Erich looked amused. Luckily Emmy appeared with Niles.

"I'm on my way to give Niles a tour of the castle," she said to Kelley. "Do you want to come along?"

"Yes, I'd love to see it."

"Don't show her the dungeon," Erich called as they walked off. "She doesn't like to believe there's a downside to royal living."

Kelley turned away without answering. What was the use?

In spite of her preoccupation, Kelley was fascinated by the historic old building. Emmy led them through grand reception rooms with fan-vaulted ceilings and parquet floors that glowed from years of polishing. Every hallway was lined with paintings, marble pedestals holding graceful sculptures and cabinets filled with priceless china figurines.

A winding stone staircase led up to the top of one of the crenellated towers, where an old oak door opened to a balcony. The view outside was breathtaking. They could see for miles in every direction.

When Niles commented on the fact, Emmy said, "That's one of the reasons Dornberger Castle survived. An invading army couldn't creep up on it. By the time the enemy got through the woods, the home guard was ready for them."

"Is there really a dungeon here?" he asked.

"Not anymore. It was converted into a wine cellar and storage space long ago. One of the walls still has a couple of chains bolted to the stone blocks, though. I'll show it to you if you like."

When they reached the ground floor and started down a corridor, Kurt appeared. "Where have you been?" he asked Kelley with barely restrained annoyance. "I've been looking all over for you."

"Emmy was giving us a tour of the castle."

"I would have done that." He pouted. "I've barely seen you all day."

"Henrietta and I went for a walk," Kelley answered, controlling her irritation. "It's the first time we've been able to spend any time together."

"She came back ages ago. You couldn't have been touring the castle all this time."

After a look at Kelley's mutinous face Emmy said, ''If we're going to the wine cellar we'd better get started. It's almost time for cocktails.''

Kurt joined their little group, which didn't delight Kelley. She refrained from saying anything, however.

The former dungeon was at the bottom of a narrow flight of precipitous stone steps. Unlike the rest of the castle, the ceiling here was low, adding to the sense of oppressiveness. The vast expanse had been wired for electricity, but before that it must have been dank and frightening.

Heinrich was down there inspecting the awesome collection of bottles. Wine racks lined an entire long wall from floor to ceiling, and each cradle held a dusty bottle lying on its side.

''You've come at a good time.'' He smiled. ''I was just selecting the wine for dinner. Does anyone have a preference?''

''I can't speak for the others, but I adored that gewürztraminer you served the last time I was here,'' Emmy said.

''You have excellent taste, my dear. That's what we'll have.'' He moved down the row and began to take bottles from their slots.

''Can I carry those upstairs for you, sir?'' Niles asked.

''As soon as I dust them off. You're a handy young man to have around.''

''While you're doing that I'll show them the remains of the dungeon,'' Emmy said.

The iron manacles at the end of long chains were a sobering reminder of past cruelties. Men with no hope had lain on these clammy stones, chained like animals. Kelley shivered.

"Fortunately people don't hurt each other like that anymore," Heinrich said quietly. He had come up behind them.

That wasn't strictly true, Kelley thought somberly. They merely inflicted pain in a different way.

Dinner was an uncomfortable affair for Kelley. Erich alternated between asking her innocent sounding but barbed questions, and smiling at Magda, who fawned over him sickeningly. Kurt reacted by being annoyingly attentive to Kelley.

Emmy and Niles were the only ones who thoroughly enjoyed the excellent dinner. They seemed to be hitting it off well.

After they'd all had coffee in the drawing room, Emmy asked if their hosts would excuse Niles and herself for a short time.

"He wants to see if our wine taverns are anything like English pubs," she explained. "I thought I'd take him into the village for an hour."

"That's an excellent idea," Henrietta said. "But don't hurry back. Heinrich wants to play cards. Do you play bridge?" she asked Kelley.

"If you're not tournament class players," Kelley answered.

"Don't I wish! We just play a friendly little game. Heinrich will be my partner and you can have Erich." Henrietta seemed oblivious to the consternation she was causing a couple of her guests.

"I'm really not very good," Kelley said quickly. "Why not let Magda take my place?"

"We're not leaving her out. She and Kurt are such good friends. I'm sure they have a lot to say to each other," Henrietta said serenely.

Kelley felt trapped. Couldn't Henrietta see how Erich felt about her? The prospect of having him snipe away at her all night was agonizing, but there was nothing she could do about it.

Kelley was so tense at first that she made foolish mistakes. But the others were kind and Erich never got irritated. He passed off her errors as mere bad luck. Eventually she relaxed and started to enjoy the game.

She was playing four spades doubled when Magda stopped by to say an acerbic good-night. Henrietta replied absentmindedly as she gathered in a trick.

Kurt didn't get any more attention when he hovered over them a few minutes later. He fidgeted for a while, then finally said to Kelley, "There's a full moon out. Maybe we can take a walk when your game is over."

She frowned. "Please, Kurt, you'll make me lose track of trump."

"I certainly wouldn't want to be responsible for *that*," he remarked sarcastically. When no one answered, he sighed. "Since I seem to be in the way, I'll go to bed."

The others murmured a vague good-night and continued with their game.

By the time the evening was over Kelley felt completely at ease with Erich. Although they'd lost to Henrietta and Heinrich, they shared a team spirit. Nobody took the game seriously anyway.

"This was very pleasant," Heinrich said as he gathered up the cards.

"For you two," Erich joked. "You won."

"You scored a few points yourself," Henrietta observed dryly.

Their eyes held for a moment before he turned to Kelley. "Shall we take a belated look at the moon before we turn in?"

Kelley was reminded of the last time she'd taken a walk with Erich in the moonlight. "I don't know where you get your energy," she answered lightly. "I'm asleep on my feet."

"Just for a few minutes? Lightning rarely strikes twice," he said softly.

That's what Erich's compelling kiss had been like—a lightning storm that had shaken her to the core. "I'm going to bed," she said abruptly.

Chapter Five

Kelley slept late the next morning because she'd lain awake half the night trying to figure Erich out. He'd been utterly charming all through the bridge game, and if she'd gone for a walk with him afterward he would undoubtedly have tried to make love to her. Would he put all that effort into one-upping Kurt? It didn't seem likely. Or did she just want to believe some deeper emotion was involved?

A knock at the door brought her soul-searching to an end. It was probably the maid. Henrietta said anyone who cared to could have breakfast in bed. What service!

"Come in," Kelley called happily, sitting up against the headboard. Her expression changed when Erich appeared in the doorway. "What do you want?" she asked sharply.

"I'm sure you know the answer to that." He chuckled.

As he walked toward her, his gaze moved from her flushed cheeks to her bare shoulders. Under the sheer chiffon nightgown her nipples curled into little coral rosettes.

She hastily pulled the covers up to her chin, her eyes flashing violet fire. "What makes you think you can just walk into my room?"

"You asked me in."

"I thought you were the maid," she muttered.

"I'll be glad to pinch-hit. Would you like me to run your bath?" His eyes sparkled with mischief.

"No, I would not!"

Kelley felt terribly vulnerable, although she knew Erich would never try to force himself on her. That was the whole trouble. He didn't have to. Her entire body heated as she gazed up at his handsome face.

"It's very annoying to have you stand over me like that," she snapped irritably.

"I'm sorry. Is this better?" He sat on the edge of the bed, facing her.

Kelley sighed. "What are you doing here, Erich? Besides trying to ruin my weekend."

His face sobered. "Do you honestly think that's my intention?"

"I've given up trying to figure you out."

His smile reappeared. "I don't know why. I've been very open about my feelings."

"Have you?" She stared at him searchingly.

"I've never wanted any woman as much." He put out his hand and smoothed her tousled hair.

Kelley reached up and combed her own fingers through her hair. "I must be a mess," she murmured, because she couldn't think of anything else to say.

"You're beautiful." His fingers trailed across her cheek to trace the shape of her mouth. "I wish I could have been here next to you when you awakened, warm and drowsy in my arms. Someday it's going to happen, sweetheart. Can you doubt it?"

"I...I don't know." She faltered, transfixed by the brilliance of his eyes.

"I'm a patient man." He smiled. "I can wait until you're sure. I don't want you to have any regrets."

Would she have more regrets if she continued to deny her feelings for him? It was more than mere passion. Kelley finally admitted the truth to herself. She had fallen hopelessly in love with Erich.

As she gazed up at him, parting her lips, another knock sounded at the door. Erich hadn't closed it securely, so it swung open when Kurt knocked. He stood on the threshold, peering into the room.

For a moment they all remained motionless. Then Kurt said coldly, "I seem to have stopped by at an inopportune time."

"You didn't interrupt anything," Kelley said hastily. Her heart was pounding as she clutched at the covers once more.

Erich got up from the bed. "I came to ask Kelley if she'd like to go to the flea market in the village."

"If I'm not mistaken, you have a date of your own. Although I realize one woman has never been enough for you," Kurt added nastily.

Erich's eyes glittered dangerously. "At least that's the story you've been spreading about me. This is the first time you've had the guts to say it to my face, you lying little weasel."

As he took a step toward the other man, a maid appeared carrying a breakfast tray. She stopped uncertainly when she noticed the two men glaring at each other. "Should I come back later, miss?"

"No, the gentlemen were just leaving," Kelley said firmly.

"That's giving him the benefit of a doubt," Erich growled. "He's lucky he's able to walk out of here."

Kelley's nerves were still jangling after they all left. The nasty scene between the two men was unfortunate, but she couldn't honestly blame Kurt for jumping to conclusions. If he'd happened by five minutes later, his suspicions might have been a reality.

Was someone trying to send her a message? She still didn't know how Erich felt about her, beyond the fact that he wanted her. Sighing deeply, she threw back the covers and got out of bed.

By the time Kelley was dressed and had gone downstairs, everyone was milling around the hall.

"I was about to send someone up to see if you were awake," Henrietta said.

"I'm sorry," Kelley mumbled. "I guess I overslept."

"No problem. The others are going to a flea market, and I thought you'd like to join them."

"Aren't you going?" Kelley asked cautiously.

"No, Heinrich and I are going to laze around here." Henrietta smiled at her husband. "It will be the six of you."

Kelley was in a quandary. It was obvious her hosts wanted to be alone, but could she count on Erich and Kurt to act civilized? She didn't want to be the catalyst that would start an explosion.

"Do come," Emmy urged. "It's lots of fun. I've gotten some fabulous antique jewelry at these things."

"How can I pass up an opportunity like that?" Kelley smiled.

Erich drove Heinrich's Rolls so they could all go in one car. The tension was minimized by the presence of Emmy and Niles, but Kelley was glad it was only a short drive to the flea market.

Once they got there, everybody wandered off in different directions, stopping at the displays that interested them. Kelley prudently avoided the two men and stayed with Emmy and Niles. Kurt tried repeatedly to get her alone, but she managed to elude him.

In spite of all her maneuvering, Kelley really enjoyed the fair. She found a lovely heart-shaped onyx and marcasite brooch, and Emmy bought a chiffon scarf. Even Niles bought a strand of amber beads.

"For my mother," he explained hurriedly.

"I'll bet!" Emmy teased. "You probably have an entire harem at home."

"How can I answer that?" he asked plaintively. "I want you to think I'm popular, but not fickle."

"All men are," she assured him.

"You just haven't met the right man," he said, gazing into her eyes.

Kelley was pleased to notice that Emmy didn't discourage him. Maybe she was starting to come to her senses.

They all met up again at the Viennese sausage stand, where they devoured sausages, and washed them down with German beer.

"Mmm, those are delicious," Kelley proclaimed. "They're even better than American hot dogs."

"Or English bangers," Niles agreed.

"I think we've made two converts." Emmy laughed.

"I've been trying," Erich murmured.

"I hope Henrietta isn't expecting us for lunch," Kelley said hastily.

"No, we're on our own," Emmy replied. "They want some time alone together."

"Isn't it nice that they still feel that way? I hope I have a marriage like theirs someday," Kelley said wistfully.

"Who doesn't?" Emmy's eyes were suddenly bleak.

Kurt looked soulfully at Kelley. "Any marriage can be perfect if two people work together toward a common goal."

"And one of them can afford it," Magda commented sarcastically.

Emmy looked at Kelley and rolled her eyes. "If everybody's seen enough, let's go to a *heuriger.*"

"What's that?" Kelley asked.

"It's a wine bar, like the one Emmy took me to last night," Niles said.

"Next time we'll go to Grinzing. That's where you can see the really picturesque ones," she told him. "It's on the outskirts of the city."

"I'm free anytime you are." He smiled.

Magda stared moodily at the young couple. "If we're going, let's get started. There isn't anything more to do here."

The village had a collection of small shops, including a bakery with a few tables in the back. As they walked toward the wine shop, Kelley stopped to look in the window at the delectable pastries.

"Is that a Sacher torte?" she asked, pointing to a chocolate cake.

"Yes, haven't you ever tasted one?" Emmy asked.

"No, but it's on my list of things to do."

"There's no time like the present," Erich said.

"You should wait till you get back to Vienna and go to the Sacher Hotel. That's where it originated," Kurt said to

Kelley, pointedly ignoring Erich. "This one is bound to be inferior."

"She might not be able to tell the difference. Some people are remarkably tolerant of inferior quality," Erich drawled.

"Let's try it," Emmy said. "Then Niles and Kelley can make their own comparison."

"One can only hope," Erich murmured, pushing open the door.

Kelley couldn't help being relieved when they returned to the castle. Under different circumstances she would have thoroughly enjoyed the afternoon, but the hostility between the two men was wearying. After chatting for a bit with her hosts, she slipped away on her own.

The woods were very peaceful after the tension filled day. Kelley strolled along a narrow path, stopping every now and then to admire wildflowers, or to watch squirrels racing by like commuters running for a train.

After a while she sat on one of the benches placed at intervals along the trail, listening to the sounds of the forest. Bird songs filled the air, insects hummed and small animals rustled in the underbrush.

At first Kelley thought the crackling sounds she heard on the path were made by a rabbit, or perhaps a deer. She sat very still and waited expectantly. Her pleasure dimmed when Kurt appeared.

"Niles said he thought he saw you heading this way," Kurt said. "What are you doing out here all alone?"

"I had enough togetherness for one day," she answered dryly.

"Certainly not with me! You avoided me all afternoon."

"You're imagining things."

"I didn't imagine seeing Erich in your room this morning," he said sulkily.

"It was perfectly innocent," she insisted. "He came to tell me about the flea market."

"He was sitting on your bed," Kurt exclaimed in outrage. "You were in your nightgown!"

Kelley gritted her teeth. "You have no right to question anything I do, but I don't want you to get the wrong impression. *Nothing happened!*"

"It's only a matter of time, though, I can tell." His expression was somber. "I never had a chance once Erich came on the scene."

"If you want somebody to tell you you're God's gift to the universe, go talk to your mother," Kelley said impatiently. "I've had it up to here with your jealousy of Erich, and I'm sick of his intolerance of you."

"You've noticed that," Kurt said eagerly.

She uttered a small sound of annoyance. "Go away, Kurt. Talking to you is like banging my head against a tree. It only feels good when I stop."

"I won't mention Erich again, I swear! But you can understand how devastated I was when I saw you together under such provocative circumstances—to say the least."

She rose from the bench. "There's only one way to end this conversation."

"Don't go." He followed her when she started down the path. "I didn't mean I believed there was anything improper going on. Not that you don't have the right to do whatever you want," he added hastily. "I simply lost my cool when I thought everything might be over between us."

"There was never anything to *be* over!" she exclaimed in frustration.

"Not even friendship?" He gave her a mournful look. "I enjoyed just being with you. It gave me pleasure to show you a side of Vienna tourists never see. I thought you enjoyed my company, too.''

Kelley knew Kurt was using emotional blackmail again, but his point was valid nonetheless. ''I do enjoy your company, when you're being yourself and not trying to score points. You don't have to compete with Erich.''

''If I promise to mend my ways, will you go to the Opera Ball with me next week? Henrietta has taken a table and Emmy will be there.'' He shrewdly dangled them as an extra inducement. ''We'll all sit together.''

Kelley supposed she owed it to him. Forcing a smile she said, ''I guess that means another ball gown. I don't know what I'll do with them when I go home. My normal life isn't that grand.''

''Then stay here. You haven't experienced a fraction of the wonderful things the city has to offer—the opera, concerts in the park, nightclubs. The Viennese know how to live.''

''Doesn't anyone work?'' she asked ironically.

''*You* won't have to. We'll spend our days and nights going to glamorous places. And if you get tired of that, I'll take you to my castle in the country.''

''The one that needs renovating.'' Her voice was expressionless.

''It needs a woman's touch.'' He corrected her. ''You'll get really excited about the project once you see the place.'' They were within sight of the house, but he pulled her down onto a bench.

''Kurt, we have to talk,'' she began carefully. ''I'm afraid you're in for a disappointment. I'm not the person you think I am.''

''I wasn't proposing anything unseemly,'' he said in a shocked voice. ''In my bumbling way I'm asking you to marry me.''

"That's really absurd! Besides the fact that we don't know each other well enough, we have very little in common."

"Neither do Heinrich and Henrietta actually, yet look how fantastic their marriage is. We can have the same thing."

"No, we can't. That's what I'm trying to tell you."

"I know you don't love me, but I'll devote my life to making you happy."

She stared at him in disbelief. "You'd marry someone, knowing she didn't love you?"

"That will come in time. I'm confident of it."

"Then why not wait till it happens?"

"I'm afraid to take the chance of losing you."

"I see." Competition from Erich had speeded up Kurt's game plan.

"Say you'll marry me," he pleaded. "We can announce it tonight at dinner."

"Don't you dare!"

His enthusiasm was slightly dampened by her vehemence, but he didn't give up. "Then at least let's get engaged. We can wait as long as you like to get married, just as long as I know you belong to me."

"People can't own other people," she said impatiently.

"I'm only asking you to make a commitment." He took her left hand and held on when she tried to pull away. Reaching into his pocket, he pulled out a ring and slipped it on her finger. "It would make me very happy if you'd wear this."

Kelley stared at the ring on her finger. A large center ruby was surrounded by sparkling diamonds. "It's gorgeous," she gasped.

"I hoped you'd think so. It was my grandmother's."

"I can't accept this." She started to take it off, but his hand closed over hers.

"I want you to have it. She would have approved of you."

"I doubt it. You have to take it back."

Before she could insist, Henrietta appeared on the lawn, waving to them. "Kurt, you have a long-distance call."

He gave Kelley's hand a final squeeze. "I'll be right back."

"Wait! Take your ring with you," she called, but he merely waved and hurried toward the house. Kelley had no alternative but to wait there until he returned.

Time passed, however, and Kurt didn't return. She was furious with him. If he thought she'd grow so attached to the ring that she wouldn't be able to part with it, he was badly mistaken. It *was* beautiful, though. She turned her hand from side to side, watching the diamonds glitter in the sunlight.

As it grew later, Kelley became more annoyed. She had to dress for dinner and she wanted to take extra pains because Emmy had said Sunday nights were always black-tie affairs. But first she had to get rid of the confounded ring!

Finally she simply had to get dressed. As Kelley started toward the house, she noticed Erich lounging on a lawn chair reading a book. Of course it was too much to hope he wouldn't notice *her*. When he rose to greet her, she stuck her hand in her pocket.

"Did you have a nice walk?" he asked pleasantly.

"Yes, but I'm afraid I stayed out too long. I have to rush and change for dinner."

Erich chuckled. "Emmy and Magda went up ages ago. What takes you women so long to get ready?"

"We have a lot more to do to ourselves. All you men have to do is shave and put on a dinner jacket."

His eyes roamed over her delicate features. "I've seen you without makeup. You don't need anything to make you beautiful."

Kelley's pulse beat faster, remembering that morning. "Yes, well, tonight I'm going to try to be glamorous." She turned away without giving him a chance to reply.

Instead of the lingering bubble bath she would have liked, Kelley took a quick shower. She needed time to catch Kurt before he went down to dinner.

It didn't take long to make up her face, despite what she'd told Erich. Her black lashes were naturally long and thick, so tonight she used only a touch of violet eye shadow. Instead of outlining her mouth with a deep rose pencil and filling in with a lighter pink lipstick as planned, she settled for one color, swearing at Kurt the whole time.

After zipping up her dress, Kelley fastened long dangling rhinestone earrings to her lobes, looking at her reflection in a full-length mirror. The long black gown was completely unadorned except for wide satin cuffs embroidered with tiny seed pearls and crystal beads. It was a deceptively demure looking dress. The skirt was slit to midthigh, displaying a long expanse of leg whenever she moved.

Would Erich think she looked sexy? That had never been a problem. When she recalled the predatory gleam in his green eyes, her breathing quickened. Picking up the ruby ring, she hurried down the hall to Kurt's room.

He didn't answer her soft knock, so she was forced to knock harder. When he still didn't respond, she called in a low voice, "I have to see you, Kurt. I've been waiting all afternoon." Kelley's temper got the better of her when that didn't produce results, either. She banged on the door with her fist. "Damn it, Kurt! Stop trying to avoid me."

Erich came sauntering down the corridor. The smile on his face was more like a sneer. "Trouble in paradise?" he drawled.

Kelley was so startled she jumped visibly. Which of course made her look guilty of something. "I didn't hear...I mean, this must look..." She stopped and took a deep breath.

"Did you and Kurt have a tiff?"

"No, certainly not! Why should we argue?" She clutched the ring more tightly in her sweaty palm.

"Perhaps you couldn't convince him that we didn't make love this morning." He trailed a forefinger insolently along the neckline of her gown. "That's understandable. He might have been right if we hadn't been interrupted."

So Erich knew she was poised on the brink! What he didn't realize was the reason—and that was something he must never know. Let him continue to think only sex was involved.

She pushed his hand away. "Your ego is working overtime."

His face darkened. "If you prefer a moral bankrupt like Kurt, I suppose it must be."

"You've decided we're having a passionate affair simply because you found me knocking on his door. That really *is* damning evidence," she said sarcastically.

"Hearing you begging him to talk to you gives it a little more credibility."

"I was not begging, and there's a perfectly simple explanation."

"I'd be interested in hearing it."

"Your own mind is so much more inventive. I wouldn't dream of spoiling your pleasure." She stalked back to her own room and banged the door shut.

Kelley had clenched her fists so hard that the circle of diamonds was biting into her palm. The discomfort finally penetrated her anger. What was she going to do with the damn ring? The servants were undoubtedly trustworthy, but she didn't feel comfortable letting it out of her possession. The ring must be enormously valuable, besides being a family keepsake. The only solution was to wear it—on her right hand. That increased the chance of somebody noticing, but she certainly wasn't going to wear it on her engagement finger!

Everyone had gathered in the drawing room for cocktails by the time Kelley went downstairs. Everyone but Kurt.

"How lovely you look, my dear." Heinrich handed her a glass of champagne while gazing at her admiringly.

"Your gown is to die over," Emmy agreed.

"When you have a figure like Kelley's," Henrietta said. "You can't wear a dress like that if you have anything to hide."

"I disagree," Erich drawled. "What better way to distract someone's attention?"

Emmy laughed. "A man's maybe. Women examine each other with an eagle eye."

Kelley unobtrusively transferred the glass of champagne to her left hand and glanced around the room. "Where's Kurt?" she asked casually.

"Poor soul, he had a crisis at his apartment," Henrietta answered. "A broken pipe, I believe. He had to go back to Vienna."

"He's gone?" Kelley couldn't hide her dismay.

"Yes, but he'll be back. I told him not to bother, that we'd understand, but he insisted. He said not to wait dinner for him, though."

Everything seemed to be conspiring to make Kelley's life miserable, but at least Kurt was coming back. When he did appear she wasn't going to let him out of her sight until he took back his ring.

Dinner was an elegant affair of many courses served on fine china and accompanied by several different wines. Kelley tried to take part in the conversation, but she was uncomfortably aware of Magda's interest in the ruby ring. Kelley was prepared to say it was a costume piece she'd bought herself, but the other woman didn't ask her about it. When Kurt showed up halfway through dinner, Kelley breathed a sigh of relief.

"Did you get everything taken care of?" Henrietta asked.

"Plumbing is one of those mixed blessings of modern life," Heinrich commented sympathetically.

Magda didn't join in the conversation. She waited with a little smile on her face until the subject had been exhausted and she was sure of everybody's attention. Then she said to Kurt, ever so casually, "I've been admiring Kelley's ring. It looks exactly like the one you inherited from your grandmother. It couldn't be, though, because you sold that one quite a while ago, didn't you?"

Kurt's face turned a dull red. "No, of course not!"

"You told me you did," she said relentlessly. "Why would you say that?"

"You must have misunderstood. What I said was—yes, now I understand why you got that impression. A friend of mine fell in love with the ring. I, uh, happened to show it to her. She asked if she could borrow it to wear to a gala party, so I loaned it to her. She kept it an unconscionable amount of time."

Kelley was appalled at Magda's cruelty. It was obvious that Kurt had been forced to pawn his grandmother's ring at some point. How could Magda embarrass him by revealing the fact in front of his friends?

The others had sat silently throughout his ordeal. Even Erich looked uncomfortable. Finally Henrietta came to his rescue.

"The amount of jewelry some women wear to those big parties is downright vulgar," she said.

"Somebody should tell them more isn't necessarily better," Emmy agreed.

In their well-bred way they made Magda aware of their disapproval, but she continued to look pleased with herself.

Kelley couldn't wait for dinner to be over. When everyone trailed out of the dining room, she took hold of Kurt's arm and forced him to lag behind with her.

Taking off the ring, she put it in his palm and closed his fingers around it. "There! I was never so glad to get rid of anything in my entire life."

"You didn't believe those spiteful things Magda said? How can you think I would give you a cheap imitation?" Kurt looked shocked.

"That never entered my mind. I simply want you to take it back. I told you I couldn't accept it, and I meant it."

"Just wear it for the weekend," he begged.

"*No.* I don't wish to discuss the matter any further. Come on, let's not give the others any more to talk about." She walked away from him.

Kelley didn't know what entertainment Henrietta had planned, but she didn't intend to be partners with Erich in anything, no matter what excuse it took. As it turned out, Kelley's determination was unnecessary. Henrietta asked Emmy to play the piano.

"Nobody wants to hear an amateur perform," Emmy protested. "That's right up there with having to watch home movies of somebody's vacation."

"Nonsense. You play beautifully. You could have been a concert pianist if you'd stuck with it."

Emmy's mouth curved mockingly. "That's the story of my life."

Her hostess had made up her mind, and the younger woman knew it was useless to argue. She sat down at the grand piano with a rueful look at the others.

Henrietta hadn't been passing out idle compliments. Emmy played expertly. Her Valse Triste was sweet and haunting.

The melancholy music echoed Kelley's mood as her thoughts drifted to her insoluble problems. When she finally fell in love, why did it have to be with someone unattainable? After tonight's fiasco she and Erich weren't even friends anymore. When the weekend was over she'd never see him again. At least that would be less painful than enduring his contempt. She glanced up to find him staring at her with a frown on his face.

Why couldn't Erich just ignore her and let it go at that? Kelley felt herself growing more and more tense under his condemning gaze. Luckily she was sitting near the door. When her nerves threatened to reach the breaking point, Kelley rose and slipped unobtrusively out the door to the terrace.

She drifted over to the rose garden, where the flamboyant blooms were now almost colorless in the darkness. They reminded her of other flowers that had looked pale in the moonlight. The music wasn't sad that night. It was a romantic Strauss waltz, and it wasn't played on a piano. Kelley turned away, then drew a sharp breath. Erich had followed her noiselessly.

"I saw you leave. Are you all right?" he asked.

"I'm fine. I just needed a breath of fresh air."

He smiled faintly. "Emmy will be sure her playing drove you away."

"No, she's very good. She really might have been a concert pianist."

"People make choices in life," Erich answered evenly. "They aren't necessarily the right ones."

"I guess a person has to find that out for herself."

"True. You can give advice, but when it isn't taken you have to back off."

They both knew they were no longer talking about Emmy. Kelley changed the subject determinedly. "It's been a lovely weekend."

"I suppose it has, for you." Erich glanced at her hand. "Where's your ring?"

"I gave it back to Kurt. That's what I was trying to do before dinner. Not that I expect you to believe me," she added wearily.

He stared at her, frowning. "You didn't know it was a fake at that time."

"You never give up, do you?" she asked angrily. "Kurt's embarrassment tonight must have delighted you."

"On the contrary. I thought Magda's performance at dinner was disgraceful, and so did everyone else."

"Somebody ought to put a muzzle and a leash on that woman," Kelley muttered.

"Possibly, but it was poor taste for Kurt to give you the ring tonight."

"So, it was all Kurt's fault. Is that what you're saying?"

"I was merely suggesting that he might have anticipated trouble. Why didn't he wait until the weekend was over? It's almost as if he was flaunting your relationship in Magda's face."

Kelley couldn't tell Erich that *he* was the one Kurt was sending a message to. "Emmy told me Kurt and Magda used to go together, but the relationship is obviously over for him. Any woman with a shred of dignity would accept the fact and let him go."

Erich's face darkened at her continued defense of the other man. "I agree. She should be counting her blessings, and *you* should have your head examined!"

"For refusing to believe slander about a friend?" Kelley asked disdainfully.

"Is that what you want everyone to think he is? Just a friend? I suppose that's the reason you wore his ring on your right hand. Or did it bother you to accept a fake engagement ring?"

"It's a perfectly beautiful ring," she said indignantly. "What *didn't* bother me was the fact that Kurt had to pawn it temporarily. People do find themselves strapped for cash on occasion, but you wouldn't know about that."

"It's a permanent condition with him. He's sold off everything of value. Why would he redeem the ring?"

"Anybody could figure that out. It has sentimental value for him."

"Kurt has as much sentiment as the pawnbrokers he deals with," Erich said bitingly. "You can be sure he had a copy of the original ring made for an eventuality like this—to make a rich, trusting woman like yourself think he's a great catch."

"I don't believe you," Kelley said heatedly, to cover her own misgivings.

Kurt had been the first one to bring up the question of the ring's authenticity. Why? Unless he was afraid someone else might suggest it to her. His timing in the woods was suspect, too. Kurt considered Erich a serious threat after finding him in her room this morning. That was really funny in a hurtful sort of way.

"You don't want to hear the truth. You're too dazzled by a title," Erich said grimly. "It's a good thing you can afford him. Kurt has big plans for your money."

This was the time to tell Erich the truth about herself, but how could she? He'd think she was an opportunist, too.

"I don't share your opinion of Kurt, but that's beside the point. He did ask me to marry him, and I turned him down. Contrary to what you think, all American women don't yearn to be a baroness or a countess—or even a duchess," she added deliberately. "When I marry it will be for love, and I won't care if he pumps gas for a living. So I'd appreciate it if you'd save your advice for someone who needs it."

"Why did you accept the ring in the first place?" he asked slowly.

"Kurt put it on my finger, and then he was called away before I could make him take it back."

After a moment's silence Erich slanted a wry glance at her. "I feel like a complete jerk."

"You deserve to."

"I don't suppose you'll ever forgive me?"

"An apology might help."

"It's yours. I'm not usually so judgmental." He ran his fingers through his thick hair. "Kurt has a way of getting under my skin. I never should have accepted Henrietta's invitation."

"Didn't she tell you he was coming?"

"Among other people." Erich gazed steadily at her.

"Don't pretend you came on my account!" Kelley's frustration boiled over. "You're as big a phony in your own way as Kurt is. Both of you want something from me, and *your* objective isn't any nobler than his.''

He smiled slightly. ''If you're referring to my desire to make love to you, that scarcely makes me a scoundrel. A lot of men must have felt the same way.''

''They didn't sulk and make accusations when they weren't successful.''

''What you consider sulking was merely concern for you,'' he answered quietly. ''I hated to see you being taken in.''

''If I'm stupid enough to fall for a snow job, that's *my* problem.'' Kelley knew she was being unreasonable. Erich was trying to show he cared. It wasn't his fault that concern wasn't what she wanted from him. She turned away. ''We'd better go back inside.''

He took her arm. ''Don't go yet. We have to talk.''

''I think we've both said enough.''

He held her an instant longer, staring into her eyes. Finally he sighed and released her arm. ''Maybe you're right.''

As they walked back to the house, Kelley could almost feel her heart breaking into little pieces. This was the last time she would ever be alone with Erich. She stole a quick look at his autocratic profile. Forever after, moonlight and roses would remind her of this poignant moment.

Emmy had just ended her recital when Erich and Kelley reentered the drawing room, so everyone noticed their return.

''I told Henrietta my playing would break up the party,'' Emmy joked.

''You played beautifully,'' Kelley protested. ''I just stepped outside for a breath of air. I could still hear you out there.''

Emmy grinned. "What I lack in skill, I make up in volume."

"Stop putting yourself down. I thought you were great." Niles looked at her admiringly.

"We all did," Henrietta said. "Now, who would like a nightcap, or perhaps a cappuccino?"

As the others named their preference, Kelley managed to get Emmy aside. "Are you returning to your parents' house when you leave here?"

"No, I have to go back to Vienna. Stavros is coming in tomorrow. We have a luncheon date." Emmy's animation died.

"Will you give me a ride into town?"

"Certainly. I'll be happy to have company, but what are you going to tell Kurt? I'm sure he expects you to drive back with him."

"I'll think of something." Kelley sighed. "I've had a lot of practice at evading the truth the last couple of days."

"It's been quite a weekend, hasn't it?" Emmy's eyes sought out Niles.

"I know *I'll* never forget it," Kelley answered bleakly.

Chapter Six

Breakfast the next morning was an informal affair. Guests helped themselves from a buffet where eggs, sausages and bacon were kept warm in large chafing dishes. The long sideboard also held pitchers of freshly squeezed orange juice, toast, muffins and a large bowl of strawberries with a pitcher of heavy cream. Next to the coffee urn was a tray of Viennese pastries.

Kelley helped herself sparingly, girding for the inevitable argument with Kurt. She managed to avoid him until breakfast was over by taking a seat next to Heinrich, where she encouraged her host to talk some more about his roses.

"You must invite this charming young lady back again," he told his wife. "She's the first guest who's known the difference between a rose and a ranunculus."

"I'm really a fraud." Kelley smiled. "I don't know anything about roses, but I loved hearing about yours and seeing your beautiful home."

"We enjoyed having you," Henrietta said graciously.

"It was great, as usual," Emmy joined in. "I hate to leave, but we must get going. Are you ready, Kelley?"

"*I* brought Kelley," Kurt said sharply.

"Yes, well, I thought I'd ride back with Emmy. She's going to...uh...take me to her hairdresser," Kelley said lamely. "I really must have my hair done."

"I can drop you there," he persisted.

"You'd never find the place." Emmy stepped in helpfully. "My luggage is already in the car. Where is yours, Kelley?"

"It's in the front hall. I'll just run upstairs to get my purse and I'll be right down."

When Kelley came out of her room, Erich was walking down the hall toward her. Kelley's heart sank. She'd hoped to avoid a private meeting with him. They had nothing further to say to each other, so it was bound to be awkward.

She nodded and kept on walking, but he blocked her way. "Were you going to leave without saying goodbye?"

"I...um...I thought I'd do that downstairs."

He stared at her moodily. "The weekend has been a real disaster, hasn't it?"

She glanced away. "I prefer to call it informative."

"I'm sorry you had to find out about Kurt in such a painful manner."

She shrugged. "I'll survive."

"That shouldn't be a problem, since you said you aren't in love with him." Erich watched her covertly.

"Falling in love doesn't fit in with my plans right now," she answered lightly. "I have places to go and things to see."

"You're leaving Vienna?"

"I never expected to stay forever."

"Where will you go?"

"Oh, I don't know—maybe Istanbul or Venice. A gondola ride on the Grand Canal sounds romantic."

"I thought you weren't looking for romance."

"I said I didn't want to fall in love. There's a difference."

"I never realized that," he said ironically. "Perhaps you can enlighten me."

"Romance lights up your life like a thousand Roman candles. You wake up smiling every day—even though you know it won't last."

"Funny, I thought the condition you described was love. But unlike you, I *do* expect it to last."

"Hope springs eternal," she said mockingly. "That must be why you keep on looking."

Before he could answer, Emmy's voice floated up the staircase. "Are you almost ready, Kelley? I hate to rush you, but we have a long ride ahead."

"I have to go," Kelley said to Erich. "If I don't see you again..." She paused to gaze at his handsome face one last time.

"Is that what you want?" he asked quietly.

She couldn't bring herself to say yes. Turning away, she murmured, "Goodbye, Erich." *My love,* she added silently.

Niles carried Kelley's luggage out to Emmy's car. After stowing it in the trunk he came around to the driver's side and bent down to look in at Emmy.

"Don't forget, we have a date to see the statue of Strauss in the park," he said.

She hesitated. "Perhaps I'd better find someone else to take you. I'm going to be tied up for a few days."

"I can wait."

"Well, actually I may be busy for longer than that. My...a friend is coming from out of town and I won't have much free time."

"If you don't want to see me, I'd prefer that you come right out and say so." He gave her a crooked smile. "I thought we got along great, but that might only be wishful thinking on my part."

"It isn't, Niles. I enjoyed your company very much. I just wish it were that simple." She sighed.

"I don't want to complicate your life." He gently tucked a lock of hair behind her ear. "I'd simply like to be a small part of it."

She gazed up at him wistfully for a moment, then her expression hardened. "I'm sorry, but that's impossible. Goodbye, Niles. It's been fun." She put the car in gear and drove away with a set face.

They left the castle behind and drove through the woods in silence. When they had almost reached the highway, Emmy slanted a glance at Kelley.

"Aren't you going to say anything?"

"I didn't think you felt like talking," Kelley answered.

"You know what I mean. You think I'm being foolish. Go ahead and say it."

"You already know how I feel."

"It was the kindest thing to do," Emmy insisted. "What's the point in letting him think we could ever be anything more than friends?"

"If you're serious about getting engaged today, then you did the right thing."

Emmy gripped the wheel hard. "I have a feeling Stavros is going to insist on an answer. I can't stall forever."

Kelley uttered a sound of annoyance. "Will you listen to yourself? You sound like somebody facing a life sentence at hard labor."

"A lot of women would love to trade places with me," Emmy answered defensively. "Stavros is very generous. I'll have everything money can buy."

"I won't use that trite expression, 'money can't buy happiness.' Maybe it can for some people. I just don't think you're one of them." Kelley drew on her own experience. She didn't possess great riches, but what she did have had created more problems than it solved.

"It's possible to marry someone your own age and not be happy," Emmy said. "Nobody can give you a guarantee. This way, at least I know I'm making several people happy."

"You might have to keep reminding yourself of that," Kelley remarked sardonically.

"Stavros isn't a monster," Emmy protested. "He's a very charming man. You really have to give him a lot of credit. His family was dirt-poor. Stavros came up the hard way, and now he hobnobs with the rich and famous."

"How did you meet him?"

"It was last New Year's Eve, at the opera. I was in the duke and duchess Von Wernbrun's party. The holiday season is very gala in Vienna, and the opera house was packed. I can't remember who performed, because the real fun comes during intermission in the bar." Emmy grinned. "Everybody gathers to look at each other's gowns and jewels."

"That's not a male pursuit. What do the men do?"

"Try to fight their way to the bar. Or else they stand around and ogle the more gorgeous women. Stavros was there with Carlina, that glamorous Swedish model who wears those outrageously revealing clothes."

"He had flamboyant tastes back then," Kelley commented.

Emmy glanced over wryly. "Meaning, what does he see in me?"

"Not at all. His taste has definitely improved."

"You don't have to be polite. I've asked myself the same question. Stavros has been linked to some very exotic women."

"Who introduced you?" Kelley asked.

"Nobody, actually. Stavros was part of the countess Schlagel's party. Myrna comes from a very old family, but she's always been a rebel. She runs with a racy crowd and has been involved in some messy scandals. The old guard are outraged by her behavior, especially the duchess."

"The one you were with?"

Emmy nodded. "Myrna should have known she was asking for trouble when she brought Stavros over to our party. That's probably why she did it. When Myrna tried to introduce him, the duchess looked right through her and walked away. It was very embarrassing. I didn't think it was right to snub an innocent person, so I held out my hand and introduced myself."

"That was a nice thing to do. He must have appreciated it."

"Stavros was too poised to be upset by the incident, but it made *me* feel better."

"Did he ask you for a date that night?"

"No, we just chatted for a few minutes. I thought that was the end of it. Even when he phoned the next day and invited me to a party, I assumed it was his way of acknowledging a courtesy. I accepted because I decided it would be fun to meet a lot of celebrities."

"You must have had a good time if you continued to go out with him."

"It was like entering a different world. Stavros and his friends think nothing of flying to another city just for dinner. They travel by private plane and limousine, and they cruise on luxury yachts."

"You'll lead a pampered life if you marry him, anyway."

"Yes." Emmy stared through the windshield at the road.

"Will you live in Greece?"

"Stavros has an apartment in Athens and an estate on Crete, but he intends to buy a house in Vienna, too. So I guess we'll be spending some of our time here."

"That will be nice for you. You'll be near your family and friends. Although, Stavros might not want to hang out with the nobility after being snubbed so publicly."

"You wouldn't think so, but he's been more than forgiving. He's gone out of his way to make them like him. For my sake, I suppose, since he couldn't care less about their opinion. It's really very sweet of him."

"What has he done specifically?" Kelley wasn't ready to award any Brownie points.

"When I first started to go out with him we spent all our time with his friends, but after he asked me to marry him, that changed. Instead of partying with the jet set, he gave small elegant dinners and invited my parents and their friends."

"I suppose he thought they'd object, and he wanted to show them he's really a solid citizen."

"He certainly succeeded, and not only with my parents. Stavros had those stuffy grande dames eating out of his hand. They forgot how shocked they were by his excesses," Emmy observed mockingly. "He obviously but-tered them up for my sake. Why would he care about being accepted?''

Kelley finally had the answer to something that had been puzzling her. Emmy was an outstanding person—pretty, intelligent and thoroughly nice. But Stavros had a reputation for collecting gorgeous, sexy women. Perhaps he was initially attracted to Emmy because she was a refreshing change, but why would he want to marry her?

Because she could give him the one thing his money and power couldn't buy, entrée into the closed ranks of aristocracy. His humble beginnings had left a mark on him that even great wealth couldn't erase. Stavros had indulged in every excess, but now he was getting older. Maybe he wanted children to carry on his name, and he wanted those children to be accepted into a world that still didn't welcome him. What better person to open the door than Emmy?

"Stavros might be ready to settle down, but are you?'' Kelley asked slowly. "There's a whole world out there, and it's filled with interesting men. You were attracted to Niles this weekend. Doesn't that make you think twice about your choice of a husband?''

"You were attracted to Erich. That doesn't mean you want to marry him. At least, I assume you don't.''

"You assume correctly.'' It was Kelley's turn to stare out at the road.

"You two spent a lot of time together.'' Emmy glanced over speculatively.

"That's ridiculous! We were always with the group.''

"Not when I was playing the piano,'' Emmy teased. "Although I don't blame you for cutting out. You *were* gone a long time, though. Kurt was furious at Erich.''

"That's a permanent condition between the two of them,'' Kelley answered wearily. "It has nothing to do with me. What time is your luncheon date?'' she asked to change the subject.

Emmy's smile faded. ''One o'clock. The traffic has been heavier than I anticipated. I'll just make it.''

''You can drop me off anywhere when we get to the city. I'll take a taxi to the hotel.''

''I'm not in that big of a hurry. Stavros will wait.''

''Are you sure? Or are you hoping he'll get angry and leave?'' Kelley asked quietly.

Emmy frowned. ''Give it a rest, Kelley.''

''You're right. I'm way out of line. I won't say another word.''

''I'm sorry. I didn't mean to be rude. I know you mean well, but I'll really have an exciting life. As I told you, Stavros isn't an ogre. You'd realize that if you met him.''

''I'm sure he's very charming,'' Kelley said politely.

''Why don't you have lunch with us today? Then you could make up your own mind.''

''I couldn't do that. He wants to be alone with you. He'd be less than delighted if you brought along a total stranger, and I wouldn't blame him.''

''He won't mind, honestly. Stavros is always pleased to meet my friends. It's all settled. I won't take no for an answer.''

Kelley argued, but Emmy was adamant. It was Kelley's private opinion that Emmy wanted to postpone making a commitment, but since a chance to meet the mysterious Stavros Theopolis was irresistible, Kelley let herself be persuaded.

Stavros was already sitting at a table when they arrived. He was an impressive looking man with prematurely gray hair and strong features. Kelley couldn't judge his height, but he had the bulky shoulders and thick torso of a man who had done manual labor in his day. It was a fleeting impression that was belied by his elegantly tailored suit, silk tie and the fabulously expensive gold watch on his wrist.

He rose with a smile when he saw them. "My dear little Emmy, late as usual."

She turned her head at the last minute, so his kiss landed on her cheek. "I'm sorry. I had to drive up from the country. I was at Henrietta's for the weekend."

"Then you're forgiven." Stavros looked with interest at Kelley.

"This is Kelley McCormick. She was at the house party, too, so I asked her to have lunch with us."

"I hope you don't mind," Kelley said out of courtesy. He couldn't very well say so if he did.

"On the contrary." His practiced gaze took in both Kelley's face and curved figure, lingering for a moment on the latter. Something flickered in his eyes as he raised her hand to his lips. "I enjoy being surrounded by beautiful women."

She could believe that. The man oozed sensuality. "You're very kind," she murmured.

A waiter seated them, then presented menus. For the next few minutes they all concentrated on making their selections.

When the waiter had departed with their orders, Stavros turned to Emmy. "I've been trying to telephone you. You're very hard to reach."

"I haven't been home much," she admitted.

"I gathered that," he said dryly. "What have you been doing?"

"Well, as I told you, I was away for the weekend."

"Who else was there?"

"A lot of people you don't know," she answered evasively.

He gazed at her impassively, then turned to Kelley. "Emmy hasn't mentioned you before. Did you meet this weekend?"

Stavros seemed determined to ferret out every detail, one way or another. Kelley was a little disturbed by his possessiveness. He wanted to know every move Emmy made. If he was like this *before* they were married, what would her life be like afterward?

"We met last week—at a charity ball," Kelley added, anticipating his next question. "That's where I met Henrietta, too."

"You should be flattered to have been invited to her country home on such short acquaintance. I haven't been fortunate enough to make the guest list yet." His voice was heavy with irony.

"You wouldn't have enjoyed yourself," Emmy said swiftly. "We did funky things like visit a flea market and wander around the village."

He covered her hand with his. "Being with you would have been pleasure enough for me, my beloved."

She laughed self-consciously, withdrawing her hand. "Don't be too sure. Henrietta made me play the piano, and all the guests were terribly bored."

"She's just being modest," Kelley told him. "She's really very good."

"I didn't know you played the piano," he said to Emmy. "I'll have to buy you a concert grand. We'll go shopping today and you can select one. I keep discovering new things about this dear girl every day," he told Kelley.

"Emmy has a lot of potential," Kelley answered. "I keep telling her that."

"Oh good, here's our lunch," Emmy exclaimed. "I'm starving."

During the meal, Stavros turned his attention to Kelley. "What brings you to Vienna?"

"I guess you could say a search for adventure," she answered. "I'd never been to Europe before."

"Vienna is a nice city, but it doesn't have the romance of Greece. You must come for a visit. On the island of Crete, the sun sparkles on the blue Aegean, scarlet flowers climb up the white walls of houses, and everyone gathers in the *tavernas* to drink and dance."

"But the men dance with each other." She smiled. "That isn't very romantic."

Holding her gaze, he said in a honeyed voice, "Believe me, dear lady, you would have no cause for complaint."

It might have been just an idle comment, except for the suggestive look in his eyes. Or was she just imagining things? Surely Stavros wouldn't come on to her in front of Emmy. Still, Kelley was uncomfortable.

"Emmy told me you have a home on Crete," she remarked. "I suppose that accounts for your partiality."

"Emmy will have to bring you for a visit so you can judge for yourself. It isn't a castle, but her friends are always welcome." He gave Emmy a sardonic smile.

Stavros obviously felt slighted at not having received an invitation to the house party. Kelley already knew Henrietta didn't approve of Stavros, at least not for Emmy. Now she realized that he was also aware of the fact, and it annoyed him. Although Henrietta was only titled by marriage, her social position was impeccable. Stavros's battle for acceptance would be ruthless—with Emmy caught in the middle.

"Your European custom of inviting people for the weekend is so hospitable," Kelley said. "I'm afraid we regard houseguests as a nuisance in my country."

He shrugged. "If you have a large home, it's pleasant to share it with others."

"Maybe that's our problem. People don't have big estates anymore. They can't afford the servants to staff them."

Stavros flicked a glance at Emmy. "The same problem exists over here. Many of the stately old homes are being sold for nonpayment of taxes."

"I was discussing that with someone," Kelley said. "What can be done with a castle once it's repossessed?"

"I suppose it could be turned into a private school or a hotel," he replied with disinterest. "Although I don't know who would pay to stay in a drafty old place with inadequate plumbing."

"Those would be minor inconveniences to me and thousands of other Americans. I'd take a castle over one of those sterile modern hotels any day."

"They aren't all like Henrietta's," Emmy pointed out.

"That's correct. Tell your little friend about the joys of bathing in frigid water," Stavros said.

"Hot water heaters can't be that difficult to install," Kelley insisted.

"You're quite right. All it takes is money. Isn't that true, my dear?" he asked Emmy.

She gave him a brittle smile. "You know more about buying things than I do."

"My little kitten has claws," he murmured. "I like spirit in a woman."

Kelley barely heard them. The germ of an idea was percolating in her mind. Emmy spoke to her twice before getting her attention. "I'm sorry. What did you say?"

"I asked if you wanted to go to the powder room with me," Emmy repeated.

"Yes, I'd like to." Kelley pushed her chair back.

"Must you both desert me at the same time? I can never understand why women indulge in this form of group activity." Stavros chuckled.

"It's a female bonding ritual," Kelley told him. "Like football players dousing each other with champagne."

When they reached the powder room, Emmy slanted a look at Kelley. "Well, what do you think of him?"

"He's about what I expected."

"Most women think Stavros is charming."

"He's very pleasant, but I wouldn't want to be married to him—in spite of all his millions."

"That's easy for *you* to say. I can't count on winning the lottery."

This was a perfect opening, but Kelley didn't want to waste time on her own situation. She had only a few minutes to persuade Emmy not to make a mess of her life.

"Don't you see what Stavros is doing to you?" she asked. "He wants complete control over you. You'll have to account for every minute of your time—where you went and who you were with. Can you live like that?"

"Things will be different after we're married," Emmy said defensively. "Stavros is a little insecure because I haven't given him a definite answer yet."

"Don't do it today," Kelley said urgently.

"I know what I intend to do, so what's the point in putting it off?" Emmy stared at her image in the mirror. "It isn't fair to him, and I'll feel better after everything is settled."

"I doubt it, and I wouldn't worry about Stavros. He's a lot tougher than you are."

"He has feelings, though," Emmy protested. "I'll admit I don't want to marry him, but I'm fond of Stavros. He's a very generous man."

Kelley doubted that he ever did anything without a guaranteed return, but she didn't have time to argue. "Listen to me. I have an idea, but some of the details need to be worked out. Just promise you won't give Stavros an answer today."

Emmy rested her head on her hand. "I know you mean well, but nothing is going to change."

"Don't be too sure. Anyway, we're only talking about one day."

"I'm running out of excuses," Emmy said helplessly. "What will I tell him?"

"You'll think of something. Do as I ask and I'll call you later this afternoon."

"All right, if you insist." Emmy sighed. "Although I don't know what good it will do."

"You never can tell." Kelley grinned. "It's like chicken soup. It can't hurt, and it might help."

When they returned to the table, a stunning brunette woman was sitting in Emmy's seat. She was talking animatedly while Stavros listened with an indulgent smile. They both glanced up when Kelley and Emmy arrived, but the brunette didn't relinquish her chair.

Emmy took the vacant place at the table, greeting the woman tepidly. "Hello, Claire. I didn't know you were in town."

"Didn't Stavros tell you?" The brunette widened her eyes in mock surprise. "I was visiting on Crete, and he gave me a lift here in his plane."

"We've been so busy chatting with our guest that I didn't have time to mention it," Stavros said smoothly.

"Permit me to introduce Kelley McCormick. This is one of your countrywomen, Claire Dumont," he told Kelley.

"Didn't I see your picture on the cover of *Vogue?*" Kelley realized why the woman looked vaguely familiar.

"Is it finally on the stands?" Claire asked. "I posed for that cover months ago."

"I loved the gown you were wearing," Kelley remarked politely.

"Wasn't it fabulous? But the price tag! All I want for Christmas is a man who can afford to buy me goodies like that." Claire gave Stavros a meaningful look.

"How is David?" Emmy asked abruptly.

"You're *way* behind the times, darling. We split up weeks ago."

"I'm sorry," Emmy murmured.

"Don't be. I've been having a ball."

"Will you join us for dessert and coffee?" Stavros asked, managing to sound courteous while effectively changing the subject.

"I wish I could, but I'm already late for a pedicure." Claire rose in one sinuous movement. "Thanks—for everything." She put her hand lightly on Stavros's shoulder.

It was an innocent gesture, yet it spoke volumes to Kelley. Stavros might be a pillar of rectitude in Vienna, but he was still living it up on the island of Crete. Had he hosted his own house party this weekend? Or was it only a party of two? In either case, he wasn't acting like a man who was tired of la dolce vita. Marriage wouldn't change him, either. After he had Emmy safely under his thumb, Stavros would continue to lead his same profligate life—only more discreetly this time.

When Claire had left them, Kelley remarked innocently, "What a vivacious woman. She must be great fun at a house party."

"I'll invite you both together and you can judge for yourself. Emmy can make the arrangements." Stavros's reply was pleasant, but his earlier seductive manner toward her had vanished.

"I don't like that woman," Emmy stated. "Under the glitzy facade, she's really quite common."

"We can't all be barons and baronesses," he said mockingly.

"My aversion has nothing to do with a title and you know it! I simply don't enjoy being in her company."

"Then you won't have to," he said soothingly.

Kelley watched his performance with contempt. Finally she couldn't take anymore. "It's been a lovely lunch. Thank you both for including me."

"You're not leaving?" Emmy asked. "We haven't had dessert yet. They have wonderful pastries here."

"Yes, do stay." Stavros's request didn't have her urgency. He hadn't gotten where he was by misjudging people. He recognized Kelley as an adversary.

"You're very kind, but I really must go."

"It's early," Emmy protested. "What will you do all afternoon?"

"Your friend will think you don't want to be alone with me, my love." Stavros's smile didn't quite conceal his annoyance.

"Don't worry about it." Kelley stood. "We both know how Emmy feels about you."

Instead of looking for a taxi to take her back to the hotel, Kelley started to walk. She had a lot of thinking to do. The conversation at lunch had sparked an idea that could be Emmy's salvation and her own.

It was true that Americans were inordinately interested in royalty, perhaps because titles didn't exist in America.

Not that anybody wanted them to, but they were fascinated by all the trappings that went along with them—the castles and suits of armor, the extensive parklike grounds.

There were dozens of castles dotting the countryside, and many people would jump at the chance to stay in one if accommodations were available. Why didn't the owners who were in dire straits, like Emmy's parents, open their homes to a select clientele of well-paying guests? It would be the perfect solution.

The only problem, as Stavros had pointed out, was the lamentable condition of so many of the historic old places. Where would the money come from to make them livable? Because heat and hot water were two amenities tourists would demand.

Where did any business get money when they needed it? From a bank, of course. She could talk to the manager on Emmy's behalf and explain why it would be a good investment. Certainly better than foreclosing and getting stuck with a white elephant.

A little thrill ran through Kelley's veins as she planned her strategy. First they had to find out what a heating system and hot water heaters cost. There would be other expenses, but those were the big ticket items. Once the figures were in she'd be able to draw up a cost accounting sheet and balance it against potential revenue. That was her field. She knew exactly how much income was needed to offset debits and show a profit.

Her original idea had been to provide Emmy with an escape hatch. But the more Kelley thought about it, the more excited she got. This could turn her own life around, too. She and Emmy would be partners. They'd start with her family castle, then after it was a success, Emmy could persuade others of the impoverished old guard to follow their example. By that time she'd be knowledgeable about plumbers and carpenters, and she could charge a consulting fee.

Kelley would supply the guests from her end, and she knew just how to go about it. Personal letters to the memberships of country clubs, dignified ads in upscale magazines, the potential was limitless. It would be an exciting new career for her. One where she'd get to meet people and travel.

Kelley knew her plan would work. Now she had to convince Emmy—and soon! For the first time, Kelley became aware of her surroundings. She was in a part of the city she'd never seen before and there wasn't a taxi in sight. By the time she finally flagged one down her nerves were twitching. If only Emmy had stood firm!

Kelley was about to hang up the phone when Emmy answered.

"I was sure it was going to stop ringing before I got to it," she said breathlessly. "I was just unlocking the door."

"Is Stavros with you?"

"No, I told him I had a headache—that old standby." Emmy laughed. Then her voice sobered. "He's picking me up for dinner, though. I know I promised you I wouldn't make a decision today, but I have a feeling he's going to demand an answer this evening."

"Prepare yourself for a temper tantrum. I doubt if many people say no to him."

"I intend to say yes," Emmy answered quietly.

"You don't have to." Kelley bubbled with enthusiasm as she told Emmy about her plan. It wasn't met with the delight she expected.

"It won't ever work," Emmy said drearily. "The bank will never lend us money without collateral. I'm not very knowledgeable about finances, but even I know that much."

"You do have collateral. I just explained it to you."

"Even if by some wild chance you were right, my parents would never agree to take in strangers. The very notion would send them into shock."

"But selling their daughter doesn't?" Kelley asked bluntly.

"I can't allow you to talk about my parents that way," Emmy said stiffly.

Suddenly Kelley lost patience. "Okay, you win. I'll stay out of your life. Marry Stavros like a dutiful daughter. That's what you really want to do."

"You know I don't have a choice."

"I just gave you one. Either you enjoy being a victim, or you have a martyr complex. I thought you wanted to take charge of your own life, but I was mistaken."

"That's not fair," Emmy protested. "I'd jump at the chance if I had only myself to consider."

"You owe your parents love and respect, but not this kind of sacrifice. I won't say anymore, though. It's your decision. If you change your mind, let me know. I'll be here for a few more days."

"Where are you going?"

"I haven't made up my mind yet, maybe Venice or Paris. I'm going to pick up some brochures and flight schedules."

"Isn't this rather sudden? You didn't mention it on the weekend."

"I hadn't decided then." The idyll had ended last night in Henrietta's garden. Kelley just hadn't admitted it to herself until now. "It's time I moved on and meddled in some other people's lives," she said in a heavy-handed attempt at humor.

After a pause, Emmy asked hesitantly, "Do you really think your plan will work?"

"Yes, but I can't give you a guarantee. It will take time to get estimates and do the necessary paperwork. And even if the bank okays a loan, it won't come through immediately. You can't count on keeping Stavros dangling indefinitely, and if we can't raise the money you'll lose out all around," Kelley warned.

"You're certainly changing your tune," Emmy complained. "You were all fired up a few minutes ago."

"I still am, but only if you understand the risk you're taking. Maybe I just got carried away," Kelley said uncertainly. What if she *had* been overly optimistic? Emmy was the one who would pay for any miscalculation.

After a moment's silence, Emmy said in a vibrant voice, "What the heck, let's go for it!"

Kelley's confidence came rushing back. "Fantastic! Okay, this is where we'll start."

They talked for almost an hour, making plans and dividing up the work. Emmy would get estimates from workmen, then Kelley would do the necessary paperwork. When all the figures were assembled Kelley would go to the bank and arrange for a loan.

Once Emmy had committed herself, she was bubbling over with excitement. "Are we super businesswomen or what? We have every angle covered."

"All except one," Kelley said slowly. "What if you can't convince your parents?"

"They need the same jolt of reality you gave me."

"I'm sorry for being so harsh," Kelley murmured.

"Don't be. It was true. I was living in the past as much as they were, but my parents aren't evil people. They'd be appalled to think they were pressuring me into something I truly didn't want to do. Having to scrabble around for money clouded their judgment. They wanted to spare me that.''

"I guess I can understand their concern," Kelley conceded. "All parents worry about their children."

"And vice versa. I wanted to give them back their dignity, but I chose the wrong way to do it," Emmy said simply.

"They'll have the time of their lives entertaining the commoners from across the pond." Kelley chuckled. "Your mother can put her gowns on the expense account if they dress for dinner every night."

"Which reminds me, I'd better get dressed myself. Stavros will be here shortly, and this is one date I'm looking forward to."

"Don't expect him to take it well," Kelley warned.

"I can handle the situation," Emmy said with confidence. "I'm in charge of my own life—finally."

Chapter Seven

Emmy's new maturity filled Kelley with deep satisfaction. No matter what happened from now on, she'd learned her salvation didn't depend on someone else.

When the phone rang a few minutes later, Kelley had to smile. She could anticipate a lot of these calls from now on. Emmy was really gung ho about their project.

Kelley picked up the phone, laughing. "Whatever it is, we'll discuss it tomorrow. Go get dressed."

After a moment's pause, Erich chuckled. "That's the last thing a man wants to hear from a beautiful woman."

Her mouth went dry and her knees buckled. She sat down abruptly, unable to utter a word.

"Kelley? At least we were on speaking terms the last time I saw you. Why am I getting the silent treatment now?"

"I...I was just surprised to hear from you," she said breathlessly.

"You didn't expressly tell me not to phone."

"No, I . . . how have you been?" she asked inanely, thrown into complete confusion by his unexpected call.

He laughed. "You mean since this morning."

Kelley took a deep breath to compose herself. "I don't mean to be rude, but I'm rather busy. What can I do for you?"

"Why do you keep asking me that when you have no intention of doing it?" he teased.

She marveled at his ability to act as if they were still the best of friends. Unfortunately she didn't share his talent. "As you pointed out, we just saw each other this morning," she said crisply. "Was there something you forgot to tell me?"

His voice sobered. "That's the whole problem. I never got to tell you anything."

"I seem to remember you saying a great deal—all of it critical."

"Not all of it," he said softly. "I might not have mentioned how sensational you look in a nightgown, but I'm sure you knew what I was thinking."

Kelley was glad he couldn't see her pink cheeks. Her heart beat faster every time she remembered what almost happened. "That incident was a mistake—like everything else about the weekend."

"I acted like a jackass," he admitted.

"If you're expecting me to disagree with you, don't hold your breath."

"You have every right to feel the way you do. I owe you an explanation."

"You've already explained and I'm sick of hearing what a jerk Kurt is, and how you were only trying to save me from the clutches of a fortune hunter."

"That part's true, but it isn't the entire story."

Kelley sighed. "Can't we simply forget about it? In a minute we'll be having another full-blown argument."

"I didn't call to talk about Kurt. You're right. We'll never agree on that subject."

"Then why *did* you call?"

"Because I never got a chance to tell you something at Henrietta's. Every time I tried, you either walked away from me, or somebody interrupted us."

"That was usually a good thing. What more could you possibly have to say?"

"I can't tell you on the telephone."

"That's the only way I'll listen. I don't want to see you again, Erich." It would be self-destructive to keep on torturing herself.

"I was afraid you'd feel that way," he said somberly. "But it's something I have to say. You deserve the last laugh."

"I'm not a vindictive person. I can understand why you thought I was a title-happy American. You didn't have to be so brutal in your condemnation, but I realize I was only a pawn in your ongoing feud with Kurt."

"Is *that* what you think?"

"You might have convinced yourself that you wanted to prevent me from making a costly mistake, but your rivalry with Kurt was the primary issue," she said sadly. "You couldn't stand to see him win."

"Our misunderstanding is even greater than I thought," he exclaimed. "You really do need to hear what I have to say. I'm in the lobby. Come down right now or I'm coming up."

"I honestly don't want to," she said plaintively. Kelley had learned what that note in Erich's voice meant. He would get his own way at any cost.

"Okay, I'll be there in a couple of minutes."

"No, wait! I'll come down." That was the lesser of two evils. He could scarcely take her in his arms in the lobby.

Erich was waiting when the elevator doors opened. He looked grim, which wasn't a good sign.

Kelley decided to go on the offensive. Thrusting her chin in the air she said, "All right, I'm here. Kindly make this brief, because I have things to do."

"I won't keep you any longer than necessary." He took her arm and propelled her through the lobby.

"Where are we going?" She tried to pull away, but his grip merely tightened.

"Someplace where we won't be interrupted."

"I don't want to go anywhere with you. What's wrong with right here?"

"I just told you."

Kelley continued to object, but Erich hustled her outside and into his car.

As he drove away she asked, "Where are you taking me?"

"It isn't far."

"That's not what I asked you," she exclaimed in exasperation.

He turned his head to glance at her briefly. "Why do you have to turn the slightest thing into a confrontation?"

"Because you're a very devious man. If you were taking me someplace I wanted to go, you'd tell me."

"You wouldn't willingly go anywhere with me," he answered moodily. "You made yourself quite clear."

"Since you're aware of that, why don't you accept the fact?"

A muscle jerked in his jaw. "We have some unfinished business."

"I can't imagine what it is."

Her displeasure had no effect on him. Erich continued to follow his original plan—whatever that was. Finally he pulled into a parking lot on the waterfront and cut the engine.

Kelley glanced around in bewilderment. Moored below them was a collection of boats, some little more than dinghies, others quite elaborate.

"What are we doing here?" she asked.

"We're going aboard my boat where nobody will bother us."

She followed him silently, only partly because it was futile to argue. Another reason was curiosity. Erich had never mentioned owning a boat.

It was a luxury cabin cruiser, gleaming with white paint in the waning light. He held out a hand to help Kelley on board, then led her into the main cabin. The furnishings there were comfortable rather than elegant. A couch and several chairs were covered in a cheerful print, and tables scattered around held books and magazines.

Kelley glanced at the watercolors on the walls and the wide windows that gave an unobstructed view of the Danube. "This is charming," she remarked, forgetting for the moment that they were adversaries.

"It's a welcome change from all the usual formality. I enjoy the change of pace."

"I didn't know you liked boats. Why didn't you ever mention it before?"

"I never had a chance to. We spent most of our time arguing about Kurt."

"Whose fault was that?" she challenged.

Erich sighed. "I didn't bring you here to fight the same battle all over again. I followed you outside last night to apologize for jumping to conclusions. It wasn't enough evidently. You walked away from me.''

''Without any protest from you,'' she answered bitterly.

''You weren't in a mood to forgive me. I tried to talk to you again this morning, with the same result. You as much as said you never wanted to see me again.''

''Your persistence amazes me. Is your ego so great that you have to score with every woman you're even casually attracted to?''

''There's nothing casual about my feelings.'' He thrust his hands into his pockets, staring at her morosely. ''I'm in love with you.''

Kelley drew a sharp breath. ''Do you expect me to believe that?''

''No. I've never been able to convince you of anything. It happens to be true, though.''

''Is that why you didn't call me after we almost . . . after that night in the park?''

''I was afraid I'd scare you away permanently. The force of your own feelings frightened you. I knew you wouldn't want to see me again so soon.''

She remembered all too vividly the molten desire that had almost clouded her judgment. ''You're a very experienced man,'' she murmured, unable to look at him.

''I didn't seduce you, Kelley, whether you're willing to admit it or not. There's an awesome chemistry between us. It ignites without a word or a touch.''

''That's merely sexual attraction. You must experience it regularly. How can you call it love?''

''Because I want more than a night or a weekend with you. I want all of you, all the time. When we're apart I can't get you out of my mind. That's why I couldn't pass up a chance to be with you this weekend, although bringing Magda was a mistake, I'll agree.''

"You did it to embarrass Kurt. You counted on her to make a scene."

"I expected her to confront him, but not so publicly. The way she did it was in very poor taste, however Kurt brought it on himself. He and Magda have gone together for years. Everyone, including Magda, expected them to get married eventually. He dumped her without warning because you were a better prospect. I hoped, when you found out, you'd realize what a self-serving worm he really is.''

"Henrietta simply asked him to drive me down. There was no romance involved," Kelley insisted.

"Maybe not on your part. *His* feelings were obvious to everybody. What I can't understand is why he didn't wait till the weekend was over to ask you to marry him. When Magda saw Kurt's ring on your finger it drove her over the edge. How could he have been so stupid?''

"He was desperate. Kurt was afraid I was falling in love with *you.*"

Erich gave a bark of harsh laughter. "That's really funny, isn't it?''

"Not really," Kelley murmured.

He stared at her with a slight frown. "It is to me, in an ironic sort of way. I had to practically kidnap you to get you here today."

Happiness was beginning to explode inside of Kelley like a shower of meteorites. She hadn't believed at first that Erich was in love with her. Men sometimes said that to get what they wanted. But he hadn't tried to touch her, although he knew from experience how vulnerable she was. That would be his most potent weapon. As impossible as it seemed, Erich actually loved her!

She gave him a dazzling smile. "If you'd told me the truth instead of playing silly games, you wouldn't have had to browbeat me into coming with you."

"I'm not sure I understand," he said warily.

Kelley walked slowly toward him. "Maybe you're not as knowledgeable about women as I thought."

Dawning hope lit up his face. "Does that mean you're more than just attracted to me?"

She put her arms around his neck and gazed up into his strong face. "I'm crazy in love with you. Is that clear enough?"

"My dearest one!"

His arms closed, straining her against his taut body while his mouth took such fierce possession that she could hardly breathe. Erich's kiss revealed the depth of his desperation and longing. Uttering low sounds of satisfaction deep in his throat, his hands roamed over her body, urging her even closer, although they were almost fused together.

Kelley returned his kiss with equal fervor. Her hands moved frantically over him, too, tracing the width of his shoulders, the bunched muscles in his back. This had seemed such an impossible fantasy that she needed to be sure he was real.

Their hearts were beating wildly when he tangled one hand in her long hair and gently tugged her head back. Staring down at her with naked desire he said huskily, "Tell me this isn't a dream."

She gave a throaty laugh. "Are your dreams always this vivid?"

"They are about you."

She traced the inner curve of his ear suggestively. "Tell me about them."

He scooped her into his arms. "They begin like this."

His lips brushed tantalizingly across hers as he carried her down to a cabin on the lower deck. Moonlight shining through the portholes revealed a bed and some other furnishings, but Kelley was only aware of Erich. His arms, his lips, the warmth of his body were setting her on fire.

He stood her on her feet by the bed and removed the jacket of her pants suit. "In my dreams I undress you slowly," he said in a low, hypnotic voice.

The silvery lace bodysuit fit like a second skin. Erich paused to cup her breasts in his palms, sending a shudder of delight through Kelley. She caught her breath when he kissed each hardened peak while unfastening the waistband of her slacks. When they slithered to the floor she stepped out of them and unbuttoned his shirt with shaking fingers.

"This wasn't in my dreams," he said in mock protest, making no attempt to stop her.

"You weren't the only one who had fantasies." She pushed the shirt off his shoulders and leaned forward to kiss his flat male nipples.

Erich uttered a hoarse cry and gathered her close. They kissed with torrid intensity, moving against each other in sensuous invitation. As their desire mounted, his fingers moved over her back, searching for a zipper or buttons.

Kelley laughed softly at his muttered curse of frustration. "You have to know the combination." She drew away and reached between her legs for the hidden snaps.

"Whoever designed this thing was a sadist," Erich growled, brushing her hand aside so he could replace it with his.

He took his time, sending liquid fire racing to the juncture of her thighs. When the garment was finally unfastened, Kelley's legs were trembling. Erich stripped off the lace bodysuit and held her at arm's length. His eyes glit-

tered like emeralds as he gazed at her nearly nude figure.
She was wearing only sheer panty hose.

"I knew you'd be perfection." His palms glided from
her collarbones over her breasts and down to her hips.

Kelley held out her arms to him. "Hold me," she whispered. "Love me."

"That's a promise."

He rolled her panty hose down her hips, kneeling to remove them completely. Kelley anchored her fingers in his
hair to steady herself as he kissed the soft skin of her inner thigh. She gasped when his warm mouth moved higher.

"This was the part of my dream that drove me crazy,"
he murmured.

"You're doing the same thing to me!" She sank beside
him and tugged at his belt.

"My sweet passionate angel." He rose and carried her
to the bed.

Removing the rest of his clothes took only an instant. He
joined her on the bed, covering her body with his. The
scorching contact was so inflaming that she parted her legs
and wrapped her arms around his waist.

Erich's control fled and he plunged deeply, bringing
Kelley such joy that she arched her body and called out his
name. He held her tightly, gripping her buttocks as she met
his thrusts with wild abandon.

Their damp bodies met and parted repeatedly in a dance
of love that grew in intensity until every muscle was taut.
When the exquisite torment was too much to endure, a final burst of sensation jolted through them, bringing utter
fulfillment.

Diminishing spasms of pleasure accompanied their slow
spiral down from the heights. They clung to each other,
savoring the aftermath of ecstasy.

Finally Erich moved his head just enough to kiss Kelley's temple. "And this is the way the dream always ends."

"Are you tired of me already?" The words were joking, but it made her uneasy to even think of the dream ending.

"You can't be serious!" He raised on one elbow to gaze down at her. Stroking her cheek he said, "You're mine now, and I won't ever let you go."

Kelley's heart did a funny little flip. Was Erich talking about marriage? She needed to find out—but carefully. Covering her uncertainty with a little laugh she said, "You'd better not make any rash statements."

"You can't have any doubts after what we just shared?"

It wasn't the answer Kelley wanted, but maybe it was too soon. Erich had said he loved her, and he'd certainly showed it. No woman could ask for a more tender, thoughtful lover. She just needed to have a little patience.

"I won't ever get enough of you." He cradled her in his arms and urged her head onto his shoulder. "You're God's most inspired creation—an absolutely perfect woman."

She smiled. "Nobody's perfect."

"You are. You have the body of a siren and the face of an angel."

"How about my mind?" she teased. "Did you notice I have one?"

"It's one of your great attractions." He tipped her chin up and gazed at her fondly. "You have everything. In addition to being incredibly sexy, you're a very kind person."

"I hope so, but how would you know that?"

"I found out a lot about you this weekend. The way you dealt with Kurt, for instance. He made a nuisance of himself, but you tried to let him down gently."

"Poor Kurt." Kelley sighed. "He's not really a bad person. His values are just skewed. You could be a little more tolerant, too," she said mildly. "You're everything he wants to be."

Erich frowned. "I don't wish to discuss him."

"You were the one who brought up the subject."

"That was a mistake. We always wind up in an argument, so let's just agree to disagree. We've ironed out all of our misunderstandings and I want to keep it that way," Erich stated firmly.

"I suppose that would be prudent, since you can't think of one good thing to say about him."

Erich's frown changed to a smile. "I'm in his debt for introducing me to you—however inadvertently. If Kurt wasn't a tacky fortune hunter we'd never have met."

Kelley stirred uneasily. She couldn't put off telling Erich the truth about her financial status any longer. There was no reason to be nervous about his reaction. He was almost sure to think the mixup was funny.

"You don't really know a lot about me," she began tentatively.

"I'd say I knew you intimately." He chuckled richly, gliding his hand over her body.

"That's not what I mean."

"What surprises do you have in store for me?" He scissored his legs around both of hers and dipped his head to kiss the tip of her breast. "Tell me everything."

"I'm trying to," she answered faintly.

"I prefer to find out for myself," he murmured.

Kelley felt herself melting under his sensuous exploration. She tried to stem the rising tide. "Please, Erich, I can't think when you do that. I really want to talk to you."

"Whatever you say, my love." He trailed a forefinger down her spine while his hardened body moved erotically against hers. "What would you like to talk about?"

It didn't seem important at that moment. "It can wait," she whispered, parting her lips for his deep kiss.

Erich's lovemaking was leisurely this time, compared to their first overwhelming need for each other. He searched out every pleasure spot on Kelley's body, learning what pleased her the most.

She gasped with delight as his kisses and caresses aroused her to a fever pitch. Then he gratified her desire so thoroughly that she was filled with glowing contentment.

Afterward, Erich pulled the covers over their relaxed bodies and they drifted off to sleep in each other's arms.

It was very quiet in the cabin when Kelley awakened sometime later. For a moment the unfamiliar surroundings confused her. This wasn't her hotel room. Then the warmth of Erich's body brought back vivid memories. She relaxed and her mouth curved in a smile of absolute bliss.

He opened his eyes and gazed at her tenderly. "This is part of the dream, too. Waking up and finding you in my arms."

After they kissed sweetly she said, "It's so quiet out. It must be very late."

"What difference does it make?" He chuckled. "You're not going anywhere."

She glanced over at her clothes, lying in an untidy heap on the floor where they'd been discarded. "I should hang up my clothes. They'll be terribly wrinkled."

"Does it really matter?"

"I don't want to look a complete mess when I walk through the lobby tomorrow."

Erich wrapped his arms more securely around her. "I'm not letting you get away that soon."

"Your stamina is awesome." She laughed. "I believe you *could* stay in bed for a week."

"You'll find out."

"I'll have to take your word for it. We can't all be grand dukes with unlimited time to indulge our every whim," she teased. "Some of us live in the real world."

"You think my life is one long pursuit of pleasure, don't you?" he asked slowly.

"I wasn't criticizing," she said hastily. "Why shouldn't you enjoy yourself?"

"That would make me a very shallow person. Everyone should contribute something, not simply take up space."

"I'm sure you're very charitable."

He shrugged. "It's easy to give money when you have a lot of it. I've tried to do more than that."

"In what way?"

"I told you about the children's home I founded. I'm the director of that. It isn't merely a title. I'm actively involved in its operation. I also sit on the board of several charities. Again, these aren't simply organizations I lend my name to. I participate in the fund-raising, a job that requires equal parts of arm-twisting, tact, and subtle blackmail if necessary."

Kelley looked at him with new respect. "I had no idea. I thought those formal balls were your natural environment."

Erich grimaced. "Most of the time I'd prefer wearing jeans to a dinner jacket."

"You could do anything you like. I think it's wonderful that you have such a sense of responsibility toward your fellow man."

"I wasn't looking for a pat on the back. I just didn't want you to think I'm a frivolous playboy, interested only in sybaritic pleasure and compliant women." A grin lightened his serious expression. "Not necessarily in that order."

She gazed at him with pure love. "I knew you were special the moment I saw you in the middle of that crowded ballroom, surrounded by people who all wanted to be close to you. I can't believe you even noticed me."

"I've been waiting for you all my life, sweetheart."

They kissed lingeringly, murmuring tender endearments and caressing each other affectionately. Inevitably their passion rose and they made love again with the same stirring result.

When they were totally spent, Erich stroked Kelley's hair languidly. "This is going to be a week to remember."

"You aren't serious!"

His chuckle had a deep male sound. "Don't worry. I won't keep you in bed all week. We'll go ashore in Bratislava. It's a town in Slovakia, only a few hours from here. Then we'll leave the boat there and fly to Budapest. Would you like that?"

"I'd adore it!"

"Good, then we'll leave first thing in the morning."

"More likely around noon," she said. "I have to go back to the hotel and pack."

"Why? I'll buy you everything you need when we get where we're going."

"I have to get my passport, and so do you."

"I'd forgotten about that," he admitted. "See how much I need you?"

"I intend to keep reminding you," she answered lightly.

"Okay, I'll drop you off at the hotel and swing by my place to pick up a few things. Don't dawdle, though. We want to get as early a start as possible. The scenery along the Danube is lovely."

"It won't take long to throw a few things into a suitcase," she promised. "That's all I have to do except telephone Emmy."

"I didn't know you two were that friendly."

"We've gotten to be on short acquaintance. She's very direct. I like that."

Erich smiled fondly. "Yes, Emmy is a good kid. I just wish she'd do something with her life."

"I'm pointing her in the right direction," Kelley said confidently.

"How can you do that?"

"At Henrietta's luncheon, Emmy told me about her family's lack of finances. I was appalled that her solution was to marry a man older than her father."

"Henrietta and I both told her she's out of her mind, but she won't listen. Who knows? Maybe the life of a jetsetter appeals to her."

"Have you ever met Stavros Theopolis?"

"I've been introduced to him, that's all. He seemed fairly pleasant. Maybe they'll be happy in spite of the age difference."

"That's not the only problem Emmy will face," Kelley said succinctly. "Stavros is a womanizer, and he's not about to change. Would you believe he gave me the eye right in front of Emmy?"

"That doesn't surprise me," Erich answered affectionately. "I can't imagine any man resisting you. Just tell him for me that if he comes near you I'll break both his legs, regardless of his age."

"I'm serious, Erich. You were taken in by his phony charm. He would make Emmy's life a living hell."

"I hope you're wrong, because there's nothing anyone can do about it if she's made up her mind. We've all tried talking to her."

"I did more than talk. I gave her an out," Kelley said smugly.

"What do you mean?"

She told him about her plan, growing more animated by the minute. "It's more than just her salvation, it will give her a career. This project will take years. If at any time it slows down, Emmy will have learned so much that she'll be able to branch out into a number of fields."

Erich hesitated. "I don't want to dampen your enthusiasm, but you have no idea how much money it would take to get your project started."

"We will have after all the estimates are in. Emmy will be working on that this week. We'll be able to show the bank exactly how the money will be spent."

"They're more interested in income than outgo," he observed dryly.

"I'll have that calculated, too, as soon as we see how many rooms we're talking about. The number of guests has to be kept low because we're selling exclusiveness, but we can charge more for the privilege, so it evens out."

"It will take years to pay off the kind of loan you'll need," he warned.

"What difference does it make? We can keep the payments manageable by amortizing the cost of the repairs over a number of years. We should also qualify for a tax break, and the interest on the loan is deductible. Banks tend to look more favorably at a business whose indebtedness isn't unwieldy."

Erich was looking at her admiringly. "I'm impressed. You really know what you're talking about."

"Did you think I was just another pretty face?" She laughed.

He kissed the tip of her nose. "There aren't any other faces as pretty as yours. You could sell *me* your Brooklyn Bridge, but bankers are born with computers for hearts. Even if your fact sheet is convincing, they're apt to question your ability to deliver the requisite paying guests."

"I plan to approach so many sources that the law of averages will guarantee results." She told him the methods she intended to use.

His reaction was a puzzled frown. "That isn't the easiest job in the world. Why would you go knocking on doors when you don't have to?"

"I don't know the market for upscale lodgings here in Europe, but I do know there's an untapped pool of potential customers in America. After Emmy's castle is a success and we start on others, I'll look into the possibilities here."

"That doesn't answer my question. Why are you getting so involved?"

"It was my idea, and she can't do it alone," Kelley answered simply.

Erich cupped her cheek in his palm tenderly. "Is there no end to your good qualities?"

Kelley knew she'd been evading the issue. The perfect opportunity had presented itself when he asked why she was devoting herself to the project so wholeheartedly. Certainly part of her enthusiasm was for Emmy's sake, but the success of their venture was crucial to her own finances. At the rate she was spending it, her money wouldn't last long. He had to be told right now.

"I wish I were as noble as you think I am, but I'm not," she began carefully. "You have a lot to learn about me."

"And I plan to enjoy every minute." He smiled. Before she could continue, Erich's stomach growled loudly. He glanced at the luminous clock on the nightstand. "No wonder my stomach is complaining. It's after midnight and we haven't had dinner."

"It's too late to go out now. I don't feel like getting dressed."

"I don't want you to." He leered playfully as he tossed back the covers. "I'll go see what I can whip up in the galley."

"I can't believe the Grand Duke Erich Von Graile Und Tassburg knows how to cook," she teased. "You probably had some four-star restaurant prepare a sumptuous meal."

"I wish I'd thought of it, but I never expected the night to turn out like this." He flashed her an incandescent smile.

"I didn't, either," she said softly, watching him pull on jeans and a T-shirt. She swung her legs to the floor. "I'll come and help you."

"You don't think I'm competent?" he asked in mock outrage.

"I think you can do anything." She put her arms around his waist.

Erich caressed her bare bottom. "On second thought, are you really hungry?" he murmured.

"Yes, I'm starving." She laughed. "Go get started and I'll join you in a couple of minutes."

Kelley's laughter faded as she got dressed. Once more she'd failed to tell Erich the truth, although it wasn't her fault this time. Actually she'd tried repeatedly to talk to him, but he always seemed to change the subject.

She paused in the act of zipping up her pants. Had Erich already found out somehow? That would explain why he never wanted to listen. He thought she might be embarrassed at having accepted Henrietta's invitations under false pretenses. It *had* bothered her, although she hadn't lied about being an American. That was Henrietta's initial interest in her. Dear Erich, he was a real treasure. Kelley was glad she'd finally gotten his message. She wouldn't bring it up again. The past didn't matter, only the future, and hers was bright.

Erich's broad-shouldered body almost filled the compact galley. He was whistling while he stirred something in a pot on the stove.

Kelley sniffed appreciatively. "That smells good. What are we having?"

"Not much, I'm afraid. I only stock the boat when I'm taking it out, which I haven't done recently. All I could find was a couple of cans of spaghetti. Is that all right?"

"Perfect. Can I set the table?"

"No, just sit there and look beautiful." He reached over her head to get two plates out of the cupboard.

"Okay, I'll get out of your way. There isn't room enough for both of us."

"There's always room for you," he answered meltingly, dishing up the spaghetti.

It was the most memorable meal Kelley had ever eaten. She glowed with happiness as she sat across from Erich at the small table. This was the way it would be if they were married. Was that too much to hope for? Why should it be? She'd never expected to hear Erich say he loved her. The world was full of miracles!

He interrupted her reverie. "I can't believe my cooking deserves a smile like that. Can I hope my other talents had something to do with it?"

"Stop fishing for compliments. You know how you affect women."

"I'm not interested in any other woman." He reached over and squeezed her hand. "I only want to make *you* happy."

"You have, my love," she answered softly. "So happy I'm afraid something will happen to spoil things."

"Nothing will," he promised. "All of our misunderstandings are behind us."

Kelley packed rapidly, leaving most of her couture wardrobe behind. The jeans, sweaters and running shoes she'd brought from home were more appropriate, if not as glamorous. After a moment's hesitation she included one dinner dress, just in case. When her suitcase was all packed, she telephoned Emmy.

"You certainly got out early," Emmy said. "I phoned at nine o'clock and you'd already gone."

"Yes, I got your message," Kelley answered noncommittally.

"Where were you at that ungodly hour of the morning?"

Kelley's mouth curved in a tender smile. She'd been curled up in Erich's arms. They'd slept late after their strenuous night.

"I wanted to talk to you," Emmy continued, without waiting for an answer.

"You're not waffling on our deal, are you?" Kelley asked in sudden concern.

"No way. I broke up with Stavros last night."

"How did he take it?"

"Not gracefully. Stavros doesn't take rejection well," Emmy said dryly. "When he saw he couldn't change my mind he got quite ugly."

"Are you all right?"

"I'm ecstatic! If it weren't for you I would have married him without realizing what I was letting myself in for. He's a very cruel man under that surface charm. Why didn't I see it?"

"He's fooled more experienced people than you. Put him out of your mind and go on from here."

"That's why I called you. I spoke to a plumbing and electrical contractor, and he told me what kind of furnace we'll need. I'm on my way out now to price them. I'll phone you when I get back this afternoon with the figures."

"Oh, well... I won't be here."

"That's okay, I'll catch you this evening."

"Well, the thing is, I'm going away for a while."

"You haven't changed your mind about helping me?" Emmy wailed.

"No, nothing like that. I was just asked to... uh... go on a little cruise." Kelley was afraid to give undue importance to Erich's invitation. He hadn't actually committed himself yet. "You won't need me for a week. You'll be busy getting estimates. I'll be back by the time you have all the information."

"That's a relief," Emmy said fervently. "I'm counting on you."

"I won't let you down," Kelley promised.

Now that her concern was allayed, Emmy was curious. "Whose yacht are you going on? Maybe I know them."

"It isn't really a yacht."

"Well, who are you going with?" Emmy couldn't see why Kelley would mind telling her.

"Erich invited me," Kelley said reluctantly, knowing the questions wouldn't stop.

"When did all this happen? You certainly hid your feelings during the weekend. Half the time the tension between you two was pretty thick."

"We had a couple of run-ins, nothing heavy. Neither is this week. Erich offered to take me on a cruise down the Danube, and it was an offer I couldn't refuse," Kelley said lightly.

"I'm relieved to hear you haven't fallen in love with him. Erich is a living doll. Women find him irresistible— too many women. Who wants to be a face in the crowd?"

"You don't think he'll ever settle down?" Kelley asked wistfully.

"I suppose anything is possible." After a moment's silence Emmy said, "Maybe I should mind my own business, but I don't want to see you get hurt."

"Not to worry," Kelley said breezily. "I enjoy Erich's company, but I don't care to get involved any more than he does."

"Then you should have a ball. Enjoy your trip and call me when you get back."

Kelley's euphoria was considerably dimmed after her conversation with Emmy. Erich couldn't be called a womanizer—he was too thoughtful and caring for that. But there were a lot of beautiful women in the world, and he was only human.

When he knocked on the door a few moments later, Kelley greeted him with a forced smile. At first he didn't notice.

"Sorry I took longer than I expected. I had to return a few urgent phone calls. Are you all ready?"

"Yes."

"Do you have your passport?"

"It's in my purse."

He looked at her more closely. "Is anything wrong, Kelley?"

"No, of course not." She smiled brightly. "Shall we go?"

"Not until you tell me what's bothering you." He framed her face in his palms and looked searchingly at her. "I don't want anything to come between us. You're very important to me."

"I'd like to believe that," she whispered.

"How can you doubt it? Didn't last night tell you anything?"

Kelley remembered not only the passion, but also the caring and tenderness of their lovemaking. Emmy couldn't know about that. She didn't know that love could change a person.

"What happened in the hour I was away from you?" he persisted.

She gave him a misty smile. "I missed you."

"Dear heart!" He crushed her in his arms. "Don't ever do that to me again. I don't know what I'd do if I lost you now."

"That's not very likely." She kissed the point of his chin. "I'm ready if you are."

Chapter Eight

Kelley was fascinated by the Danube. The water was more green than blue, a wide placid river that flowed through many countries before reaching the Black Sea.

The imposing United Nations Headquarters Building overlooked the water, along with the huge DDSG Shipping Company and a converted grain storage house that had been turned into a gracious hotel.

But when they left Vienna behind, the scenery became rural. Long stretches along the bank had only an occasional house, and some of these were merely little boxes on stilts. Many had fishing nets spread out on a strip of narrow beach.

Kelley perched on a stool next to Erich, gazing delightedly at the scenery while he steered the boat. "This is so charming," she remarked. "I love a big city like Vienna, but it will be great fun to wander through an unspoiled little village."

He smiled. "I'm sorry to put a damper on your expectations, but Bratislava is the second largest city in Slovakia. It has a population of almost half a million."

"Too bad. I was hoping to see lots of local color."

"It has plenty of that, including one of those castles you're so enamored of," Erich teased. "Trust me. You won't be disappointed."

His prediction was correct. Kelley was entranced when they reached Bratislava some time later. Standing on a bluff and dominating the landscape was a gray stone castle straight out of a picture book. It was built in the shape of a square, and each corner was topped by a tower with a cone-shaped turret. The fading light gave an added mysticism to the ancient edifice.

"It's too bad we got such a late start," Erich commented. "We won't be able to do much sight-seeing today."

"We'll just have to get up early tomorrow morning," Kelley said.

"Depending on when we get to sleep tonight." He hooked a hand around the back of her neck and pulled her closer for a kiss.

"I can tell I'm not going to see much of Bratislava," she said plaintively.

"Which one of us would you choose?"

Kelley gazed up at his handsome, virile face. Erich was almost overwhelmingly masculine in tight jeans and a baggy sweatshirt that failed to camouflage his broad shoulders.

"No contest," she said softly. "You'd win, hands down."

"That's the answer I was hoping for." He hugged her to his side. "Just for that, I'll restrain my passion and take you sightseeing."

"You don't have to go to extremes," she murmured.

He laughed. "There's no pleasing you, woman."

"You've done awfully well so far."

"If you keep looking at me that way I'm apt to run the boat aground. Go out on deck," he ordered.

"It won't be the same without me," she warned.

"I found that out already," he answered in a husky voice.

Kelley hung over the railing, drinking in the exotic sights and sounds. In the distance were Gothic church spires, and she could just make out a baroque clock tower.

Erich joined her at the railing after docking the boat. "Would you prefer to stay in a hotel tonight?" he asked. "The cabin is rather cramped."

"I like it that way." She smiled. "We have to cuddle."

He put his arms loosely around her shoulders. "Shall we try it now, and then make up our minds?" When she hesitated, glancing toward the dock he said, "I was only joking, honey. We'll go ashore and walk around a little before the last of the light is gone."

They didn't get to see much before darkness fell. Erich led her into a wine cellar, promising they'd make up for it the next day.

"This is what I was hoping for," Kelley exclaimed, glancing around the cavernous room.

The brick walls and domed ceiling gave an old-world ambience to the place, and a string quartet lent an air of gaiety. The musicians wandered throughout the room, stopping to serenade the patrons.

"I wish I'd brought a camera," Kelley lamented as they sat at a table and sipped their wine.

"This is just a commonplace Slovakian wine cellar," Erich said dismissively.

"That's why I'd like a picture of it. But it's just as well. You'd probably be terribly embarrassed if I acted like a typical tourist."

"Why should it bother me? That's what we are."

"*I* am, but you're scarcely typical."

"How did you reach that conclusion?"

"I doubt if many of the patrons here are grand dukes."

"I'm just a man like any other. You should know that," he murmured.

"I need reminding every now and then," she answered demurely.

"Is tonight soon enough?"

"That sounds about right."

"How do you feel about an early dinner?" The candle-light made his eyes glow like green coals.

"I'd better agree or I'll have to settle for a plate of spaghetti in the middle of the night." She grinned.

"I hope I provided compensations."

She looked at him with starry eyes. "Couldn't you tell?"

Erich sat back in his chair. "If you expect to get a proper dinner we'd better change the subject. I have very little willpower where you're concerned, and you're taxing it to the limit."

Kelley's willpower was also shaky at this point. How was it possible to love someone so much? "Let's talk about our plans. How long will we be here?"

"As long as you like, but there's more to do in Budapest. I suggest we hit the high spots of Bratislava tomorrow and fly to Budapest the next morning."

"What will you do with the boat?"

"I've arranged for someone to take it back to Vienna. We'll stay in a hotel in Budapest. Do you think you can cuddle in a regular-size bed?" He smiled.

"With a little cooperation from a friend."

"I believe in very close friendships," he said in a deep velvet voice.

Kelley gazed at him through long lashes, remarking ingenuously, "To get back to tonight—there's a lot to be said for early dinners."

They left the wine cellar and strolled hand in hand down the street till they came to a small restaurant.

It had the picturesqueness that so delighted Kelley. A fire burned in a large brick fireplace blackened from much usage. Grouped around it were tables covered with blue-and-white checked cloths centered by a small vase of flowers. The finishing touch was a gypsy violinist who played soulfully.

"It's the Hungarian influence," Erich told her. "Bratislava was the capital of Hungary until the late 1700s."

"It must be a very old city."

"Let's see if I can remember my history. The Slavs settled here in the fifth century, but Bratislava dates back to a Roman outpost. It was called Posonium, I believe."

While they dined on goulash and drank red wine, Erich told Kelley interesting bits of history.

"You're remarkably well-informed," she commented.

"It's my part of the world. You must be knowledgeable about your own history."

"That's easier. We don't go back as far."

"I'd like to travel in America. It seems incredibly vast to a European."

"Haven't you ever been to America?"

"Only to New York City and your capital, Washington, D.C. I realize that doesn't even scratch the surface."

"No, it leaves out the south and west, among other regions. You can come home with me and I'll show you Los Angeles in depth."

Erich frowned. "Surely you're not thinking about going home so soon?"

"In a couple of weeks, I hope."

"I thought you were enjoying yourself," he said evenly.

"I am, but I have to go back and scout around for rich tourists. We discussed that already."

"I guess I didn't think of it as being imminent."

"It might not be. After Emmy and I have a solid proposal to present, we'll have to wait for the bank to make a decision. I can only hope your loan divisions move faster than ours."

He looked at her with a hooded expression. "Do you plan to come back to Vienna after you've accomplished your purpose at home?"

Kelley's hopes shriveled and died. If Erich had marriage in mind, now was the time to mention it, or at the very least try to persuade her to stay. Instead of that, he was letting her go. She stared at the table, carefully lining up her silverware.

"I suppose I'll be back some day," she answered carefully. "We hope to tap the European guest market after we're established."

Erich's eyes had turned bleak. "I'll miss you," he said quietly.

"I'll miss you, too," she whispered. He must never know how much!

"We'll just have to make the most of our time together." He mustered a smile. "We have this week anyway."

"Yes, I'm looking forward to seeing Budapest. I suppose you know it well."

They made polite conversation during the rest of the meal and on the way back to the boat. All spontaneity had fled. They were like two casual acquaintances. When Kelley went below to the cabin, Erich didn't follow. Muttering something about checking the pilothouse, he left her.

Kelley got undressed disconsolately. What did Erich want from her? He had only to say the word and she'd stay—or at least return as soon as possible. Was he one of those male chauvinists who expected a woman to be there for him when he wanted her, without any commitment from him?

When he came in sometime later, Kelley squeezed as far over in the narrow bed as possible and pretended to be asleep. Now she regretted her choice of the boat over a hotel. Lying next to him would be agony.

She stifled a groan, watching through her lashes as he got undressed. Moonlight streaming through the porthole bathed his nude body in a silvery light. He looked like one of those impossibly perfect statues of a Greek athlete. Would she ever forget that perfection? She closed her eyes hastily when he got into bed next to her.

"We have to talk, Kelley." He knew she wasn't asleep. "I want to apologize for acting childish when you spoke about going home. I'd hoped—well, never mind. I'm sorry."

She didn't pretend there'd been no tension. "You knew I'd have to leave sometime," she said in a small voice.

He didn't answer for a moment and when he did it was obliquely. "I realize how much this venture means to you."

"Not only to me. Emmy can't do it alone. She needs me."

"So do I, but evidently that's of secondary importance."

Kelley sat up in bed, wrapping the sheet around her breasts. "Now you *are* being childish. You're doing work that satisfies you, how can you begrudge me the same opportunity?"

"I don't. I just hoped you'd make room in your life for me, too," he answered quietly.

She looked at him uncertainly. "I didn't think you cared that much."

"What do I have to do to convince you?" He sat up next to her and smoothed her hair tenderly. "I've tried to show you how I feel."

Kelley's lashes drooped. "We have very satisfying sex."

His hand fell away. "If that's all it is to you, then I've failed. I thought we were making love," he said harshly.

"I guess love means different things to people," she said in a low voice.

"Obviously." His tone was biting. "But at least *I* told the truth."

"I did, too, even though you don't believe me." Kelley sighed. "Last night was so perfect, yet here we are at each other's throats again. Maybe we ought to admit we just aren't right for each other."

"Don't say that!" He gripped her shoulders hard. "We can work this out. We've had misunderstandings before."

"Too many of them. Love is supposed to make you feel good, not take you on a roller coaster of ups and downs."

Erich smiled wryly. "I believe that's a classic description of the tenderest of emotions. Didn't one of your countrymen say, love is hell?"

"I think the correct quote is, *war* is hell." She couldn't help returning his smile reluctantly.

"Unfortunately it seems to be the same thing with us." He gently traced the shape of her mouth. "I don't know why. All I want to do is make you happy."

"You do, most of the time." Kelley felt herself falling under his spell again. If this was all she was destined to have, wouldn't she be foolish to spoil it?

He gathered her into his arms and cradled her head on his shoulder. "I guess I expected too much, but I don't want to lose you, sweetheart. I hate to see you go, but I understand why you have to. I won't say a word if you promise to come back to me."

"Maybe you'll find someone else while I'm gone," she murmured.

"Nobody could ever take your place." His embrace tightened convulsively. "Don't leave me, Kelley."

"Never for long, darling." That's what she'd yearned to hear. Fierce exultation filled her. How could she have doubted his love?

Their kiss expressed all the anguish both had felt, and the gratitude that it was over. They tried to reassure each other, muttering broken words of endearment as their legs twined together and their bodies strained to get closer.

Erich scattered frantic kisses over Kelley's face and neck, then continued down her body, trailing a fiery path. She arched her hips as the storm built, bunching the sheet in her clenched fists.

He knelt over her with blazing eyes. "I do know how to satisfy you, don't I?"

"I never knew it could be so wonderful," she gasped.

"It's never been like this for me, either." He cupped her breasts in his hands and leaned down to touch the sensitive tips with his tongue. "I love the taste and feel of you. I want to leave my mark on every inch of you. You're mine!"

"And you're *mine*," she cried out triumphantly.

"All of me," he promised deeply.

Kelley reached out blindly for him, running her hands over his lean hips, digging her fingers into his buttocks. How could she ever do without this man? Her hand closed around his manhood, guiding it toward the pulsating core of her desire.

Erich's breathing quickened and he clasped her tightly in his arms, joining their bodies. They were welded into one person, giving and receiving pleasure so intense that they writhed in ecstasy. The throbbing crescendo exploded inside both of them at the same time, followed by aftershocks of diminishing intensity. Their taut bodies were bathed in a warm glow as straining muscles gradually relaxed.

When his heartbeat returned to normal, Erich murmured, "How can making love to you be more fantastic every time?"

Her mouth curved in a smile of pure bliss. "Maybe all couples in love feel like this."

He settled his head on her breast. "I wouldn't know. This is a new experience for me."

"You've known a lot of women, Erich. Weren't you ever in love with any of them? You can tell me the truth."

"I won't deny that I've had close relationships—although not as many as I'm credited with. They were charming women and I was very fond of them. But I never went into a blind panic at the thought of losing one of them." He tilted his head to look up at her. "How about you?"

"I can't match your record." She smiled ruefully. "I suppose I should invent some torrid romances to make you jealous, but there weren't any. I've been waiting all my life for someone like you."

"Do you know how happy that makes me?" He kissed her tenderly. "It proves we were meant to be together."

"I hope so," she answered soberly.

"Good Lord! If tonight didn't convince you, I don't know what more I can do."

"It's always wonderful when we make up. I just wish we didn't argue so much."

"We're not going to anymore." Erich's tone was firm. "Our problem was a lack of trust, but that's all over with. You do believe I love you, don't you?"

"Oh, yes!" It was like a miracle, but he'd succeeded in convincing her.

His eyes lit with mischief. "And I've bamboozled you into thinking I'm perfect, so all of our problems are solved."

"You *are* perfect." She touched his features lightly with her fingertips. "I like everything about you."

"Let's hope you don't discover any of my bad habits this week." He chuckled.

"Whatever they are, I can live with them."

"I'm excessively cheerful in the morning," he warned. "I even whistle on occasion."

"That's okay, I'll put a pillow over my head."

"Not tomorrow, you won't. I intend to bring you breakfast in bed, and then we're off to see Bratislava."

"I guess we should go to sleep if we plan to get up early."

Pinpoints of light appeared in his eyes as he caressed her body. "I don't think another half hour will make that much difference, do you?"

She put her arms around his neck. "I'd be willing to give up a whole hour."

Erich fell asleep in her arms soon afterward, but Kelley remained awake, reliving the rapture. All of her doubts were a thing of the past. Erich still hadn't asked her to marry him, but maybe he didn't want to use marriage as a bribe not to leave him. Or the answer could be that the thought of marriage spooked him. Erich had been a bachelor for a long time.

Kelley smiled in the darkness. He'd get used to the idea. Much as she hated to be separated from him, perhaps it was a good thing. He'd find out what it was like to be without her when she went back to California. All she had to do was be patient.

Her eyes grew dreamy. Grand Duchess Kelley Von Graile Und Tassburg. She quickly stifled the laughter that welled up in her. It didn't exactly flow off the tongue. Maybe she'd have to change her first name too. Snuggling closer to Erich, Kelley closed her eyes and drifted off to sleep.

Their day in Bratislava went by in a whirlwind of activity. They started in Old Town, dominated by the imposing Gothic-baroque Town Hall and the ornate clock tower. Across the square were some large homes—although they were really too grand to be mere houses. Kelley questioned Erich about them.

"Those were palaces built by wealthy burghers in the 1700s."

"They're so well taken care of. In my country we tear down lovely old structures to make way for a supermarket or a hamburger stand."

"Your buildings don't have centuries of history."

"That's true. We have to settle for sixty or seventy years. The Brown Derby restaurant in Los Angeles was declared a historic landmark because it dated back to the 1920s." Kelley grinned.

They visited the impressive St. Martin's Cathedral, where Hungarian kings were crowned for three hundred years. Then they gazed at the carefully preserved Michael Gate, the only remaining tower gate left from the fifteenth century city fortifications.

By late afternoon Kelley was dragging a little. "I don't think I can absorb much more," she groaned.

Erich consulted his watch. "It's time to go to the airport anyway."

"Can we take Budapest in smaller doses? Everything runs together when you see it all at once."

"We'll take our time," he promised. "All we'll do tonight is go out to dinner."

Kelley's interest revived when they flew into Budapest. It was a magnificent city, much larger than she expected. Erich had told her it was originally two cities, Buda and Pest, separated by the broad Danube. They were united now by many bridges.

Her head swiveled back and forth on the taxi ride to the hotel. "What are those gorgeous buildings on both sides of the river, more castles?"

"The one on the left bank, or Pest side, is the Parliament Building. The one on the right side is Buda Castle. You can spend all day there. The complex houses three large museums and the National Library."

Kelley flexed her tired feet. Maybe we'll save that for later in the week."

Erich laughed. "I think that's a good idea."

The hotel he took her to was the ultimate in luxury. Their suite was elegantly furnished and the tall windows overlooked a park. Kelley wandered around the room delightedly sniffing the bouquet of roses on the coffee table, and peering inside the small, well-stocked bar.

"Let's relax and have some champagne," Erich suggested. "We don't have that much to unpack."

"I didn't know Budapest was so Continental. It's lucky I decided at the last minute to take a dinner dress. I'm afraid I'll have to wear it every night, though."

He uncorked a bottle of champagne and filled two glasses. "You can buy anything you need here in the hotel. They have some excellent shops."

"With prices to match, no doubt."

Kelley thought about her depleted finances and the need to conserve. She wouldn't have a regular paycheck coming in anymore, and it would be months before she could count on any money from their venture.

"My frugal little darling." He ruffled her hair fondly. "When are you going to learn that money's to spend?"

She looked at him uncertainly. Could she be wrong? Was it possible Erich *didn't* know her situation?

"Why don't you lie down and take a little rest?" he suggested. "I'm going downstairs for a few minutes."

Kelley took a long, relaxing bubble bath instead. Much as she cherished their time on Erich's boat, it was a luxury to stretch out in a large tub.

He was gone more than a few minutes. She had finished with her bath and was wrapping herself in a long terry-cloth robe when he called to her from the bedroom.

"Where have you been? I was wondering what happened to you." She came out of the bathroom and stopped in surprise. The bed was covered with boxes. "What's all that?"

"I did a little shopping."

"It looks like you gave the Hungarian economy a giant boost. What did you buy?"

"Open them and see."

The boxes were filled with dresses and accessories. The first one held a red satin coatdress with rhinestone buttons down the asymmetrical closing, and a sparkling half-moon buckle on the wide belt. In the second box was a pale blue silk chemise with a long scarf that circled the neck, then floated free over one shoulder.

"They're absolutely stunning," Kelley gasped.

"I hoped you'd like them. The next one may be a little much for here, but I couldn't resist," he said.

The short sheath was completely covered with handsewn silver beads. From the front it was deceptively simple, but the back dipped almost to the waist in a draped cowl. Completing the outfit were shimmery panty hose and a pair of high heeled silver sandals.

"I don't know what to say, except you shouldn't have," Kelley said helplessly. "I know the price of designer clothes. These must have cost a fortune."

He brushed that aside. "The shop has a good selection if you'd like to exchange anything."

"I love all three," she assured him. "You have wonderful taste, but I still think you were too extravagant."

"Making you happy is all that matters." He tugged her hair playfully. "I knew you couldn't justify buying them for yourself."

So she was right the first time. Erich did know she wasn't wealthy. Kelley was glad now that she hadn't rehashed the whole story. He might have thought she was hinting when she mentioned bringing only one dress.

"Which one are you going to wear tonight?" he asked.

"I'll let you choose."

"The red one would be nice." He started for the bathroom, unbuttoning his shirt. "I'll take a quick shower and then we'll go out to dinner."

Kelley was dressed by the time Erich came out of the bathroom with a towel wrapped around his middle. She twirled for his inspection, knowing he'd approve. The red dress was very becoming. Its short, full skirt stopped just above her knees, and the wide belt called attention to her narrow waist.

"Do you like it?" she asked.

"You look fantastic! I can't decide whether you're more beautiful dressed or undressed."

She laughed softly. "We'll make the comparison later and you can take your choice."

He gathered her in his arms, saying throatily, "I'm afraid there wouldn't be any contest."

Erich and Kelley got an early start the next morning because there was so much to see. They began with St. Stephan's Basilica, stopping to admire the lofty front doors decorated with bronze busts of noted composers set in vertical rows of circular frames.

Kelley was awed by the magnificent interior with its vaulted ceiling, mosaics and the huge marble statue of St. Stephan in the sanctuary. "The workmanship is incredible," she exclaimed. "Did you notice the different shades of marble on the walls and pillars?"

"More than fifty different kinds, supposedly, but you can't stop to count them all." Erich smiled. "We have a lot more to see."

Their next stop was Heroes' Square. The broad plaza, decorated with white rectangles and squares bordered in gray, was dominated by a tall column bearing a statue of the Archangel Gabriel. The base was surrounded by seven statues of Magyar chieftains on horseback.

"What a lovely, peaceful spot," Kelley remarked. "I love all this wide open space. Those buildings on either side are beautiful, too. What are they?"

"The one on the left is the Art Gallery and the other is the Museum of Fine Arts. I suggest we leave those for another day, however. I want to take you to the Fisherman's Bastion, and afterward we can have lunch at the Hilton Hotel nearby. It's quite fascinating."

"A modern hotel?" she asked doubtfully.

"This one was built on the site of a medieval church and monastery of the Dominican Order. When they started to excavate for the hotel, workmen uncovered the remains of some of the ancient walls. Instead of bulldozing them, the plans were altered to use them as part of the design."

Each new place delighted Kelley, but the Fisherman's Bastion topped the list. It looked like a castle straight out of Disneyland. White cone-shaped towers were ringed by balconies on different levels. The parapets were curved and decorated with arches and round cutouts. Broad flights of stairs spiraled up from the street to a promenade, then continued up to the arched entrance.

"It's like an enchanted castle." Kelley looked around with shining eyes. "I expect a beautiful princess to appear any minute."

"She's already here," Erich answered, brushing a strand of long hair off her forehead.

He could barely tear her away after she discovered the view. On their right was a church with peaked roofs covered with colorful tiles in an intricate geometric pattern, and across the Danube was the Parliament Building. The river broadened out to the left, and in the middle was an island densely covered with greenery.

"I see some buildings." She pointed. "Do people live there?"

"That's Margaret Island, named after Princess Margaret, the daughter of King Béla IV. It has two hotels, but it's mostly used for recreation. I think we'll go there tomorrow for a change of pace."

Kelley and Erich slept late the next morning, due to their strenuous day and night. After dinner they'd gone to a nightclub.

She was more than willing to spend a quiet day just relaxing. Erich had arranged for the hotel to pack them a picnic lunch, and they planned to stroll around the island leisurely.

Kelley wasn't prepared for the beauty of Margaret Island. From a distance, the trees concealed all the lovely little glens. In one area a waterfall cascaded down a hill into a tranquil pond dotted with water lilies.

A larger pond had ducks swimming around on its surface, quacking contentedly. The rococo Water Tower at the far end of the island overlooked a broad green lawn. That was where Kelley and Erich decided to eat lunch.

She helped him spread out a tablecloth on the grass. "This is a feast," she commented as he brought out a roast chicken, triangles of pastry filled with potatoes and mushrooms, and a bottle of white wine. "At home I have a tuna fish sandwich for lunch. If I keep eating like this I'll grow out of my new clothes."

"Save room for the Dobos Torte," he said imperturbably, holding up a multilayered cake iced with chocolate.

She groaned. "How do you expect me to have any willpower when you tempt me like this?"

"I don't." He raised her hand and kissed the palm. "I want you to lose all your inhibitions with me."

"You got your wish days ago," she murmured.

After they'd eaten and packed away the leftovers, Erich stretched out on the grass with his head in Kelley's lap. "Mmm, this is nice." His eyes were closed and he had a smile on his face.

She stroked his thick hair, loving the clean, crisp feel of it. "You're usually such a dynamo. I've never seen you this relaxed."

"You mean with my clothes on?" He opened his eyes and gazed mischievously at her.

"Behave yourself," she ordered. "We're in a public place."

"That doesn't stop me from wanting you." He captured her hand and held it to his cheek.

She smiled. "That's one of the few things I know about you."

"I'd say you knew me quite intimately." He chuckled.

"But no other way. You never talk about yourself."

"Enough people do it for me." His voice became a trifle grim.

"Don't put me off, Erich. I know more about Emmy's life than I do about yours. Tell me about your family, to start with. Do you have any brothers or sisters?"

"I don't have any family to speak of, only an elderly aunt and uncle. My parents died a long time ago. They were killed in a private plane crash."

"How very sad!"

"It was pretty devastating. I was away at college when it happened."

"That's a terrible tragedy to cope with when you're so young," Kelley said sympathetically.

Erich looked pensive. "It was a difficult time. I was too old to live with relatives and too young to get married and establish my own household. I grew up in a hurry, but that wasn't necessarily a bad thing. When you're all alone in the world you learn to be self-sufficient."

That explained a lot, Kelley thought. Erich no longer needed the security of a family. His great charm and noble lineage made him welcome anywhere. A wife wouldn't provide anything that wasn't already available to him. She sighed unconsciously.

"I didn't mean to depress you." He stood and extended a hand to pull her up. "Let's go see if we can rent a couple of bicycles."

* * *

The week flew by all too quickly. Every day they wandered through museums and castles, and visited other historic places on both sides of the Danube. At night they had dinner in gourmet restaurants, or in quaint out-of-the-way little cafés that served native dishes and local wines.

It was usually late when they returned to their suite, but they were never too tired to make love. All the fascinating sights paled in contrast to the sight of each other. With whispered words of endearment that turned to moans of pleasure, they brought each other rapturous fulfillment.

The night before they were due to leave, Kelley cuddled closely against Erich. "The time went by too fast. I wish we didn't have to leave."

He kissed the top of her head. "That means you enjoyed yourself."

"You know I did. I don't want to see it end."

"It won't," he said fondly. "This is just the beginning. There are so many places I want to show you."

"It won't be the same, though. This week has been like a honeymoon," she said wistfully. When she felt his body tense, Kelley added hastily, "Not that I have the slightest desire to get married."

Erich's expression was unreadable in the darkness. "Really? Most women want a home and children."

She hastened to put his fears to rest. "I might someday, but certainly not now. I have too many things to do first."

"Such as?"

"Well, launching my new career for one thing. Emmy should have all the preliminary work done by the time I get back, and then it's up to me. I have to estimate the cost of the project so I can present the figures to the bank."

"It sounds like a big job," Erich commented impassively.

"Yes, but I love the fact that I'll be working for myself."

"Why is that important?"

"It's a challenge. I have to prove I can make it on my own."

"That doesn't mean you have to put your personal life on hold. A lot of women handle a career *and* marriage."

Kelley wasn't taken in by his casual tone. What did it take to convince him? "I'm sure that's possible, but right now I'm having too much fun to even consider marriage," she said dismissively.

"It's gratifying to hear I'm keeping you amused." His tone was caustic.

She laughed softly. "That isn't exactly the word I'd use."

"It describes our relationship, though. Is that enough for you, Kelley?"

"I feel the same way you do about commitments," she lied.

"You'll be able to walk away from me without a second thought when you decide it's over?" he persisted.

"Or *you* do."

Erich kept insisting he loved her, and maybe he did in his own way. But only in the heat of passion was she confident their affair would lead to marriage. If he was serious, wouldn't he propose instead of being so wary every time the subject came up?

"Do we have to talk about it now?" she asked. "We're here together and everything is wonderful. I don't want to think about the future."

"But *I* do." He propped himself on one elbow and stared down at her. When she turned her head away he cupped her cheek to make her face him. Whatever he was going to say was forgotten. "Are you crying, Kelley?"

"I never cry." She blinked her eyes rapidly.

Erich wasn't fooled. He folded her in his arms tenderly. "It's all right, sweetheart. We won't talk about anything that bothers you. I want this week to be perfect for you."

"It is!" She flung her arms around his neck and hugged him tightly. "I'll remember it always."

He clasped her just as tightly, muttering, "I don't want memories, I want *you.*"

"I couldn't be any closer," she murmured, moving sensuously against him.

Erich's response was immediate. As his hands caressed her body and he parted her lips for a deep, possessive kiss, Kelley stopped worrying about the future. No matter what came afterward, at this moment Erich belonged to her completely.

Chapter Nine

Kelley and Erich returned to Vienna in the late afternoon. As Erich hailed a cab outside the airport he said, "Would you mind if we stopped by my place before I take you to the hotel? I want to try to catch someone before his office closes."

"I don't mind," she answered. "I'd like to see where you live."

"I'd ask you to stay, but I know you're anxious to get together with Emmy."

That wasn't going to take up her nights. Erich must realize that, so there was no point in mentioning it. "I do have to get in touch with her," Kelley said, hiding her disappointment. "Emmy probably thinks by now that I abandoned her."

"I won't keep you long," he promised. "I just have to make one quick phone call."

"No problem. I'm not in that big a hurry."

Erich's town house wasn't as large as Henrietta's, but it was equally elegant. A round inlaid marble table in the foyer was centered under a crystal chandelier, and the walls were hung with priceless paintings in gold frames.

"What a beautiful entry." Kelley walked over to look at a French impressionist done in misty pastels. "I'd love to see the rest of the house."

He glanced at his watch. "If you'll wait a few minutes, I'll give you the grand tour."

"Go ahead and make your phone call. I'll wander around by myself."

"Feel free to—" Erich paused, looking toward the staircase with a puzzled expression. Music was filtering down from upstairs. "That's funny. Someone must be up there."

"Don't you have servants?"

"I gave them the week off. Besides, my staff isn't in the habit of playing rock music."

"They probably didn't expect you back yet."

"Possibly." He didn't look convinced. "Stay here while I find out what's going on. The music suddenly got louder, as though someone had opened a door. "Who's there?" Erich called sharply.

A young woman appeared at the top of the stairs. She had a long mane of sun-streaked blond hair, velvety brown eyes and flawless skin. Although she was only in her late teens, there was nothing immature about her. A tight T-shirt revealed fully developed breasts, and designer jeans clung like wallpaper to her rounded hips and long legs.

"Elisabeth!" Erich exclaimed in delight. "Why didn't you tell me you were coming?"

"I wanted to surprise you."

"You succeeded. Come down here and let me look at you." He held his arms open wide.

She ran lightly down the stairs and into his arms as Kelley watched, feeling her heart turn to lead. The look on Erich's face told how he felt about this girl.

"Where have you been?" Elisabeth demanded, noticing the luggage by the front door.

"I took a little trip down the Danube. Do you think I spend my entire life waiting for you to pop up?" Erich teased. He turned and included Kelley belatedly, introducing the newcomer as Elisabeth Kronenburg.

The two women acknowledged the introduction with an equal lack of warmth. "You aren't Viennese, are you?" Elisabeth asked.

"No, I'm American."

Kelley was acutely conscious of the rumpled state of her own hair and clothes in contrast to Elisabeth's perfection. She looked like one of those impossibly gorgeous girls in a jeans ad. No wonder Erich was so captivated by her. What man wouldn't be?

Elisabeth didn't even try to hide her disapproval. "You must be a new acquaintance of Erich's. I never heard him mention your name before."

Kelley forced a smile. "You came as a big surprise to me, too."

"That's Elisabeth's specialty." Erich chuckled. "Right now she's supposed to be at school in Switzerland. Would you like to explain what you're doing here?" he asked her. "I'll fix us a drink while you're trying to think of an innovative excuse."

"I thought you'd be glad to see me." Elisabeth pouted as she led the way to the library, a handsome room with richly bound books and fine leather furniture.

"I'm always ecstatic over your visits—even more so when you give me a little warning," he added dryly.

"If I'm in the way I'll leave," she answered sulkily.

Erich ruffled her hair fondly. "Stop acting like a spoiled child and tell me what you've been up to."

"Nothing interesting. I don't know what I'm doing at that stupid school anyway."

"Supposedly learning to be a proper wife."

A warning bell went off in Kelley's head. Was this teenager being groomed to be *Erich's* wife? Was that the reason he hadn't formed any lasting relationships with women? He'd chosen Elisabeth long ago?

"I don't need to go to school to get a husband," she said confidently. "I've had lots of proposals already."

"That should keep you happy." He smiled indulgently.

"You don't believe me?" she challenged.

"I think we can find a better time to discuss it." Erich walked over to Kelley. "Is your drink all right? Do you need more ice?"

"No, thanks, it's fine. Didn't you want to make a phone call?" she reminded him.

"I'm afraid it's too late now. I could have dropped you at the hotel, after all."

"That's okay. I *would* like to get out of these clothes, though." Kelley mainly wanted to get away from Elisabeth and her proprietary attitude toward Erich.

As he hesitated imperceptibly, Elisabeth said, "Go ahead with whatever you were going to do. Don't worry about me. I have some phone calls to make anyway."

"All right. I'll be back after I take Kelley to her hotel."

"I might not be here," Elisabeth announced.

Erich sighed. "Don't be unreasonable, Elisabeth."

"I don't know what you're talking about." She gave him an innocent stare. "I only meant that Klaus Coblentz told me to call him the next time I was in town. We'll probably go out to dinner."

Erich frowned. "You know how I feel about Klaus. He's an irresponsible rich man's son. I don't want you to have anything to do with him."

"You're too hard on Klaus," she protested. "Just because he got into one little scrape."

"He was arrested for drunk driving," Erich said crisply. "That's not a boyish prank. He was lucky no one was injured, or he'd be in prison right now. I want you to promise me you'll never get in a car with him."

Erich's solicitude for the other woman was more than Kelley could bear. She set her drink down and stood, murmuring, "Why don't I just take a taxi?"

"I'll take you as soon as I settle this," he answered with a touch of impatience.

"I don't mind, really." Kelley left the room without giving him time to argue.

As he gazed after her indecisively, Elisabeth reclaimed his attention. "Everybody deserves a second chance."

"Not if it means putting your life in jeopardy," he replied grimly. His expression softened as he gazed at her. "I don't want anything to happen to you, little one."

She came over and put her arms around his waist. "Darling Erich, you do love me, don't you?"

"In a very special way." He folded her in his arms and kissed the top of her head.

A triumphant smile curved her mouth as she rubbed her cheek against his solid chest.

Kelley paced her hotel room in a state bordering on shock. How could her idyllic week have ended this way? She and Erich had been so happy together in Budapest. They'd made love only this morning! Not once during the entire week had he given any indication there was another woman in his life.

Elisabeth Kronenburg wasn't even a woman! She was a self-centered teenager—with the face and figure of a sex goddess, Kelley reminded herself drearily. Was that enough for a mature man like Erich, though? He'd known many beautiful, intelligent women. What did he have in common with a youngster?

Maybe there was some other explanation. Maybe she was a relative. Or perhaps he was just being kind to a teenager with a crush on him.

Even as Kelley tried to convince herself, she knew she was grasping at straws. Erich didn't have any family and his manner was more loving than kind. She should know. He'd looked at *her* that way all week.

That was what really hurt—Erich's deceit. How could he make love to her with such passion when his heart wasn't involved? Men were certainly different than women, Kelley thought bitterly. Sex was a form of recreation for them. No deeper emotion need be involved.

The telephone rang, immobilizing her. She didn't want to talk to Erich in her present state of mind. But if she didn't answer, he'd know she was avoiding him—and why. It would be humiliating for him to think she was jealous. Kelley reached quickly for the phone.

She'd prepared herself needlessly, because Emmy's voice greeted her. "I can't believe I finally reached you! I thought you were never coming back."

"I told you I'd be gone a week," Kelley answered distractedly.

"I know, but I have so much to tell you."

Kelley forced herself to concentrate. "Good news, I hope."

"Some good and some bad. I had no idea things like bathtubs and sinks could cost so much. Or that the price of copper tubing is out of sight. I don't even know why we need so much of it."

"Did you get written estimates?"

"Lots of them, and that's another thing. You'd think they'd all be close in price to each other, but they're not. There's a difference of thousands between the highest and lowest estimate. I guess that makes the decision easier."

"Not necessarily. The lowest bid isn't always the best choice. We have to be sure we're dealing with a reliable contractor who will stand by his work."

"How can we know for sure?" Emmy asked dubiously.

"More legwork. I'll be here to help you, though."

"That's what I'm counting on. I don't know what kind of questions to ask. Are you free for dinner tonight? I'd like to show you what I've got so far."

Kelley hesitated for only a moment. Erich didn't intend to spend the evening alone, and neither did she. "Dinner sounds fine. Where shall I meet you?"

Emmy had done a good job of gathering information, although the results were a little dismaying. She was right about the cost of renovation. It was out of sight.

"We'll just have to cut corners where it won't show," Kelley declared.

"Furnaces and plumbing don't show, but we have to have them," Emmy pointed out.

"I was thinking of the decor. We want the property to look smashing for our brochure—like the first glimpse of Henrietta's castle. People will be standing in line waving checks if we can achieve that kind of effect."

"You're talking about millions of schillings!"

"It won't take a fraction of that to spruce up the out-side. You'd be surprised at what a splash some inexpensive bedding plants can make. Does your castle have a circular driveway like hers?''

"No, ours is straight and it ends in a courtyard."

"How about garages for the guests' cars?"

"I suppose they could use the old stables around the back."

"What condition are they in?" Kelley asked.

"Bad, like the rest of the place." Emmy sighed. "I think you'd better come down and see for yourself what we're talking about."

"That isn't a bad idea. Would your parents mind?"

Emmy hesitated. "I'm afraid they won't be wildly receptive. I had to beg, plead and threaten before they finally agreed to our plan."

"Then maybe I'd better stay away."

"You'll be working in the dark if you don't see firsthand what the problems are. I can't guarantee you a warm welcome, but I still think you should come."

"Okay, I will. I can take rejection." Kelley's smile faltered as she remembered her earlier experience with it.

"It won't be that bad. My parents are really nice when you get to know them."

"I'm sure they are," Kelley answered politely. She changed the subject. "Has Stavros tried to contact you again?"

"No, he left town in a huff after our breakup. He's probably sulking on his yacht or his walled estate. I don't think he ever struck out before."

"It's pitiful what some women will overlook for money."

"I was one of them," Emmy said soberly.

"Not really. You were just misguided."

Emmy shivered. "I didn't know how much I was dreading the prospect until I was free of him. How could

I even have considered going through with it? If I had to marry for money, I should at least have picked someone gorgeous like Erich." She smiled.

"I thought we agreed he wasn't husband material." Kelley made sure to keep her tone light.

"I suppose some woman will get him eventually. I'm sure he wants a son to carry on the line."

"That means he'll probably marry someone young and gorgeous. Who fits that description?" Kelley hoped to find out more about Elisabeth without coming right out and asking.

"That could describe all of Erich's dates." Emmy grinned. "Like you, for instance. Did you have a good time this week?"

"Yes, it was very nice," Kelley answered neutrally.

"Where did you go?"

"To Bratislava, and then on to Budapest."

Emmy didn't seem to notice her friend's terse replies. "Isn't Budapest charming? I hope you got to see more than just museums and churches. They're impressive, but there's so much more to the city."

"We didn't miss a thing."

Kelley had tried to avoid talking about her week with Erich, but Emmy kept asking if she'd been to certain restaurants and nightclubs. Once Kelley started telling her where they went, all the good memories came rushing back. The days and nights had been a pure delight.

Gradually the band around Kelley's heart eased. Erich had been a joyous companion and a considerate lover. Surely he'd felt something for her. It couldn't have been only sex for him.

By the time she returned to her hotel room, Kelley's spirits had lifted. This whole tempest in a teapot had been brought on by Elisabeth's calculated intention to make trouble. But Erich wasn't responsible for her behavior. If she hadn't acted equally childishly by stalking out, all this misery could have been averted.

She was tempted to phone him right this minute, but it was almost midnight. First thing in the morning, though, she'd call and set things right between them.

Erich's phone rang for a long time the next morning. Kelley was about to hang up and call again, thinking she'd dialed wrong, when Elisabeth answered. Shock rendered Kelley speechless at first.

"Hello," Elisabeth repeated impatiently. "Who is this?"

Kelley clutched the receiver so tightly her fingers were white. She mustn't jump to conclusions again. "Is Erich there?"

"Is this Kelley?"

"Yes, may I speak to Erich?"

"He's in the shower right now. We haven't been up very long. I'm not supposed to answer his phone, but it rang so long I thought it might be important."

"No, it isn't important," Kelley said dully.

"We just finished having breakfast together. Erich should be out in a few minutes. It never takes him long when he showers alone." Elisabeth giggled.

Kelley realized the young woman was deliberately rubbing salt in the wound, but it hurt anyway. "Well...I won't keep you."

"Do you want to leave a message?"

"No. Don't even bother telling him I called."

Kelley hung up the phone with lifeless fingers. So much for a misunderstanding. Elisabeth had spent the night with Erich, and it wasn't the first time. Kelley had known the truth about them yesterday, even though she'd fought against it. Elisabeth had a key to Erich's house. How else could she have gotten in when all the servants were gone? Their affair was of long-standing duration, in spite of her youth.

Kelley felt empty inside. Reality had crushed her dreams and the future looked bleaker than it ever had. She desperately wanted to leave Vienna with all its broken promises, but she had an obligation to Emmy. Forcing her chin up, she walked across the room to the closet.

Kelley was dressed and ready to go down to the lobby when Erich phoned.

"Good morning, angel." He was bubbling with good cheer. "Did you get a good night's rest?"

"Probably better than you did," she answered tightly.

"Actually you're right. I didn't sleep well. I missed having you beside me."

Anger started at Kelley's toes and spread through her like wildfire. "How gullible do you think I am?"

"I don't understand."

"I don't, either. How many women does it take to satisfy you?"

After a moment's pause, Erich asked, "What's this all about, Kelley? Are you angry because I didn't drive you to the hotel yesterday? I did offer, if you remember."

"Very halfheartedly."

"That's not true. I merely wanted to make an important point with Elisabeth before I left."

"You made it perfectly clear that she comes first," Kelley said stiffly.

"Surely you're not jealous of Elisabeth. She's just a child."

"That *child* wears a bigger bra size than I do!"

He laughed softly. "Quantity will never take the place of quality."

"Don't try to turn that phony charm on me," Kelley stormed. "You've razzle-dazzled me for the last time."

"Would you mind providing some specifics?" Erich's cajoling tone cooled. "I thought we had a rather spectacular week together."

"I did, too. I didn't realize I was only the warm-up act for the main event."

"You're not making any sense. You can't be referring to Elisabeth."

"Oh, can't I? Do you deny you spent the night with her?"

"Are you asking me or telling me?" His voice was ominous.

"Don't try to lie your way out. She very kindly provided me with the details." That wasn't strictly true, but Kelley's imagination had supplied what Elisabeth implied.

"I don't know what she told you, but I've never lied to you, and I don't appreciate being accused of it. How can you condemn me without a hearing?"

"I heard—and *saw*—all I cared to. She's in love with you."

"She has a schoolgirl crush," he protested. "She'll get over it."

"Giving her a key to your house should help," Kelley said sarcastically.

"You don't understand about Elisabeth and me. I would have told you about her if I'd known you were going to meet."

"When you have a love life as extensive as yours, there's bound to be a slipup now and then."

"You make me sound like a womanizer," he said evenly.

"That's the way Kurt described you the first time we met, but I was too dumb to believe him."

"And now you do?" Erich's voice was dangerously expressionless.

"What would you call a man who tells a woman he loves her just to get her into bed? I believed you!"

"I'd be more impressed if something other than your pride was involved. You went away with me because you wanted to. It's that simple."

Kelley was caught in a Catch-22 situation. If she admitted she loved him, her pride was destroyed. If she let him think she only went for what he could do for her, that made her as shallow as he was.

"I made a mistake and I deeply regret it," she said in a low voice.

"Don't worry about it," he drawled. "I won't tell anyone if you don't."

Pain seared through her at his insolent tone. Erich was finally showing his true colors. She was right about him the first time. He'd never cared about her. Kelley didn't trust herself not to break down.

"There's no point in continuing these recriminations," she said quietly. "It won't change the facts."

"You're certain you *have* all the facts?"

"Enough to know it's over for us. Goodbye, Erich."

After a moment's silence he said, "Goodbye, Kelley, and . . . good luck."

Kelley was still sitting motionless on the side of the bed when Emmy phoned from the lobby half an hour later.

"I'm downstairs. Are you ready to go?"

"What?" Kelley asked vaguely. "Oh . . . yes, I guess so."

"Are you all right? You sound funny."

"I'm fine. I was just . . . uh . . . going over the figures you gave me."

"That's enough to put anyone in a fog," Emmy said wryly.

"They're not so bad. Give me five minutes and I'll be right down."

Kelley ran a comb through her hair, then after a glance in the mirror she used blusher on her pale cheeks. Squaring her shoulders, she picked up her overnight bag and went out the door.

Fortress House, the Rothstein family seat, was undeniably shabby. Ivy had grown over some of the windows, and a few of the flagstones in the courtyard were cracked. The grass in the meadow fronting the house was shaggy and dotted with clover, instead of being mowed to neat perfection. But for all the signs of neglect, the turreted stone castle retained its dignity and old-world ambience.

"This is charming," Kelley exclaimed. "What fun you must have had here as a child."

"Yes, my friends and I used to play tag on the lawn. It was as smooth as a putting green in those days. Now it looks disreputable."

"Not really, it just needs mowing." Kelley glanced around. "Those flowers beds could stand weeding, too."

"You should have seen the grounds when we had a staff of gardeners. They were outstanding."

"They will be again," Kelley promised.

"I wouldn't bet on it. You have no idea how much gardeners cost, or how many of them it takes just to keep that much lawn mowed."

Kelley eyed the large expanse speculatively. "I've heard of sheep being used to keep hillsides cropped. That would be a nice bucolic touch for the tourists and also keep maintenance costs down."

The front door opened and a tall man with sandy hair came out. He was dressed casually in slacks and a sweater with leather patches on the elbows, but he had an unmistakably aristocratic bearing.

"I thought I heard voices out here." He smiled at Emmy.

"Hi, Dad." She went over and kissed his cheek. "I'd like you to meet my friend, Kelley McCormick."

Kelley braced herself for hostility, but the older man merely looked at her curiously. "So you're the young woman our daughter has been telling us about."

"I don't suppose I'm your favorite person at the moment, but I hope you'll change your mind." Kelley extended her hand. "Thank you for letting me visit."

"Emmy's friends are always welcome," he answered noncommittally.

"Is Mother at home?" Emmy asked.

"Yes, she's been waiting for you." His eyes met his daughter's, conveying some kind of message.

Emmy stifled a sigh. "Well, let's go in and get it over with."

The entry hall was lofty and impressive, but cool. The thick stone walls of the castle retained the previous evening's chill, even though it was now almost noon.

Kelley followed her host down a corridor to a sitting room with a roaring fire in a stone fireplace. This room was evidently used regularly by the family. Books and newspapers were stacked on tables, and the couches and chairs had seen better days, although they were originally of top quality.

Emmy's mother was sitting by the fire with her feet on a needlepoint footstool, reading a book. She was a handsome woman with a firm jawline and an imperious stare that she turned on her visitor. Kelley finally met the hostility she'd been expecting.

After the introductions had been made, Giselle Rothstein said to Emmy, "I'm glad your friend is here because I have something to say to both of you. Your father and I have reconsidered your preposterous proposal. Under no circumstances will we agree to it."

Kelley had a hunch the decision was made by the baroness rather than the baron. He seemed like an easygoing sort with a sense of humor that would permit him to adapt to most situations with grace. Emmy's mother was the fierce traditionalist.

Emmy groaned. "We've been through all this. It's either try Kelley's plan or lose Fortress House entirely. You can't afford to live here without outside income."

"I don't intend to acquire it by becoming a common innkeeper," Giselle snapped. "What would our friends say?"

"Would you rather have them come visit you in a little flat somewhere?" Emmy asked in exasperation.

A flash of fear showed on the older woman's face, but she forced it back.

"That's nonsense. Fortress House has been in your father's family for hundreds of years. This is our home—which you don't seem to understand. It is not some public place for crass tourists to tramp through."

"What you refuse to admit is you're living in four unheated rooms, scrimping to make ends meet, and taxes are still bankrupting you."

"That's not something we need to discuss in front of a stranger," Giselle said austerely.

Emmy ran slim fingers through her long hair. "Ignoring your problems won't make them go away. One of these days the bank will send someone out here to evict you."

"That's absurd! They wouldn't dare. This property was a land grant to the Rothsteins by Henry II in the twelfth century. The Turkish advance was stopped by these very walls."

Kelley made a mental note to incorporate that into her brochure. It was the kind of thing tourists were impressed by.

"Can't you talk some sense into her?" Emmy appealed despairingly to her father.

"It wouldn't do any good. You need her cooperation, not just her grudging acceptance," he said shrewdly.

"Don't make *me* the villain, Ernst!" His wife turned on him indignantly. "You don't like the idea any better than I do."

"I have a few reservations." He directed them to Kelley. "You're asking us to go even further into debt with no guarantee of success. Why would anyone choose to stay here rather than a luxury hotel? The competition seems rather unequal."

Kelley had been waiting for the right moment to make her pitch. Now that she'd seen Fortress House she was convinced her plan would succeed. "I'd be in total agreement if all you were offering was lodging. But the people who come here will be more than paying customers, they'll be your guests."

The baron raised an eyebrow. "Isn't that a matter of semantics?"

"Not at all. You're right about luxury accommodations. We have to offer more. Our targets are wealthy people who have been everywhere and done everything. Although they pay handsomely for service, it's always impersonal. They're outsiders wherever they go. You're essentially inviting them to a private house party where they'll get to meet the local gentry."

Giselle looked shocked. "You're not actually suggesting we introduce them to our friends?"

"In a general sort of way," Kelley answered carefully. "Part of the package will include a garden party made up of your friends and neighbors. The presence of a mere dozen outsiders will scarcely be noticed. Of course the cost will be charged to the corporation. Including the caterer and servants to pass sandwiches and pour tea," she added. "You won't have to do a thing except see that everyone has a good time."

Giselle's expression was wistful. "We used to have parties like that," she murmured, almost to herself.

"You'll also host a welcoming cocktail party for the guests, and a formal dinner on the last night of their stay. The brochure will mention black-tie events, so they'll come prepared. Naturally you'll have to hire an excellent chef," Kelley said artlessly. "These people will expect gourmet food at the prices they'll be paying."

Dawning excitement was shining in the older woman's eyes. "That certainly wouldn't be a problem. One thing I do know about is handling a large staff."

Ernst was gazing at Kelley sardonically. "What position did you hold in America, snake oil saleslady? You're making a lot of promises."

"I think they're justified. Speaking from my own experience, if a vacation like I described had been available, I would have jumped at it."

"You really think a tea party and dinner with strangers will bring people knocking at our door?"

"You bet, when the tea party is at a castle and the dinner is hosted by a baron and baroness." Kelley grinned. "But there will be other amenities. A chauffeured car will be available, and Emmy will wangle them tickets to social events like charity balls. You can do that, can't you?" she asked her friend.

"No problem, as long as they have the cash."

"Where do you expect to recruit all these delightfully wealthy tourists?" Ernst asked.

Giselle didn't bother listening while Kelley explained her strategy. She broke in impatiently to say, "I only have silver and place settings for twenty-four. Will that be enough?"

"Plenty. I don't think you should accept more than a dozen guests at a time. It's better to turn a few people away rather than be too available."

"You honestly think this will work?" Ernst asked slowly.

Emmy answered for Kelley. "I'm sure of it, Dad. I never would have sent Stavros packing if I hadn't been."

"At least that's one good thing," he said. "I never really liked the man."

"You and Mother encouraged me to marry him!" Emmy exclaimed.

The older Rothsteins exchanged a glance. "He offered you the security we couldn't," Giselle said quietly. "It's a scary world out there. You don't know that because you've never had to make your own living. We didn't want you to wind up as we have, worrying about the future."

Kelley realized she'd misjudged Emmy's parents. They hadn't urged an unsuitable marriage on her for their own gain. They wanted her to have security in a world that frightened them.

"None of us has to worry about the future anymore." Emmy smiled brilliantly. "By this time next year Fortress House will be a showplace and we'll all be rolling in money."

Chapter Ten

As Emmy was driving Kelley back to town the next morning she said, "You're a real miracle worker. I thought we were sunk when Mother announced that she'd changed her mind."

"She just didn't understand how much easier her life will be."

"Even so, when she makes a decision, usually dynamite won't move her. This goes against all her convictions of how the aristocracy should behave."

"She'll have a ball." Kelley grinned. "I can see them now, presiding over dinner in elegant evening clothes. The tourists will eat it up. Now all we have to do is qualify for a loan."

"I'm convinced you can do anything," Emmy said fervently.

"Thanks for the vote of confidence. I'll make some appointments as soon as I get back to the hotel."

The phone in Kelley's room rang before she could use it. Kurt was on the other end. That was no big surprise, since there had been numerous messages from him in her box.

"I've been trying to get you all week," he complained. "Are you avoiding me?"

"Of course not. I was out of town."

"You didn't mention any plans on the weekend. Where did you go?"

"I took a little sight-seeing trip." She changed the subject before he could question her further. "I'm rather busy at the moment, Kurt. Did you want something special?"

"I haven't seen you since the house party at Henrietta's," he said in an aggrieved tone.

"I told you, I was away." She sighed. "I haven't seen anybody."

"Not even Erich?"

"If I *were* avoiding you, your ridiculous fixation about Erich would be the reason. I don't happen to share your interest in him. In fact, I don't want to hear his name again. Is that clear?" she asked tautly.

"I'm sorry. I won't mention him again, I promise. I'm really delighted that you finally saw the light. He's completely untrustworthy where women are concerned."

"Is this your idea of not mentioning him?" Kelley asked ominously. "Goodbye, Kurt."

"No, wait, don't hang up! I called for a reason—to remind you of the Opera Ball next week. You said you'd go with me, remember?"

Kelley didn't. "How many of these things do you people have?"

"Dozens, but this is the important one. All of society will be there."

"You said that about the last one."

"They're all well attended, but this is the prestigious one that everybody wants to be seen at. The tickets are almost impossible to come by if you're not on the A-list." Kurt paused to let that sink in.

"If it's such a big deal, you should take someone who appreciates the honor," she said ironically.

"Our customs might seem laughable to you, but they're a matter of tradition to *us*," he said stiffly.

"I wasn't making fun of them." Kelley had been, but she regretted it. Kurt took his social life seriously. "I honestly think it would be better if you took somebody else. I might not even be here by then." It was unlikely that she'd get her loan approved that fast, but anything could happen.

"Where are you going?" he asked in alarm.

"I have some business to take care of back in the States."

"You're not going home for good, are you? You'll be back?"

"I don't know at this point."

"Don't go, Kelley. You could have a wonderful life right here," Kurt said urgently. "Not many newcomers are accepted as fast as you were. Henrietta was really taken with you, and I can introduce you to more people like her."

"Everybody has been very kind to me, especially you, but I never expected to stay forever."

"Why not? What do you have in America that we can't offer you here? You know *I'd* do anything to make you happy."

"Please don't start that again, Kurt. We've been through all this before. I'm not ready to make a commitment."

"You don't have to! I'm willing to wait."

"What does it take to get through to you?" she asked in exasperation. "I don't love you, Kurt."

"Are you in love with anyone else?"

Kelley's fingers curled rigidly around the receiver. "No."

"Then there's hope for me. All I want is to see you now and then. Is that too much to ask? Have dinner with me tonight."

"I really can't. I'm working on a business deal and I have to get all my figures together."

"Tomorrow night, then."

She hesitated. "I'm not trying to put you off, but I have a lot on my mind right now. I wouldn't be very good company."

"Just being with you would be enough for me. I warn you, I don't intend to give up. I'm available for breakfast, lunch, whatever's convenient for you."

Kelley cast about for a way to get rid of him. She did have to set up some appointments. "I'll make a deal with you. Give me this week to get my business affairs in order and I'll go to the ball with you."

"But it's a whole week away," he protested.

"That's the best I can do."

"Couldn't we at least have lunch one day?" When she didn't answer he sighed. "All right, if that's the way it has to be. You won't disappointment me?"

"No, we have a date. And now I truly must go," she said firmly.

Kurt was deeply disappointed by Kelley's indifference to him. His mood wasn't improved by a telephone call from Magda later in the morning.

"I haven't heard from you in over a week," she said tentatively.

"Did you expect to after that disaster at Henrietta's?" His voice was frosty.

"Whose fault was that?" she demanded, her conciliatory tone vanishing.

"How can you ask after the disgraceful scene you made? I can assure you, you'll never be invited back there again."

"Is that supposed to ruin my day? I wasn't invited *this* time. I came as Erich's guest."

"How could you have accepted? You knew he invited you expressly to embarrass me."

"Now I've heard everything!" Magda said explosively. "You broke our date so you could take another woman to Henrietta's for the weekend, and *I'm* supposed to feel guilty about showing up with Erich?"

"I couldn't very well turn Henrietta down when she asked me to bring Kelley. Henrietta is my patroness. I would have told you the truth, but I knew you'd react exactly as you did—irrationally."

"How did you expect me to act when I saw that ring on Kelley's finger? We've been going together for three years and you never offered it to me."

"Why would you want it since you don't think it's real?" he asked sarcastically.

"I know it isn't, but that's not the point," she said stubbornly.

"It seems quite pertinent to me. Why would you make such a fuss over an imitation ruby? Your actions proved the ring is genuine."

"Don't try to bluff me, Kurt. I know you too well. Remember the check I made good for you? And the Oriental rug dealer who raised such a fuss when you tried to shave his commission? I know all the little games you play."

"All right, all right, so I've been a trifle short of cash on occasion. You didn't have to publicly humiliate me."

"How about *my* humiliation? We had an understanding. When one of your deals finally came through we were going to get married."

"We talked about it," he conceded. "It was never definite."

"It was to me! Why do you think I've been waiting around all this time?" she asked in outrage.

"I can't help any misconceptions on your part. We were rather...uh...close for a time, but feelings change."

"You don't *have* any feelings," Magda answered angrily. "I was a fool to waste all these years. I should have realized I was never more than a convenience to you."

"Must we go through this, Magda? Can't we simply end it without these distasteful denunciations?"

"I haven't even begun to tell you what I think of you! You're nothing but an opportunist, and not a very good one at that. I know why you're throwing me over, but you're deluding yourself if you think Kelley will ever marry you. She's madly in love with Erich, and you know how much of a chance you have against him."

"That shows how little *you* know. Kelley told me only this morning that she wasn't interested in Erich. She absolutely refused to talk about him. What does that do to your theory?" he asked triumphantly.

"It sounds as if they had an argument. Anybody could figure that out. When's the last time you saw her?"

"She's been out of town."

"Have you seen her since the house party?" Magda persisted.

"She's been busy—working on a business deal."

"What kind of business? I thought she won a fortune in the lottery."

"She did. I suppose she's investing some of it. You can't let that kind of money sit around in a bank."

"It sounds strange to me. She could be some kind of con artist. How do you know she actually won the lottery? Claiming she had would be a good way to break into the right circles."

"Don't be ridiculous! It costs a fortune to stay at the Metropole Grande, and look at her clothes. They're all from top designers."

"Okay, so maybe she's everything she seems to be, but that doesn't mean she wouldn't jump at the chance to marry Erich. His money makes hers look like pocket change, not to mention the fact that she'd be a grand duchess. You're just spinning your wheels."

"In your opinion. If Kelley is so crazy about Erich, why is she going to the Opera Ball with me?"

"You're taking her to the ball?" Magda asked tautly.

"I just told you so."

"You asked *me* a month ago!"

"Under the circumstances you can hardly expect me to honor the commitment."

"What do you know about honor?" she asked furiously. "You let me think we had a future together, but you were only using me. I bailed you out of tight spots more than once, and now you want to throw me over for somebody who can do more for you. Well, I don't intend to let you get away with it."

"It won't do you any good to bad-mouth me to Kelley. She already knows you're a jealous, vindictive woman. She won't believe anything you tell her."

"Maybe, and maybe not. You could be in for a big surprise."

"I don't see any point in continuing this conversation. I'm just sorry things had to end like this between us."

"You're going to be a lot sorrier!" Magda slammed down the phone.

"Women," Kurt muttered as he cradled the receiver.

Kelley's eyes were bright with excitement as she walked up the front steps of the bank. Her figures were neatly tabulated in the briefcase under her arm, and she'd dressed carefully for the appointment. Her gray suit and white blouse looked businesslike, and she'd kept her makeup to a minimum.

Hans Wiegand, the man behind the polished desk asked her to take a seat. His eyes flicked over her without the male approval Kelley was used to, which pleased her. She wanted to be judged on her merits.

The banker listened while she outlined her plan. He glanced at the sheets of figures she handed him, all without comment.

"Well, that's about it," Kelley said nervously. The lack of communication between them wasn't promising, but perhaps that was just his manner. "What do you think?"

"Frankly, Miss McCormick, I'm not impressed. The countryside is full of run-down castles that are already heavily mortgaged. Throwing good money after bad isn't sound business."

"But I've shown you how you can turn them into profitable enterprises and recoup your previous investment."

"Wishful thinking, I'm afraid."

"No, it isn't! Look at the figures. We can break even the first year, and turn a profit after that."

"*If* you have full occupancy."

"We aren't planning on more than a dozen guests at a time. Signing them up will be a breeze."

"We both know how undependable the wind is," he said dryly.

"Mr. Wiegand, this isn't some crackpot scheme by an idealistic amateur. You've seen my credentials. I worked as a loan officer in a bank. I've put together this proposal very carefully. I know it's sound."

"Forgive me for being skeptical, but aren't some of your banks in trouble for granting real estate loans?"

"Not like this one." Kelley was beginning to get desperate. "Once we renovate Fortress House, the tourists will flock to it. This is a paying proposition as opposed to a liability."

"Bring me some guaranteed reservations and I might change my mind."

"I can't sell accommodations without being able to guarantee delivery!" she exclaimed. "That would be dishonest."

"And I can't risk my depositors' money on theoretical schemes."

Kelley used every argument she could think of, pointing out the public relations value to restoring a historic castle. She cited her figures again, stressing the added value to the property, but nothing moved him.

"Show me some customers and perhaps we can talk."

Emmy was waiting for Kelley in a coffee house near the bank. Her animation faded as Kelley related what had happened.

"Would it be possible to book reservations as he suggested?" Emmy asked tentatively.

"It's too risky, and it might even be illegal. Wiegand didn't actually promise me a loan, even if we had guests lined up. He merely said he'd talk about it."

"Surely he'd come through if you showed him some bona fide reservations."

"What if the renovation wasn't done in time? In a worst case scenario we could get sued. At the very least we'd have to refund the money."

"What are we going to do?" Emmy looked at her anxiously. "Don't tell me we're beaten before we even get started?"

"No way!" Kelley answered forcefully. "This was only our first try. There are lots of other banks."

"What if they feel the same way Wiegand does?"

"They can't all be that close minded. One of them is bound to realize we're offering a good deal for everybody."

Emmy relaxed. "My money's on you. If you convinced my mother, you can convince anybody."

Kelley suppressed a sigh. "Well, I guess I'd better get on the phone and set up some more interviews."

"We both need a night on the town. We've been working on this project nonstop, and it's time for a break. I'm going to call Niles."

"I didn't know you'd been seeing him."

"I haven't really had much time, but we've been out together on a couple of occasions."

"I'm glad," Kelley said. "He seems like a nice young man."

"He is. I'll give him a call and you can phone Erich. We'll double date."

"No! I mean, Erich is so busy. He wouldn't be available at the last minute."

"You can try him."

"I'd rather not." Kelley stirred her cold coffee. "I think I'd better go over our figures again tonight and see if there's any place I can cut a few more corners."

"That proposal is as lean as it can possibly be. You'll lose your edge if you don't step away from it. Give Erich a ring."

"Maybe some other time." Kelley rose.

Emmy stared at her with a slight frown. "Did you and he have a disagreement? I thought you were getting along so well. You said you enjoyed the trip."

"I did, but I have other things on my mind right now. Have a nice time with Niles tonight. I'll talk to you in the morning."

Kelley's spirits were at low ebb as she walked into the lobby of her hotel. What she'd told Emmy was true. There were a lot of other banks that would undoubtedly be more receptive. It was probably unrealistic to expect to hit a home run the first time at bat. But how much rejection could she take?

As Kelley walked toward him, Erich took a newspaper from under his arm, opened it and stepped into her path.

"I'm sorry." She stopped just short of bumping into him and glanced up. "I wasn't looking where—" The words died on her lips.

"It was my fault. I didn't see you," he answered.

They stared at each other wordlessly. Kelley hadn't thought the mere sight of Erich would affect her this way, but her heart was pounding so hard she was afraid he might hear it. Erich was impossibly handsome—and so remote. Had that hard mouth ever softened against hers, whispering passionate words of love?

She forced her gaze to a point near his left ear. "I didn't expect to see you here."

"I was supposed to meet someone." His eyes devoured her face. "You look tired." He raised his hand as though to touch her cheek, then dropped it to his side abruptly.

"I had a hard day," she said wearily.

"Is anything wrong?"

"No." She managed a smile. "Just a long day's shopping. It's hard work spending money."

He echoed her smile with a faint one of his own. "I'm glad you're learning how."

"You taught me a lot of things."

"All of them unwanted. You told me that."

Kelley could have cried. She hadn't meant the remark sarcastically, but everything seemed to provoke an argument between them.

"I didn't say they were all bad," she said in a low voice.

His expression softened as he gazed at her bowed head. "We did have a good time, didn't we?"

"I'll never forget it," she murmured.

"What happened, Kelley? We were so happy."

"We were living in a dream world," she said wistfully. "Or at least, I was. I guess I couldn't cope with reality."

"*What* reality? Nothing's changed between us."

"I can't share you, Erich. It's as simple as that."

"Do you honestly think I could want any other woman after you?" His sensuous voice vibrated deep inside her.

Kelley fought against his incredible charisma. When he was this close she wanted to forgive him everything and move into his arms. She actually ached to feel his hard muscled body against hers one more time.

Clenching her hands so tightly the nails bit into her palms she said, "You can be very convincing, but there seem to be a lot of women in your life."

"Aren't you exaggerating?" he asked gently.

"I don't know." She looked at him searchingly. "You never mentioned Elisabeth. How do I know how many other women there are?"

"You've been the only one since I caught my first glimpse of you at the ball. I've been waiting for you all my life."

"I wish I could believe that," she whispered.

"You can, my love, I swear it."

A wave of pure happiness washed over Kelley. Erich was looking at her with such tenderness it made her legs tremble. He couldn't be that good an actor. She must have misjudged him, somehow. As she was about to tell him how sorry she was, a voluptuous redhead screeched out his name.

"Erich, darling!" The woman rushed over and kissed him. "How simply marvelous to see you again." She had a pronounced English accent. "It seems like an age since we were together last."

The expression on Erich's face was almost comical, but Kelley was in no mood to laugh. He'd said he was waiting for somebody. She should have known it was a woman.

"I'd like you to meet Lady Jane Hesquith," he told Kelley in an expressionless voice.

Kelley turned on him accusingly without bothering to acknowledge the introduction. "Couldn't you at least have met her somewhere else?"

"This isn't what it looks like," he answered.

"It never is. You're always the victim of circumstances. Is that what I'm supposed to believe?"

A muscle jerked in his jaw. "You don't bother with facts. You'd much rather jump to conclusions."

"Oh, so it's *my* fault for not being more trusting! Well, excuse me for being a disappointment." Kelley was too angry to care that she was making a scene. "Goodbye, Erich. You've been an education. The next time I meet a wolf, I won't be deceived into thinking he's a lamb."

The redhead watched Kelley stalk away. "Goodness, what was that all about? I hope I didn't cause any misunderstandings."

"No." Erich's eyes were bleak. "She never understood me."

"That's her loss." Jane shrugged off the incident and turned her full attention to him. "This is such a stroke of luck, running into you like this. I was just checking in and I glanced around the lobby and there you were. The desk clerk must have thought I was completely daft the way I went dashing off. I left my credit card on the counter and everything."

"Perhaps you'd better go back and get it."

"Yes, I suppose I had. You're not by any chance free for dinner tonight?" she asked hopefully. "I'm meeting the Keitels, and I know they'd be thrilled to have you join us. You remember them, I'm sure. They were at the resort where we met. Gustave Keitel is in the steel business and he's married to that stunning German woman."

Erich waited for a break in her monologue. "I'm sorry, but I'm tied up this evening. It was nice bumping into you, Jane."

"I'll be here all week."

"Then perhaps we'll meet again," he said politely. "Goodbye for now."

Erich was lying on a couch in his den, staring out the window. Dusk had fallen, but he didn't bother to turn on any lights. When the phone rang he ignored it. After several rings the answering machine clicked on and Henrietta's voice sounded.

"Don't you ever stay home?" She chuckled. "But then, why should you? Call me when you have a minute. I'm at my town house."

Erich picked up the receiver. "I'm here, Henrietta."

"Am I disturbing you? You sound kind of distracted. Good Lord, don't tell me I caught you in bed?"

"Nothing like that," he answered impatiently. "What did you want?"

"I'm calling about the Opera Ball."

"My God, is it time for that thing again?"

"You say that every year," she replied imperturbably. "I wanted to remind you that you're sitting at my table."

"I'm not going," he said firmly. "And this time I mean it. Nothing you can say will change my mind."

"Don't be cranky, Erich. I have to fill up a table and I need somebody intelligent to talk to."

"Ask Heinrich."

"Oh, sure! I'd have better luck getting an acceptance from the pope."

"Then ask the pope," Erich said indifferently.

"Is this any way to treat an old friend? Kelley will be there," she said craftily.

Erich's long body stiffened. "I suppose she's coming with Kurt?"

"So he informed me. You'd think he pulled off a coup in a foreign country. I just don't understand Kelley."

"Join the group," Erich remarked sardonically.

"I thought you two had finally ironed out your differences. What's she doing back with Kurt?"

"She thinks he's more trustworthy than I am."

"You have to be joking! Kurt is such a loser you have to feel sorry for him. He's one of life's incompetents, although he is knowledgeable about antiques. That's what he ought to stick to, because he doesn't have credibility in any other field."

"Evidently he does," Erich said tersely.

"Don't be a horse's patoot. It sounds like you and Kelley had an argument and you're both acting stupid."

"*She* is, if she can't see through Kurt," Erich muttered.

"So you plan to sit home and sulk, leaving him a clear field."

"I'm doing you a favor. Putting the three of us in the same room is a recipe for disaster—forget about at the same table."

Henrietta laughed. "It would certainly liven up a dull evening."

"You must be very hard up for amusement," he said dryly.

"Okay, seriously. I don't know what happened between you and Kelley, but I think you should patch it up. We both know she's not interested in Kurt."

"He's not the problem. That would be easy."

"Well, what *is* the problem? You two are crazy about each other. It's obvious whenever you're together. The sparks are almost visible."

"Have you forgotten what great sex is?" he asked sardonically.

"There's nothing you can tell *me* about sex, sonny. I also know a few things about love—and that's a different matter. You and Kelley belong together."

"She doesn't happen to agree with you, and I haven't had any luck in changing her mind. Actually I'm not even sure I want to," Erich said somberly. "A healthy relationship is based on trust. Without that, it's just another affair."

"Why doesn't she trust you? I've never known you to do anything dishonorable."

"Kelley thinks I have a revolving door on my bedroom. She suspects I have women coming out of the woodwork."

"And this is all a figment of her imagination?" Henrietta asked skeptically. "You've given her no reason to doubt you?"

Erich ran his fingers through his already tousled hair. "It was all a misunderstanding."

"Uh-huh, now we're getting someplace. She does have cause for concern?"

"No! If she'd listened to me I would have explained. But she preferred to go charging off, imagining all kinds of ridiculous things. By the time I phoned the next morning, she accused me of everything except starting the war in the Middle East."

"You didn't bother to explain?"

"By then I was too angry. Why should I have to defend myself against something I hadn't done?"

"No reason, if you don't mind never seeing her again." When Henrietta heard his indrawn breath she continued, "I don't know what Kelley's plans are, but I'm sure she won't be around indefinitely. It seems a shame to part on bad terms after all the good times you had together."

"Your strategy is transparent, Henrietta, besides being ill-advised. Kelley is the one who isn't speaking to *me*. We had another misunderstanding today. She wouldn't take kindly to hearing from me."

Henrietta raised her eyes to the ceiling, but she didn't let impatience show in her voice. "I'm sorry to hear that. I still think you should come to the ball, though. By that time you'll both have cooled off. Romances end—sometimes it can't be helped—but it's always nice to remain on speaking terms."

"Kelley might not agree with you."

"I'm sure she'd be polite. She has good breeding."

"I doubt if I could take cool courtesy."

"Well, it's up to you." Henrietta sighed. "I'm really fond of both of you. I wish it could have worked out."

"No more than I do," Erich muttered as he hung up.

* * *

Kelley thought she'd hit bottom the day Erich had chosen to flaunt yet another of his girlfriends in front of her. But things went steadily downhill after that.

Every day she made the rounds of the banks, with the same result. Some of the bankers were pleasant, others were curt, but the answer was always the same. Nobody would give her a loan.

Kelley tried to project confidence for Emmy's sake, but she was beginning to wonder if she was really doing her a favor. Emmy couldn't be cushioned from reality forever, and right now the future looked grim.

"You really have to lighten up a little," Emmy told her when they were having coffee after Kelley's latest refusal. "You've lost weight and you have circles under your eyes."

"I'm not sleeping well." Kelley sighed. "I lie in bed at night trying to figure out some magic sales pitch that will get us the loan we need."

"It won't help to make yourself sick."

"You don't seem to understand. We're almost out of options. I have one more appointment tomorrow and that's it. If they turn me down like all the others, I honestly don't know what else to do."

"Something will turn up, it always does," Emmy said serenely.

"What am I going to do with you?" Kelley groaned. "This is the real world. Sometimes things just don't work out."

"Nobody can say you haven't tried." Emmy brightened. "So what if a bunch of stuffy old bankers have no vision? It only takes one. Maybe tomorrow will be our lucky day."

"And if it isn't?"

"Why worry ahead of time? Tonight we're going to get all dressed up and go out dancing. You phone Erich and

I'll round up Niles. I don't want to hear any excuses, either—you're going."

"I know you mean well, Emmy, but Erich and I...we're not seeing each other anymore."

"When did all this happen?"

"It doesn't matter when, we just aren't. So you and Niles go out and have fun. Don't worry about me, I'll be fine."

Emmy wasn't reassured. "I don't know what you and Erich argued about, but it's foolish to let a misunderstanding ruin your friendship. Why don't you call him and talk it out? I'm sure he'd be happy to hear from you."

"The telephone works both ways," Kelley responded. "Besides, Erich's not waiting to hear from me. He's much too busy with his international harem. I'll see you tomorrow." She picked up her purse and left.

Emmy had no qualms about phoning Erich, once she realized Kelley was in love with him. He might not share her feelings. Erich had gone out with some gorgeous women without forming a permanent attachment. But if there was a chance that Kelley was the exception, Emmy didn't want to stand idly by while they fouled up their lives.

"How's it going, Emmy?" Erich greeted her cordially, in spite of his black mood.

"Not so great."

"What's wrong?"

"Well, I don't know if you're aware of it, but Kelley and I have been trying to start a business together."

"She mentioned something about it," he said briefly.

"It's really a great idea, but we haven't been able to get a loan."

"That's too bad."

"Yes, it's a bummer. Kelley has been knocking herself out going from bank to bank and getting the door slammed in her face. Her spirits are really dragging, poor kid."

"I guess nobody enjoys rejection," he answered unemotionally.

"It wears you down, though. That's why I'm calling. She needs to get out and forget about everything. I thought you might ask her to go dancing tonight."

"You're a little behind the times," he said sardonically. "Kelley wouldn't let me lead her out of a burning building."

"Did you two have a fight?" she asked in mock surprise.

"It was more like World War III," he replied grimly.

"I'm sure you're exaggerating. People say things when they're angry that they don't really mean. Why not give her a call? I'm sure she'd be glad to hear from you."

"I don't mean to be rude, but you don't know what you're talking about," he said roughly. "Kelley made her feelings for me perfectly clear, and I can live with that. Anything there ever was between us is over and done with."

Emmy could tell she was fighting a losing battle, but she gave it one last try. "She really needs a friend right now, Erich. You wouldn't recognize her. She's lost all her self-confidence."

"She'll bounce back," he said indifferently.

Erich stared at the phone for a long time after he hung up. Finally he lifted the receiver and dialed a number.

Chapter Eleven

Hans Wiegand looked up from his desk and frowned at his secretary when she appeared in his office. "I told you I didn't want to be disturbed."

"I know, but I thought you'd want—"

"I pay you to follow instructions, Fraulein Spengler."

Her mouth set in a straight line. "Very well, I'll tell the Grand Duke Von Graile Und Tassburg that you're too busy to speak to him."

"Wait! Put him on immediately." The banker's perennially sour expression changed to a smile as he picked up the receiver. "This is a great pleasure, *mein herr*. What can I do for you?" The smile faded as he listened. "I really don't think..."

"I'm not asking for an opinion," Erich interrupted crisply. "That is what I'm instructing you to do."

"But I feel it's my duty to inform you it's not a risk the bank would take on its own."

"Your policies are of no interest to me," Erich answered in his most autocratic tone. "Just draw up the papers immediately. I don't want this loan stalled by a lot of red tape."

"Whatever you say, naturally."

"And remember, I had nothing to do with it. You don't even know me."

"That's understood, *mein herr.*"

Kelley telephoned Emmy, filled with excitement. "You'll never guess who just called me!"

"Kelley?" Emmy yawned. "What time is it?"

"What difference does it make? I have the most incredible news!"

"Can I call you back after I have coffee? I got in rather late last night. You really should have come with me. Niles and I—"

"Forget about that," Kelley broke in. "We got the loan!"

Emmy sat up in bed. "Do you really mean it? How? When? I thought your appointment wasn't until this afternoon."

"It isn't. Hans Wiegand just called me. He was the first person I tried. Remember I told you how insufferable he was? Well, he was like a different person."

"What do you think made him change his mind?"

"I don't know, and I don't care. The only thing that matters is *we got the loan!* We're finally on our way."

"Fantastic! How long will it take until we actually get the money?"

"That's the amazing part. Usually the paperwork takes a couple of weeks, at least. They do title searches and background checks, among other things. But Wiegand says we can come down today and sign the papers."

"It sounds almost too good to be true," Emmy said.

"You're the one who kept saying something would turn up. Well, your fairy godmother finally listened to you."

"She took her own sweet time." Emmy laughed.

"Get dressed," Kelley said. "We have a million things to do."

The rest of the week passed in a blur of activity. Kelley and Emmy hired contractors, signed purchase orders and made dozens of decisions. The days weren't long enough.

Kelley returned to the hotel at night too tired to do more than take a bath and fall into bed. Often she didn't bother with dinner. The work was satisfying, though. She even managed to push thoughts of Erich to the back of her mind. At least during her waking hours.

The nights were a different matter. He haunted her dreams, appearing in her darkened room with outstretched arms and a remembered smile on his handsome face. No words were necessary. She moved into his embrace and pulled his head down for a deep, satisfying kiss.

The dreams all followed the same pattern. Sometimes Erich carried her to the bed, sometimes they sank to the carpet together, undressing each other slowly and erotically. The culmination was always the same, though. They made love passionately, linked together in pulsating ecstasy.

Kelley awoke in the morning, her body taut with unfulfilled desire. She dreaded the dreams, yet welcomed them, too. This was all she'd ever have of Erich.

One night Kurt called as she got out of the bathtub. "Where do you go every day?" he asked. "I've tried getting you early in the morning and late in the afternoon. You're never around."

"I've had a lot of things to do." Kelley hadn't told him about her project because Kurt wasn't interested in anything that didn't concern him directly. "I just got in a little while ago."

"I know, I've been calling you."

"Any special reason?" She smothered a yawn.

"I just wanted to remind you about the ball. I'll pick you up at eight."

"It isn't tonight?" she exclaimed in alarm.

"No, tomorrow night. You did forget," he said accusingly.

"I've had a lot on my mind," she said apologetically.

"Not *me*, obviously."

"Don't be tiresome, Kurt."

"How do you expect me to feel? I've been looking forward to our date for a week, and you didn't even remember it."

"Yes, I did," she lied. "You just confused me when you said you'd pick me up at eight. I thought I'd gotten my dates crossed."

"Oh, well that's different." He sounded mollified. "My feelings were really hurt. You know how I feel about you."

"Yes, you've told me." She sighed. "Do we have to discuss it now? I've had a busy day and I'm tired."

"Get some rest, then. Tomorrow night's going to be a gala affair."

"Aren't they all?" Kelley asked ironically.

"This one will be special, you'll see."

Kelley mentioned the event to Emmy the next morning. "Are you going?"

"I have to. Henrietta is being honored for all her charity work. I can get you an invitation if you want to go."

"Kurt already asked me."

"That's great. Are you sitting at Henrietta's table?"

"Yes, he made a point of mentioning it." Kelley hesitated. "Do you know who else will be sitting with us?"

"Well, let's see. The tables seat eight and there's you and Kurt, Niles and me, and Henrietta. That's five—or six if she asks someone to even out the table. The other couple will probably be one of her committee members with her husband."

"Erich has worked on a lot of boards with Henrietta, hasn't he?" Kelley asked. "Is he one of the honorees, too?"

"Not this time." Emmy wasn't fooled by her offhand manner. Much as she hated to, she felt compelled to dampen Kelley's hopes. "Erich discourages people from nominating him. He hates awards almost as much as he hates these affairs. I'm afraid he won't be there tonight. I'm sorry," she added gently.

"What on earth for? I'm delighted. Now I can enjoy myself without worrying about Erich and Kurt going for each other's throats. I don't know which of them is the more childish, but I'm tired of both of them."

"I don't blame you," Emmy said diplomatically. "You need to meet somebody new."

"That's the last thing I'm interested in. I expect to leave here shortly."

"So soon? The work is just getting started."

"You can handle it. I have to go home and start drumming up business."

"When will you be back?"

"I don't know. You don't really need me here anymore. My part of the job is back in America."

"But what about our plans for other conversions?" Emmy objected. "And establishing ourselves with travel agents over here."

"Let's get this project off the ground first," Kelley answered. By that time maybe she could bear to be on the same continent with Erich again. Surely the pain had to subside some time.

Kelley expected to wear the ball gown she'd bought for her first date with Kurt. How long ago that seemed, and how starry-eyed she'd been. All of her dreams seemed to have come true. Cinderella had gone to the ball and met a duke who was more handsome than a prince.

A faint whiff of perfume brought back poignant memories of that evening, of waltzing in Erich's arms and gazing up into his rugged face poised over hers. She hung the gown back in the closet so roughly that she dislodged the dress hanging next to it. The other garment slipped off the hanger and fell to the floor in a shimmering heap.

Kelley reached down and picked up the silver beaded gown Erich had bought for her in Budapest. She'd never had a chance to wear it. Her eyes were bleak as she remembered how happy she'd been then, how trusting.

Should she send it back to him since it had never been worn? No, he might think she was using that as an excuse to get in touch with him again. Or worse yet, to remind him of their passion-filled week together.

It was only a dress. She'd wear it tonight with Kurt. That would prove it had no importance to her.

Kurt made more of a fuss over her appearance than Kelley would have preferred. "You look magnificent!" He inspected her minutely. "That gown is fantastic. Did you just buy it?"

She hesitated, then said, "Yes."

His eyes traveled over her long legs encased in shimmery stockings, down to the spike heel silver shoes that were part of the outfit Erich picked out. "You'll cause a sensation."

"I hope not," she said briefly.

When she preceded him to the exit he exclaimed. "I didn't see the back before. What a stunning outfit!"

Kelley regretted her choice. Every compliment was twisting the knife. "It's just a dress, Kurt. Don't get carried away."

"I was only remarking on how beautiful you look," he said in an injured voice. "I can't seem to do anything to please you."

She stifled a sigh, reminding herself that this was the last time she'd have to put up with him. "I'm sorry. I'm a little on edge tonight for some reason."

"What you need is a glass of champagne to relax you."

"How about a magnum?" She smiled without humor.

Kelley couldn't see much difference between this ball and the last one, but it was nice to be with Henrietta again.

"I was hoping Heinrich would make the supreme sacrifice, since you're being honored tonight." Kelley indicated the empty chair next to the older woman.

"Heinrich isn't into self-sacrifice. He promised to name a yellow rose after me instead."

Kelley smiled. "That's a more lasting tribute."

"I suppose so, but tonight I'd prefer a warm body in that chair. It would serve him right if I had a flaming affair with some handsome young buck."

The notion was so ludicrous that Kelley couldn't help laughing. "If you find somebody that fits the description, see if he has a friend for me."

Henrietta gazed at the young woman's lovely face. Kelley was wearing violet eyeshadow to deepen the color of her eyes, and mascara to lengthen her already sooty lashes.

The dark silky hair that swept her shoulders formed a perfect frame for her delicate features and flawless skin.

"I don't imagine you need my help in getting a man," Henrietta remarked.

"I'm looking for one like Heinrich, but the good ones are already taken," Kelley answered lightly.

"Maybe you don't appreciate a good man when you see him," Henrietta said bluntly. "I could pretend I don't know what's going on, but I believe in speaking my mind. What happened between you and Erich?"

Kelley tensed. "I don't know what you mean. Erich is simply an acquaintance."

"Hogwash! You two were crazy about each other. Everybody could see that. I don't know what you argued about, but you're very foolish if you let him slip through your fingers."

Kelley's violet eyes darkened to purple. "What makes you think any one woman could hold his interest?"

"Great balls of fire, girl! Erich could have any woman he wanted. Instead of that, he's moping around over you like a sick doggie."

"Believe me, he's not moping," Kelley said bitterly. "I happen to know of at least two women who are keeping his spirits up."

Henrietta frowned. "I'm sure you're mistaken. Erich said you'd gotten the wrong impression. You really should have more faith in him."

"He talked to you about us?" Kelley asked in outrage. "That's inexcusable! He's done some shabby things to me, but this is the worst. I'll never forgive him!" She pushed her chair back and left the table.

Emmy looked over curiously. "What's the matter with Kelley? She seemed upset."

"It was my fault." Henrietta sighed. "I forgot what happens to people who stick their noses into other people's business. They don't make a lot of friends."

Kelley was more composed when she returned from the powder room. She even managed to appear interested in Kurt when they danced. He was more encouraged than she'd meant him to be.

"You're the most beautiful woman here," he murmured, holding her closely. "All the men envy me."

"I doubt that, but you're nice to say so. She tried to put distance between them, without success.

"I'd like to be more than nice to you," he said in a throaty voice.

She forced a smile. "I have no complaints."

"Don't pretend you don't understand. You know what I'm trying to say. I want you to be my baroness, to share my life with me."

"Please, Kurt, you know it's impossible."

"Why? You'd love living here. We could have a wonderful life together."

"How can I convince you that it's out of the question?" she asked helplessly. "You're a very charming man, but I don't love you, and I never will."

"I won't accept that. You haven't really given me a chance. I know it would work. Let me take you to see my castle. You enjoyed your weekend at Henrietta's, didn't you? We can live like that, too."

If I provide the money, Kelley thought dryly. She knew it was useless to argue with him so she said, "Let me think about it."

"That's all I ask, my darling." Kurt wrapped her closely in his arms and kissed her temple.

Kelley suppressed a shudder of distaste. Glancing over at their table she said, "You really should ask Henrietta to dance." The other couple she'd invited were table-hopping, and Henrietta was sitting with Emmy and Niles.

"Yes, I suppose I should." Kurt was torn between duty and his own interests. "We'll discuss our plans afterward." He accompanied Kelley back to the table and led Henrietta onto the dance floor.

"Are you having a good time?" Emmy asked.

"Compared to what?" Kelley rested her head on her hand. "I said no to Kurt a dozen different ways and he didn't understand any of them."

"Would you like me to interpret for you?" Niles asked.

"No, he's harmless. I just wish he'd stop being so persistent."

"Tell him you lost all your money," Emmy advised. "He'd be gone like a shot."

"I doubt if Kurt is after Kelley for her money." Niles gave her an admiring look.

"It doesn't say much for him, does it? Well, that's one problem *I'll* never have." Emmy laughed. "You like me for my winning personality, don't you?" she asked Niles.

"And because you're a great dancer. Shall we? This is one of your favorites."

When Emmy hesitated, glancing toward her, Kelley said, "Go ahead, I'd really enjoy being alone for a few minutes. Nothing personal," she added with a smile.

She wasn't merely being polite. The conversation with Henrietta, plus Kurt's amorous insistence was tying her up in knots. She watched the dancers, relaxing for the first time all evening. A well-remembered voice put an end to that.

"Did Kurt desert you again?" Erich was standing over her, looking both elegant and virile in his well-cut evening clothes. "He left you alone the first night we met. The man is clearly a moron."

"He's dancing with Henrietta." Kelley could barely get the words out.

"Then he won't mind if you dance with me."

She wanted to refuse, but he took her hand and drew her to her feet. It was like her recurring dreams. She drifted into his arms, allowing her body to conform to his hard frame.

For long moments Kelley simply enjoyed the delicious pleasure of being in Erich's arms once more. The masculine scent of his after-shave filled her nostrils, along with the clean smell of his skin. She surreptitiously traced the width of his broad shoulders, reacquainting herself with his taut muscles.

"You look lovely," he murmured finally. His hand burned her bare skin as he traced the low cowl of her dress in back. "I never got to take you out in that gown."

"I thought about sending it back to you, since I never wore it."

"Why would you do that?"

"You could have given it to someone else."

His jaw tightened. "Do you really think I would do that?"

She was instantly ashamed. "No, I'm sorry. I don't know why I said a thing like that."

"Because you believe it, obviously." His face was austere. "It all comes down to basics. You don't trust me."

"Even if that were true, you must understand why."

"No, I don't," he answered stubbornly.

"You can't expect me to believe Elisabeth means nothing to you. She has a key to your house. You spent the night with her."

"We spent the night under the same roof," he corrected.

"She indicated it was more than that."

"I don't care what she said, it's what you believe."

"What reason do I have to doubt her?" Kelley asked hopelessly. "It's clear that she's in love with you. You can call it a schoolgirl crush if you like, but she's no child and you aren't doing anything to discourage her. You're as possessive of her as she is of you. You were so jealous when she mentioned going out with some boy that I became a mere annoyance in your life."

Erich had maneuvered them to the edge of the dance floor. He took Kelley's hand and led her through French doors onto a terrace that was deserted for the moment.

Turning to her, he asked evenly, "Are you quite finished?"

"Isn't that enough?"

"Now I'll tell you about Elisabeth, and this time you're going to listen. Elisabeth is my goddaughter. Her parents were my best friends. They died in a skiing accident three years ago, leaving Elisabeth all alone in the world at sixteen. I took over as a surrogate parent. I sent her to school in Switzerland as they'd planned, but her home was with me. She's always been welcome to come and go as she pleases."

Comprehension dawned on Kelley's face. "That's why she had a key."

"Precisely. I tried to provide the same loving environment she would have had with her parents. She was a lost, lonely little kid when I took over. I could relate to her trauma, even though I was older when I lost my own parents."

Kelley was greatly relieved at his explanation, but it didn't make up for everything. "Elisabeth isn't a kid anymore, she's nineteen. Maybe you don't even realize it, but your feelings for her have changed. She's become the most important woman in your life, not a ward you've pledged to take care of."

"No, darling." Erich took both of her hands. "You're right about one thing. I didn't notice Elisabeth had grown up. I still thought of her as an adolescent who had to be protected from unsuitable boyfriends." He smiled ruefully. "I was like a doting father who thinks no boy is good enough for his little girl."

"She's pretty precocious for a little girl," Kelley said grimly.

"I've spoiled her," he admitted. "Not having any experience at being a parent, I tried to compensate for her loss by giving her a lot of attention. It never occurred to me that she'd give you the impression we slept together."

"You do believe me?"

Erich's jaw set squarely. "I got the story out of her after you blew up at me. We had a long talk and got a lot of things straightened out. She understands now how I feel about her, and the way it's going to be from here on. There won't be any more incidents like the last one."

"Where is she tonight?"

"I sent her back to school with instructions to stay there."

After a moment's silence Kelley said, "I feel a little foolish."

His expression was uncompromising. "Is that all?"

"Well, anybody might have jumped to the same conclusion, given the circumstances," she said defensively.

"Not someone who knew me like you did—or should have."

"That's not fair. Elisabeth was only the first shock. There was that woman in the lobby of my hotel. Did you have to meet her there where you knew you might run into me? It was almost as if you were flaunting your conquests in my face."

Erich's austere expression softened for the first time. "That was pure, unlucky coincidence. I was so hungry for the sight of you that I hung around your lobby for over an hour, waiting for you to come in. It's a wonder I didn't get arrested for loitering. Then, when you finally did appear, Jane came shrieking over. She was checking in and just happened to see me. I barely remembered her name. She's some tiresome female I met at a resort."

"You told me you were there to meet somebody," Kelley said tentatively.

"I lied." He smiled.

"Oh, Erich, I don't know what to say. I've made us both miserable for no good reason. Can you forgive me?"

"It isn't a matter of forgiveness," he answered slowly. "What bothers me is the fact that you were so willing to believe the worst."

"You would have reacted the same way," she protested.

"No." He stared at her almost clinically. "The difference is, I believe in you. No matter how damning the evidence might be, I'd wait to hear your side of it because I know you wouldn't lie to me."

Kelley's lashes fell to hide the tears she couldn't stem. "I realize I've ruined everything between us. All I can say is, I'm sorry. I hope as time goes by you won't hate me quite as much."

"I could never hate you," he said in a husky voice. "I still want you so much it hurts."

She gazed up at him with eyes like wet violets. "How could you?"

"Because I discovered life isn't worth living without you." He crushed her in his arms and kissed her almost desperately.

Kelley clung to him, running her fingers through his hair, patting his face, trying in every way she knew how to convey her undying love.

They strained against each other, wanting to be even closer. Erich's hands wandered urgently over her body, molding her to his lean length until every muscle was taut.

Finally he dragged his mouth away and buried his face in her neck. "Let's go home before I make love to you right this minute," he groaned.

"Wait here for me. I have to go back to the table and tell Kurt I'm leaving."

"I'm not letting you out of my sight. I'll go with you."

"It would be better if you wait here. You know how Kurt feels about you. I'd like to avoid a scene."

"If that's what he chooses, I'll be happy to oblige him. I've been wanting to punch him out for a long time."

"Don't be unreasonable," she pleaded. "I'll be right back, I promise."

"I'm going with you."

The steely glint in Erich's eyes told Kelley it was useless to argue. She led the way back to the table, hoping for the best. The expression on Kurt's face when he saw her with Erich told her the hope was futile.

"I might have known you'd show up here to annoy Kelley," he told Erich angrily. "When are you going to get it through your head that she doesn't want anything to do with you?"

"That's just one of the ways you're deluding yourself," Erich drawled.

"You think you can get any woman you want with your fancy title and all your millions, but this time you struck out," Kurt said triumphantly. "Kelley told me herself she's not interested in you. If you don't believe me, ask her!"

She was very conscious of having an audience. Henrietta, Emmy and Niles were listening avidly. "Why don't the three of us go outside and discuss this?" she suggested nervously.

"What is there to discuss?" Kurt demanded. "I asked you to marry me, and you said you'd consider it."

"That's not what I said! If you remember, I told you I didn't love you."

"We discussed that," he said stubbornly. "I told you it didn't matter."

"You're really pitiful," Erich said disgustedly. "She made herself perfectly clear. What does it take to convince you?"

"Not *you!*? Kurt said furiously. "You'd like me to step aside and give you a clear field, wouldn't you? Well, I'm not going to make it that easy. We'll see who's the better man."

"Kelley already knows that."

As the two men stood toe to toe, Magda appeared at the table. Her malicious smile included all of them. "Are you two still fighting over Miss America? If you're smart, Kurt, you'll let Erich have her. This will come as a big shock, but you've been had."

Kurt scowled. "Don't try to make trouble, Magda. It won't do you any good. You and I are through."

"You mean, you're not going to borrow money from me anymore? I'm crushed," she said mockingly.

"Don't make a scene," he said sharply. "You're just embarrassing yourself."

"At least I'm not pretending to be something I'm not." Magda gave Kurt a withering look. "You and Kelley deserve each other. You're both a couple of phonies."

"Nobody's interested in your opinion. Will you please leave?"

"Gladly, as soon as I tell you about your little heiress here. She really put one over on you. I'm just sorry you couldn't persuade her to marry you. I'd like to have seen your face when you discovered she isn't rich."

Kurt frowned. "What are you babbling about?"

"Your beloved's fortune—she doesn't have one."

"That's absurd!"

"Because she's staying at an expensive hotel and wears designer clothes? It's all window dressing. Every con artist has some working capital."

They had all been frozen by surprise and embarrassment at the scene Magda was creating. Finally Erich said, "If you and Kurt have some personal problem, I suggest you settle it between yourselves without dragging Kelley into it."

Magda turned on him angrily. "You're another patsy. Why do you think she dropped Kurt for you? Because you have money and she found out he doesn't. She's just a poor working girl who came to Vienna to get a rich husband."

"That's not true," Kelley gasped.

Kurt ignored her, staring at Magda. "Are you saying she didn't win the lottery?"

"Not the millions you were counting on. I never did believe her story, so I made some inquiries. She won a paltry fifty thousand dollars, and at the rate she's going through it, that must be pretty well depleted by now."

Kurt turned to look at Kelley with dawning anger. "Is Magda telling the truth?"

Kelley felt icy cold. Everyone was staring at her with varying degrees of surprise, but Erich's reaction was the one that chilled her. His astonishment told her he hadn't known, as she thought he did. Could he believe Magda's accusations? He wasn't coming to her defense.

"I asked you a question," Kurt said ominously.

Kelley moistened her dry lips. "I never said I won the grand prize."

"You let me think you did! You strung me along all these weeks, using me and my connections. I can't believe I didn't see through you. You're nothing but a social climbing little nobody!"

Erich stirred finally. "That's enough, Kurt."

Kelley knew Erich was only defending her through innate courtesy. She couldn't look at him. Squaring her shoulders she spoke to the others. "I never meant to deceive anybody. I'm sorry if you got the wrong impression. You've all been very kind to me and I hope you'll come to realize the only thing I wanted was your friendship."

She left swiftly with her head held high, making her way through the crowd. A babble of voices erupted at the table, but Kelley outdistanced them. She was almost running by the time she reached the door.

The enormity of what had just happened overwhelmed her. Erich's incredulous expression would be burned in her memory forever. He had a right to be indignant after her lack of faith in *him*. Trust was important to Erich. His words thundered in her ears: "I know you would never lie to me."

She *hadn't* lied. It was all a misunderstanding. But would Erich believe that? Of course not. Magda's accusation was closer to his past experience. Too many women had disillusioned him.

When Kelley finally reached her hotel room she was relatively calm. It was time to go home and try to put this tragedy behind her. She got her suitcase down from the top shelf in the closet and started to pack, trying not to think about Erich. Maybe someday she could bear to remember their enchanted time together, but not now.

A knock at the door made her stiffen. Kelley remained very still, scarcely breathing. It had to be Erich, and she couldn't take any more invective in her present fragile state.

"I know you're there," he called. "I'm not going away, so you might as well let me in." When she didn't answer, he said, "Okay, if you want the entire floor to hear what I have to say it's all right with me."

Kelley moved hurriedly to open the door a crack. She'd already suffered enough humiliation. "Go away, Erich. I've apologized to you. What more can I do?"

He pushed his way inside and closed the door behind him. "What do you have to apologize for? Are you saying Magda's accusations are correct?"

"Only the one about the lottery. I honestly thought you knew I didn't have unlimited funds."

"Why would I care?"

"Because you told me a lot of women were mainly interested in what they could get from you," she said in a low voice.

He chuckled unexpectedly. "I was more than happy to give you what *you* wanted."

Kelley's heart almost stopped beating. "You didn't believe those things Magda said?"

"Don't you think I know you better than that?" Erich took her icy fingers in his big warm hands. "You don't have a devious bone in your body."

"Oh, Erich, I thought I'd lost you," she whispered.

"You couldn't get rid of me if you tried." He gathered her into his arms. "When are you going to realize that?"

"It was so horrible, everybody staring at me that way. Kurt made me feel like a criminal."

"That fortune-hunting little weasel is a fine one to talk," Erich said grimly. "I should have decked him, but I was in too big a hurry to catch up to you."

"What did Henrietta and Emmy say?"

"They felt the same way I did—that Kurt is a jerk. He didn't do himself any good. Henrietta suggested he take Magda and leave."

"I really broke up a gala event," Kelley said ruefully.

"We can have our own event," Erich murmured, leading her to the bed. He noticed the suitcase for the first time. "What's this? Were you really going to leave me?"

"I didn't think you wanted me anymore," she said simply.

"There isn't a minute of the day or night that I don't want you," he answered deeply. "I plan to spend the rest of my life making love to you, starting right now."

"I was so devastated when I thought everything was over between us. Tell me you love me," she said yearningly.

"Does this tell you how much?"

His lips touched hers in a kiss that was sweet with promise. While their mouths clung, Erich slipped the gown off her shoulders. It slithered down, leaving her bare to the waist. He cupped her breasts in his palms and dipped his head to kiss each taut nipple.

"I'm going to devote my life to making you happy," he said huskily.

"You already have," she answered, gently tugging at his tie.

Their lovemaking was passionate yet unhurried, as if they realized they had all the time in the world. They explored each other's bodies, delighting in giving pleasure. When their love play escalated into torrid desire they consummated their union, experiencing the ultimate ecstasy of two people in love.

After attaining complete satisfaction, Kelley stroked Erich's hair tenderly. "How can I leave you, even for a little while?"

His arms tightened. "You can't. I won't ever let you go very far from me."

"I don't want to, but I have to go home to round up some rich tourists."

"That can wait. Wiegand just gave you the loan. You haven't even started renovation yet."

"How did you know that?" she asked slowly.

He avoided her eyes. "I know something about construction. It doesn't move that swiftly."

"No, I mean how did you know it was Hans Wiegand's bank that loaned us the money?"

"I guess Emmy must have mentioned it." He nibbled on her lower lip. "You know what? Making love to you is like eating Chinese food. Half an hour later I'm hungry for you again."

She remained passive in his arms. "You loaned us the money, didn't you? Wiegand and everybody else in town had already turned us down."

Erich hesitated for a moment. "Does it matter where the loan came from?"

"It matters a lot. I don't want you to think I used you."

"You didn't ask for the money, darling. It was something I wanted to do. You would have found your financing somehow, because you're a very special woman, but it gave me pleasure to make things a little easier for you."

Kelley was overwhelmed by the depth of his love. Erich cared about her happiness, even after she'd destroyed his. "What did I ever do to deserve you?" she asked mistily.

"You made me happier than I ever thought possible." He drew her back into his arms. "I hope you don't believe in long engagements, because I'm not a patient man."

Kelley's happiness was complete. Her ultimate dream had come true. "How do you feel about honeymooning in California?" she asked.

"Whatever the Duchess desires," he answered adoringly.

Kelley gazed at him with starry eyes as the full import sank in. "Who says I didn't win the grand prize?" she murmured, clasping her arms around his neck.

* * * * *

A Note from the Author

I was so happy to have *Grand Prize Winner!* included in the That Special Woman! promotion, because I believe Kelley *is* a very special woman. She takes charge of her own life and refuses to let adversity discourage her, even when the future looks bleak. We all know people who whine or go to pieces over the slightest setback, but Kelley keeps her sense of humor, squares her shoulders and works out her own problems.

My goal is to have people say the same about me, although I'm afraid I don't exactly qualify for sainthood. It isn't easy being a woman, as many of us have found out. There are wonderful compensations, though. I'm grateful for so many things in my life, and I hope all of my readers are similarly blessed.

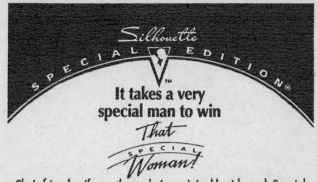

Silhouette

SPECIAL EDITION®

™

It takes a very special man to win *That Woman!*

She's friend, wife, mother—she's you! And beside each Special Woman stands a wonderfully special man. It's a celebration of our heroines—and the men who become part of their lives.

Look for these exciting titles from Silhouette Special Edition:

August MORE THAN HE BARGAINED FOR by Carole Halston
Heroine: Avery Payton—a woman struggling for independence falls for the man next door.

September A HUSBAND TO REMEMBER by Lisa Jackson
Heroine: Nikki Carrothers—a woman without memories meets the man she should never have forgotten...her husband.

October ON HER OWN by Pat Warren
Heroine: Sara Shepard—a woman returns to her hometown and confronts the hero of her childhood dreams.

November GRAND PRIZE WINNER! by Tracy Sinclair
Heroine: Kelley McCormick—a woman takes the trip of a lifetime and wins the greatest prize of all...love!

December POINT OF DEPARTURE by Lindsay McKenna
(Women of Glory)
Heroine: Lt. Callie Donovan—a woman takes on the system and must accept the help of a kind and sexy stranger.

Don't miss THAT SPECIAL WOMAN! each month—from some of your special authors! Only from Silhouette Special Edition!

When the only time you have for yourself is...

STOLEN *moments* ™

Christmas is such a busy time—with shopping, decorating, writing cards, trimming trees, wrapping gifts....

When you do have a few *stolen moments* to call your own, treat yourself to a brand-new *short* novel. Relax with one of our Stocking Stuffers—or with all six!

Each STOLEN MOMENTS title
is a complete and original contemporary romance that's the perfect length for the busy woman of the nineties! Especially at Christmas...

And they make perfect **stocking stuffers**, too! (For your mother, grandmother, daughters, friends, co-workers, neighbors, aunts, cousins—all the other women in your life!)

Look for the STOLEN MOMENTS display in December

STOCKING STUFFERS:

HIS MISTRESS Carrie Alexander
DANIEL'S DECEPTION Marie DeWitt
SNOW ANGEL Isolde Evans
THE FAMILY MAN Danielle Kelly
THE LONE WOLF Ellen Rogers
MONTANA CHRISTMAS Lynn Russell

HSM2

 **WORLDWIDE LIBRARY**

Silhouette
SPECIAL EDITION™

WHAT EVER HAPPENED TO...?

Have you been wondering when a much-loved character will finally get their own story? Well, have we got a lineup for you! Silhouette Special Edition is proud to present a *Spin-off Spectacular!* Be sure to catch these exciting titles from some of your favorite authors.

FOREVER (SE #854, December) *Ginna Gray*'s THE BLAINES AND THE McCALLS OF CROCKETT, TEXAS are back! Outrageously flirtatious Reilly McCall is having the time of his life trying to win over the reluctant heart of Amanda Sutherland!

A DARING VOW (SE #855, December) You met Zelda Lane in KATE'S VOW (SE #823), and she's about to show her old flame she's as bold as ever in this spin-off of *Sherryl Woods*'s VOWS series.

MAGNOLIA DAWN (SE #857, December) *Erica Spindler* returns with a third story of BLOSSOMS OF THE SOUTH in this tale of one woman learning to love again as she struggles to preserve her heritage.

Don't miss these wonderful titles, only for our readers—only from Silhouette Special Edition!

SPIN2

Silhouette

SPECIAL EDITION™

WILD RIVER TRILOGY

by Laurie Paige

Come meet the wild McPherson men and see how these three sexy bachelors are tamed!

In HOME FOR A WILD HEART (SE #828) you got to know Kerrigan McPherson.

In A PLACE FOR EAGLES (SE #839) Keegan McPherson got the surprise of his life.

And in THE WAY OF A MAN (SE #849, November 1993) Paul McPherson finally meets his match.

Don't miss any of these exciting titles, only for our readers—and only from Silhouette Special Edition!

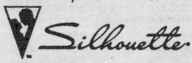

He staked his claim…

HONOR BOUND

by
New York Times
Bestselling Author

previously published under the pseudonym Erin St. Claire

As Aislinn Andrews opened her mouth to scream, a hard hand clamped over her face and she found herself face-to-face with Lucas Greywolf, a lean, lethal-looking Navajo and escaped convict who swore he wouldn't hurt her— *if* she helped him.

Look for HONOR BOUND at your favorite retail outlet this January.

Only from…

where passion lives. SBHB

SILHOUETTE.... Where Passion Lives

Don't miss these Silhouette favorites by some of our most popular authors!
And now, you can receive a discount by ordering two or more titles!

Silhouette Desire®

#05751	THE MAN WITH THE MIDNIGHT EYES BJ James	$2.89	☐
#05763	THE COWBOY Cait London	$2.89	☐
#05774	TENNESSEE WALTZ Jackie Merritt	$2.89	☐
#05779	THE RANCHER AND THE RUNAWAY BRIDE Joan Johnston	$2.89	☐

Silhouette Intimate Moments®

#07417	WOLF AND THE ANGEL Kathleen Creighton	$3.29	☐
#07480	DIAMOND WILLOW Kathleen Eagle	$3.39	☐
#07486	MEMORIES OF LAURA Marilyn Pappano	$3.39	☐
#07493	QUINN EISLEY'S WAR Patricia Gardner Evans	$3.39	☐

Silhouette Shadows®

#27003	STRANGER IN THE MIST Lee Karr	$3.50	☐
#27007	FLASHBACK Terri Herrington	$3.50	☐
#27009	BREAK THE NIGHT Anne Stuart	$3.50	☐
#27012	DARK ENCHANTMENT Jane Toombs	$3.50	☐

Silhouette Special Edition®

#09754	THERE AND NOW Linda Lael Miller	$3.39	☐
#09770	FATHER: UNKNOWN Andrea Edwards	$3.39	☐
#09791	THE CAT THAT LIVED ON PARK AVENUE Tracy Sinclair	$3.39	☐
#09811	HE'S THE RICH BOY Lisa Jackson	$3.39	☐

Silhouette Romance®

#08893	LETTERS FROM HOME Toni Collins	$2.69	☐
#08915	NEW YEAR'S BABY Stella Bagwell	$2.69	☐
#08927	THE PURSUIT OF HAPPINESS Anne Peters	$2.69	☐
#08952	INSTANT FATHER Lucy Gordon	$2.75	☐

	AMOUNT	$
DEDUCT:	10% DISCOUNT FOR 2+ BOOKS	$
	POSTAGE & HANDLING	$
	($1.00 for one book, 50¢ for each additional)	
	APPLICABLE TAXES*	$
	TOTAL PAYABLE	$
	(check or money order—please do not send cash)	

To order, complete this form and send it, along with a check or money order for the total above, payable to Silhouette Books, to: *In the U.S.*: 3010 Walden Avenue, P.O. Box 9077, Buffalo, NY 14269-9077; *In Canada*: P.O. Box 636, Fort Erie, Ontario, L2A 5X3.

Name: _____

Address: _____ City: _____

State/Prov.: _____ Zip/Postal Code: _____

*New York residents remit applicable sales taxes.
Canadian residents remit applicable GST and provincial taxes.

SBACK-OD

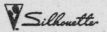